ChangelingPress.com

Flicker/Spider Duet

Harley Wylde

Flicker/Spider Duet
Harley Wylde

All rights reserved.
Copyright ©2020 Harley Wylde

ISBN: 9798643339175

Publisher:
Changeling Press LLC
315 N. Centre St.
Martinsburg, WV 25404
ChangelingPress.com

Printed in the U.S.A.

Editor: Crystal Esau
Cover Artist: Bryan Keller

The individual stories in this anthology have been previously released in E-Book format.

No part of this publication may be reproduced or shared by any electronic or mechanical means, including but not limited to reprinting, photocopying, or digital reproduction, without prior written permission from Changeling Press LLC.

This book contains sexually explicit scenes and adult language which some may find offensive and which is not appropriate for a young audience. Changeling Press books are for sale to adults, only, as defined by the laws of the country in which you made your purchase.

Table of Contents

Flicker (Dixie Reapers MC 11)	4
Chapter One	5
Chapter Two	21
Chapter Three	35
Chapter Four	48
Chapter Five	68
Chapter Six	81
Chapter Seven	98
Chapter Eight	110
Chapter Nine	126
Chapter Ten	137
Epilogue	149
Spider (Hades Abyss MC 1)	154
Chapter One	155
Chapter Two	169
Chapter Three	184
Chapter Four	198
Chapter Five	213
Chapter Six	228
Chapter Seven	240
Chapter Eight	252
Chapter Nine	267
Chapter Ten	280
Chapter Eleven	292
Epilogue	302
Dixie Reapers MC	306
Harley Wylde	307
Changeling Press E-Books	308

Flicker (Dixie Reapers MC 11)
Harley Wylde

Pepper -- My mom kept my dad a secret my entire life, only ever calling him Sarge. Now that she's gone and left me a location for the mysterious man, I'm going to finally meet him. Too bad it isn't under better circumstances. Thanks to Mom, some really bad men are after me. I'm not sure if Sarge will keep me safe or send me packing. What I didn't count on was meeting the only man to ever make me burn. Flicker. It suits him because I definitely feel like I'm engulfed in flames when he touches me. I shouldn't want him, but I do.

Flicker -- The redheaded goddess had my attention from the moment I saw her. Finding out she's Sarge's daughter couldn't even dampen my desire. He'll try to gut me when he finds out I shackled her to my bed, but I'm not letting her go. Pepper will be mine, will carry my baby, and no one will ever take her from me -- not even the henchmen from Vegas coming for her.

Chapter One

Pepper

I hated my mother for putting me in this position. I stared at the paper in my hand, hastily scribbled along with her suicide note right before she took her life. Maybe it made me a bitch that I resented her so much, but after all she'd done, it was hard to feel anything other than relief that she was gone. I'd been the product of a one-month fling, and she'd never let me forget how it had ruined her life. Or rather that I had. I didn't think she regretted her time with a man she'd only ever called Sarge, but the fact he'd left something other than memories behind had always pissed her off. I'd tried to search for my dad before, but with only knowing the name Sarge, which I highly doubted was his real name, I hadn't been able to get very far.

I looked at the address on the paper in my hand, then up at the gates ahead. It was the right place, but it wasn't what I'd been expecting. When Mom left a suicide note and instructions for me to find Sarge at the Dixie Reapers' compound, I'd expected something more military-like. This place looked more like a super-nice commune or something, but I doubted my dad was part of a cult. If the bikes across the front of a large building were any indication, he was a biker of some sort. The question was whether or not he was an outlaw or just someone who liked to ride with his buddies. This place didn't exactly scream recreational therapy or mid-life crisis, though.

At least I now understood my love of motorcycles. Must be in my blood. I shoved the paper back into my pocket, where I'd placed my mother's suicide note, and eased my bike toward the compound.

There was a man at the gates with a leather vest that said *Prospect* on the front, along with the club name. I was definitely in the right place. The large building had neon letters over the top that even read *Dixie Reapers*. Too late to turn back after I'd made it this far. Besides, there was nothing left back home. Mom had made sure of that. Vegas was no longer safe for me.

The man arched a brow as I removed my helmet and my hair tumbled down my back. Red, unlike my mother's blonde tresses, and my green eyes were far from her brown ones. I'd always assumed I took after my dad, but I would hopefully find out soon enough. I braced my feet on the pavement, but didn't get off my Indian Scout. It was an older bike, nearly as old as me, but I loved it and had paid for it with my own money.

"You don't look like the typical club whore," he said, as he scanned me from head to toe.

I snorted and rolled my eyes. As if.

"I need to see Sarge," I said.

"He expecting you?" the man asked, his tone clearly saying that he doubted it for a second.

"No, but he'll want to know I'm here. At least, I'm hoping he'll want to."

"Sarge usually doesn't go for the younger women. You might have better luck with someone else."

"I'm not here for a booty call, asswipe. Are you going to get Sarge or not?" I demanded.

He pulled a phone from his pocket and took a step back. Whoever he called, he was speaking too softly for me to hear a damn thing. He nodded a few times, as if the person on the other end could see him, then hung up.

My nape prickled and I looked over at the big building again. There was a tall, shadowy male figure, and I somehow knew he was staring at me. The man stepped into the light and my breath hitched. I couldn't see his face, only the golden blond of his hair, and the muscles in his arms. It was enough to make my heart pound a little harder, something that had never happened to me. Before I could analyze the sensation more, or the man, the prospect came back over.

"Sarge will be here in a minute. You can wait right there."

I shut off my bike, put down the kickstand, then stood up and stretched. It had been a long-ass ride, one that had taken me days. Even though I'd crashed at some cheap motels along the way, I'd never slept for long. Exhaustion tugged at me, but I hadn't wanted to put this off until morning. If the music blasting from the building behind the gates was any indication, the men here wouldn't be sober tomorrow anyway.

I kept my eye on the building, waiting for the man called Sarge to come out, but the sound of a Harley drew my attention to the right. Heading down a road that seemed to wind through the compound was the most gorgeous bike I'd ever seen. And one look at the man riding it dispelled any doubts I had as to whether or not this guy was my father. His hair was the same shade as mine, even though it was cut short, and the eyes that locked on mine were the same as the ones I saw every morning in the mirror. He was tall and lean, but had enough muscle that I doubted anyone dared to fuck with him.

He shut off his bike and dismounted, coming closer to the gates. We just stared at one another for the longest time, then I pulled the suicide note from my pocket. I shoved it through the bars of the gate and he took it, scanning it. The only hint of emotion was the tic in his jaw as his gaze lifted to mine. Mom had mentioned this guy had been in the military, and from the stoic expression I'd have to say she was probably right. He had that *don't fuck with me* look, and at the same time appeared completely disinterested in everything around him. I didn't think that was true for a moment, though. He'd probably cataloged every detail of both me and the surrounding area when he'd ridden up to the gate.

"Who was your mom?" he asked.

"Mary Ann White," I said. "The two of you met in Vegas and she said you spent a month together."

"How old are you?" he asked, his eyes narrowing a little.

"Twenty-two."

He nodded, then glanced at the paper in his hands again. "Seems we have a bit to discuss. You hungry? There's a twenty-four-hour diner in town."

"I could eat," I said, having skipped a lot of meals to get here as quickly as I could.

He looked at my bike and a faint smile curved his lips before he went and mounted his Harley again. The Prospect opened the gates as Sarge came through, and I started my bike, then followed him back into town. The club sat on the outskirts, but it didn't take long to reach the diner he'd mentioned. I parked next to him and he held the diner door for me as we stepped inside. It was a quaint little place, and I'd bet their greasy food was pretty damn good. Sarge picked a table by the window that overlooked our bikes and he claimed one side of the booth, then motioned for me to sit across from him. His gaze shot to the door behind me a moment before settling on my face.

"I'm Pepper White," I said. "Your daughter, if my mother is to be believed. To be honest, it wouldn't be the first time she lied."

He studied me a moment. "No denying I'm your dad. You look just like my mother when she was younger, and you have my eyes."

I nodded.

"Why didn't she tell me about you?" he asked.

"I'm not really sure. I guess she figured the two of you were just having fun and you wouldn't want to be saddled with a kid. Birth control must have been even more faulty back then than it is now." I pushed my shoulders back and my spine cracked a few times, then I relaxed a little. Talking about sex with a parent might freak out some people, but when your mother's occupation was sex, then it changed your perspective. I was still a virgin, only because I'd never felt that zing before. "Look, my mom is dead, if you couldn't figure that out from her chicken scratch. She wasn't the nicest person in the world, and had more problems that most. She stole something from some bad people, and now they want it back. Problem is that she said in that note that it's gone and they'll be coming for me."

"That the only reason you're here? You need protection?" he asked.

I nibbled my lower lip and shook my head. "No, I've wanted to know who my dad was for a long time. Mom only ever called you Sarge and never told me your real name. Or your location. I tried to find you, but didn't get very far."

"Did she treat you right when you were growing up? Make sure you had everything you needed?" he asked.

I snorted before I could stop myself. "Hell no. Whatever money came in she snorted or drank away. We lived in a crappy trailer that her pimp gave her when I was a few years old. It was rusted out, the heat and air didn't work, and half the time the plumbing didn't either."

"Pimp?" he asked, his eyes narrowing.

"Mom wanted to be a Vegas showgirl, but she said I'd ruined her body so no one would hire her. Martin found her wandering The Strip with me in tow. Our clothes were ragged and dirty, so he made her a deal. One she accepted. When he found out that she was hiding me under a bridge while she *worked*, he gave us the trailer. Figured it was better than nothing, I guess."

"Jesus," he muttered.

A waitress who looked like she'd been on her feet all day wandered over, a tired smile on her face. "Hey, Sarge. What can I get for you?"

"Lily, you look about ready to fall over."

She shrugged.

"I'll have whatever's on special today with some coffee. Just leave the carafe. I have a feeling I'll need it."

Her gaze strayed to mine and I arched a brow, daring her to ask the question burning in her eyes.

"Get my daughter whatever she wants," he said and Lily's head jerked back toward him so hard I wondered if she'd gotten whiplash.

"Daughter?" she asked.

"Yep."

He didn't say anything more and just looked over at me. Plucking a menu off the holder on the table, I glanced over it before ordering the steak and eggs platter and some sweet tea. I'd always wondered why I liked sweet tea when half of Vegas didn't even know how to properly make the shit, but I had a feeling it had to do with the southern twang in my dad's voice. Maybe liking sweet tea was genetic. That was a southern thing, right? Sweet tea? Couldn't think of where else I'd have picked up the taste for it. Mom certainly hadn't liked any type of tea. Just reminded me that my mom had stolen twenty-two years of time from me and my dad. I didn't know anything about him, but I wanted to.

"I'll turn your orders in to the kitchen and be back with your drinks in a moment," Lily said.

After she'd left, I glanced at my dad and noticed he was watching Lily. Or rather seemed to be staring at her ass. I snickered a little. The guy might be old enough to have a twenty-two-year-old kid, but he still had a thing for the ladies. Or at least he liked our waitress. I wondered if there was history between them.

"She's probably a sure thing," I said.

He growled as he faced me again. "Don't talk about her like that."

"Whatever. I'm just saying if you wanted to ask her out, she'd probably say yes. I can tell that she's into you."

He looked at Lily again before shaking his head. Yeah, there was a story there, but he obviously wasn't talking about it.

"So how old are you?" I asked. "You seem older than Mom, even though she looked like she was almost fifty when she died. Booze, drugs, and whoring herself out didn't do her body any favors."

"I'm forty-six," he said.

"So, you were twenty-four when I was born, and Mom was seventeen."

His eyes went so damn wide I might have laughed if he didn't look completely horrified. It seemed I wasn't the only secret Mom had kept from him.

"You didn't know?" I asked.

"She said she was twenty-one," he said. "Even showed me her ID."

"It was fake," I said. "Just like everything else about her."

"I had been discharged from the Army and just wanted to cut loose a bit before I came home to figure shit out. I'd never intended to start anything with her, much less keep it going for a month. When I told her it was time for me to leave, she seemed fine with it. I'd made no pretense of things going further with us, making sure she knew up front that I couldn't give her something more permanent."

"Which is why she never reached out to you."

"Maybe. I'd told her about my club and that I lived in Alabama. Could have found me if she wanted. Now I'm wishing I'd have called to check in on her. Maybe she'd have told me that she was pregnant and you wouldn't have had to live like that. Fuck. I'm the world's worst dad and I've only known about you for twenty minutes tops."

I grinned. "Trust me, you aren't the world's worst. I might have grown up fast, and seen way more than I ever should have, but it also made me determined not to live like that. When I turned sixteen, I dropped out of school and started working full-time, then had myself emancipated. I earned my own money, got a small studio apartment, and saved for the Indian out there. After the first month, I was able to get my G.E.D. with special permission from the state."

"And you just up and left everything behind to come here?" he asked.

"Mostly. I knew Mom was starting to get mixed up in some bad shit, and I'd planned to take off soon anyway. My lease was up on the apartment at the end of the month. I was going to hit the road and find somewhere new to call home. She just moved up my timetable a little and gave me a definite destination."

"You still working the same job all these years?" he asked.

"No. I started out washing dishes at one of the smaller casinos off The Strip. They didn't ask a lot of questions and didn't mind hiring someone my age. When I turned eighteen, I'd worked up to helping with food prep. I decided I liked the vibe in the kitchen, so I applied to culinary school. Made it through the program and I'm now a professional cook."

"So you were working as a cook when you left Vegas?" he asked.

"Yeah. I'd only had the job about six months, so I'm not sure how difficult it will be to hire on someplace new, but I explained things to my boss and he wrote me a glowing recommendation."

"Everything you own in the pack strapped to the back of your bike?"

"Yep. Well, everything I brought with me. I didn't own much to begin with. A friend is keeping an eye on my knives and a few other things I wanted to keep that couldn't fit on the bike. A good knife set isn't cheap. He promised to send them when I landed somewhere."

"He?" Sarge's eyes narrowed.

I thought it was cute that he was already trying to be a protective papa, even if I didn't need it. Not for my gay best friend anyway. He could save that for dealing with Mom's shit. If I did find the right guy, maybe that golden god back at the compound, then I wouldn't let him or anyone else stop me from having a relationship. I'd never so much as dated, too worried about what would happen. Everyone knew what Mom had done for a living and made no secret they thought I'd be the same way. I'd seen too many cases of date rape in my two years of high school to ever take the chance.

"Louis Cantrell. My best friend, who also happens to be dating the love of his life, Marcus." My lips twitched when he eased back against the booth bench. "Yes, my best friend is gay. He went through the same academy as me and is working as a cook in a classy restaurant."

The waitress, Lily, returned with our drinks and set them down, but she didn't linger. I noticed my dad waited to continue our conversation until she had moved off, and his gaze stayed locked on her for longer than was necessary. Yeah, he definitely had a thing for her.

"Guess I don't have much of a right to get upset over who you date, or don't date, since I didn't even know you existed until tonight," he said.

"What's your real name?" I asked. "Or do I just call you Sarge?"

"Lance Reid." He rubbed a hand down his beard. "But I was kind of hoping you might want to call me Dad. Shit. Your grandparents are going to freak the hell out. I'm freaking out for that matter. Never thought I'd have kids and now I have one fully grown daughter I never knew about. I don't know the first damn thing about being a parent."

"First, I don't need a parent in the sense you're thinking. I already did my growing up, but I do want to get to know you. And it's awesome that I finally have a dad. Second, I have grandparents?" I asked, ignoring his comment about him freaking out. He was allowed. If our roles were reversed, I'd probably feel the same. What my mother had done hadn't been fair to either of us. But… grandparents! I'd always envied the kids who had some. It had just been me and Mom, and she was no prize.

"Yeah. Margie and Robert Reid. My dad is from Scotland, but his accent isn't that thick these days. Mom is from Georgia. They're in their eighties. Had me late in life. Mom always called me her miracle baby."

"Do they live here?" I asked, suddenly wanting to meet them more than anything. Finding out who my dad was had been amazing, if a bit scary considering the circumstances, but discovering I had grandparents? Holy shit! That was like striking gold for a kid who had never had anyone but a junkie whore mother.

"A few towns over. Once we get some stuff figured out, I'll take you over there. For now, we need to focus on more immediate things, like do you have a place to stay?" he asked.

"Um, no, but I'm assuming even a small place like this has a motel or two."

"You can stay with me, if you're comfortable doing that. I have a house at the compound. It's not exactly big, but there's a spare room. We can decorate it however you want, if you decide to stick around for a while." He shrugged. "If you want to move on once all this mess with your mom is sorted, then that's fine too, but I'm hoping you'll keep in touch."

Our food arrived and he went quiet again. It was nice of him to offer me a place to stay, and I had to wonder if he was just being polite or if he really wanted me there. A guy who'd never thought to have kids, and hadn't known about me, might prefer to have his space. I didn't want to stay there if he was just being polite but didn't really want me under foot. I ate about a fourth of my food, glancing up at him every few bites. I could feel him watching me when I wasn't looking.

"Do you want me to? Stick around, I mean," I said.

"Yeah, I do. Might take me a few days to adjust to being a dad, or longer, but now that I know about you, I want to get to know you."

"I'd like that," I admitted.

We finished our food and he leaned back in the booth. He didn't seem in a rush to get back to the compound, so I pushed my plate away and leaned my arms on the table. I'd been right about the food. Greasy but good. It was the most I'd eaten in days and my stomach was content for the moment.

"Tell me about this trouble your mom was mixed up in, the trouble that she said would come looking for you," he said.

"Mom has -- *had* -- a bad drug habit. Heroin, cocaine, meth. She loved it all, and she wasn't above helping herself if she saw anything lying around. Except this time, she stole an entire brick."

"What the fuck did she do with a brick of coke?" he asked, his voice going dark and deep. The look in his eyes said he'd clearly kill my mom himself if she weren't already dead.

"Probably threw a party or several, and I'm sure a good bit of it went up her nose," I said. "She'd been babbling the other day about someone trying to get something from her, and that if she didn't return it, they wanted twenty grand in cash. Like my mom has that kind of money. I have no idea how long ago she took the cocaine, but it was long enough for her to go through it."

"And you didn't get more details from her?"

I sighed and looked down at my hands a moment. "You have to understand something. My mother has -- *had* -- been strung out on drugs and booze pretty much since her pimp got his hooks into her. It made it easier for her to be a whore, I guess, if she was flying high. Her abuse got worse over the years, and I'm honestly surprised she hadn't OD'd long before now. In the last five years alone, she came to me for money, claiming someone would hurt her if she didn't get her hands on some cash. Never as much as twenty grand, but it still added up. I gave it to her the first two times. The third time I got suspicious and I followed her. She used it to buy drugs and throw a party for her friends."

"So when she came crying about owing money, you figured she was lying like before," he said. "Understandable. People hooked on drugs, especially the hard stuff, will do anything for their next hit."

"I don't know who she owed the money to, so I have no idea who is coming for me. I'm hoping they can't find me here, but when she gave me your address, I knew I had to come see you. Even if you refused to have anything to do with me, I just wanted to see my dad at least once," I said.

"I'm glad you're here, Pepper." He frowned. "Why did she name you that?"

My lips curved in a smile. "She said that you liked comics and had talked about a few of the superheroes and you'd mentioned a few women. The name Pepper stuck out in her mind I guess."

He rubbed the back of his neck and his cheeks flushed pink. "Uh, yeah. I have a bit of a collection."

He didn't seem like the comic geek type, but who was I to judge? After he paid the check, and I noticed he left a ten-dollar tip on a bill that was less than fifteen dollars, we drove back to the compound. No doubt in my mind he was sweet on Lily. Maybe while I was hanging out I could give him a nudge in her direction. She'd seemed nice enough. The Prospect at the gate let us through and I followed my dad to a small bungalow that was gray with black shutters. It was very sedate compared to some of the other houses we passed, including the sprawling house next door, but I could see Sarge living here.

My dad pulled up into the small carport and I left my bike in the driveway. As I swung my leg over the seat and removed my helmet, I became aware of a figure leaning against the house just to the right of the door. My dad didn't have a light on outside, and the guy had blended with the shadows. He came closer, his gaze locked on me, and I felt my thighs clench when I got a better look. His dark blond hair was clipped short, and he had a neatly trimmed beard. I recognized him just from his hair and overall build. It was the man I'd seen earlier. The one who had made my belly clench, and not in an unpleasant way. Looking into his eyes made my legs feel like jelly. Bedroom eyes, that's what my mother had always called them. If anyone could tempt me to give up my V-card, it was this guy. Just from the way I felt under his gaze, if the man snapped his fingers and told me to bend over, I'd offer myself to him in an instant. It was such an intense feeling that it both excited and frightened me.

"Flicker, why the hell are you lurking outside of my house?" my dad asked him.

My gaze dropped to his vest and I saw his name along with a title stitched there. Treasurer. Since my dad didn't have a title under his name, I figured that meant this guy was someone important. For once, I was wishing I'd paid attention to those biker gang -- or whatever a group of bikers was called -- shows and movies people were always talking about. I was more of a cartoon watcher, though. The classics like Scooby-Doo, the Jetsons, and Droopy Dog. None of the new stuff, unless it was from the Mouse.

"Fenton said there might be trouble with your unexpected guest," Flicker said. He practically undressed me with his eyes, not that it would be all that difficult since I was in head to toe leather that was skintight. As my nipples tightened, I was glad for the extra protection. Didn't stop my cheeks from heating.

"Did he tell you who my guest was?" my dad asked.

"No. You've never been the type to go for the younger ones, Sarge. But I'm more than willing to take her off your hands for the night. Maybe for several nights." He licked his lips. "Possibly even longer. Damn."

I gasped and took a step back as my dad punched Flicker right across the jaw. The Treasurer of the club shook it off and glared at him.

"What the fuck was that shit?" Flicker demanded.

"That's my daughter you're eye fucking, asshole," my dad said, his voice nearly a growl he sounded so pissed.

Flicker jerked to look at me again, then glanced back at Sarge. He looked back and forth between us about a dozen times before he held up his hands and backed up a few steps. The sight of his cock pressing against the front of his jeans had me squeezing my thighs together. I'd never, not even once, desired a man. Why did it have to be this one? What was so special about him?

"I didn't mean any disrespect. I wasn't aware you had a daughter, much less that she was visiting," Flicker said.

"I didn't know either," Sarge said. "Her bitch of a mother kept her from me all these years. She may be in some trouble, Flicker, but I'll discuss it with you tomorrow. Stop by for breakfast?"

The Treasurer, who I was starting to think of as Mr. Drool-worthy Biker God, gave a quick nod and stalked off to the house next door. The Indian Chief Dark Horse parked in his double carport was enough to make me sigh. I'd checked out the new line-up a month ago and knew it had to be brand-new. So, gorgeous and the man had taste when it came to his ride. What more could a girl ask for? I had a feeling that being next door to him would prove challenging. My dad didn't seem to like the idea of his friend being with me, which meant I'd probably need to keep my distance.

Figured the one man who actually made me ache was off-limits. I only hoped *he* got that memo, because I had no doubt that one touch and I'd go up in flames. The man had player written all over him, but it didn't seem to matter to all the parts of my body that were currently humming in appreciation. As I watched him walk off, I had to admit the man had a fine ass.

Chapter Two

Flicker

Sarge had a daughter. A really hot, made-me-hard-in-an-instant, completely off-limits daughter. Fuck my life. I hadn't touched a woman in months. Or more accurately, my dick hadn't cooperated in months. It wasn't that I'd been a monk on purpose. I'd honestly started to worry that I would need those little blue pills to get the job done, but the red-haired siren had pulled off her helmet and got off her bike, and fuck if I hadn't had an instant hard-on. I'd thought the end to my nearly six months of celibacy was at hand, until Sarge had punched me. Any other time, I'd have knocked him on his ass, but the guy had just been defending his kid. Couldn't really get pissed at him over that.

If I hadn't known that Sarge was a dad, I wondered who else in the club hadn't known. When Fenton had said there was a woman at the gate who could be trouble for Sarge and the club, he hadn't said a fucking thing about her being his kid. Either they hadn't discussed that shit where the Prospect could hear it, or he'd just left that part out for some reason. I'd have to address it sooner or later. Fenton had slipped up more than once, but he was a decent guy. He just didn't always think things through. Some of it was probably just his age. Or maybe he was just fucking clueless. Mistakes could get people killed, though, and I knew it couldn't be tolerated.

I heard Sarge's front door slam and I peeked through the side window. His daughter was pulling a backpack off her bike. My dick pulsed in my pants as I watched her hips sway on her way back inside. I stepped back and closed my eyes, trying to think of anything that might help me soften. Road kill. Rotten teeth. Liquefying corpses. I closed my eyes tighter, but it didn't matter. One look at those curves and that sweet round ass and I was a goner.

I grumbled as I stomped through the house and went to the master bedroom. I jerked open the bedside table drawer and grabbed the lube. I nearly tore the zipper on my jeans trying to get my pants undone, and then I was slicking my cock. A groan tore through me as I stroked my shaft, my grip just the right amount of tight. Picturing the hot redhead on her knees, her lips parted as I fucked her mouth, made my balls draw up. I jerked my cock faster and harder until my cum sprayed across the bed. My chest heaved as I stared at my cock and snarled. All this time not getting hard and now the fucking thing wouldn't soften! What the hell?

It was bad enough I was getting off to visions of Sarge's daughter. Something told me only her pouty lips around my dick would be enough to tame the beast inside me right now, or her tight, wet pussy. My cock jerked and twitched. I added more lube, then stroked another one out. Didn't make a damn bit of difference, though. I had a feeling I was going to be hard as fucking steel the rest of the night and into the morning. Good thing I *hadn't* had any of those blue pills I'd thought about getting.

I rolled my head, cracking my neck, then froze as I realized my bedroom blinds were open... and so were the ones in the house next door, and one very sexy lady had just watched me. Her lips were parted, and even from here I could see how hard her nipples were. It was all kinds of wrong, and I was probably going to hell, but I started jerking off again, my gaze locked on the siren next door. She leaned in closer, practically pressing her nose against the window. I stopped, gripping the base of my dick to hold off an orgasm. The woman next door squirmed.

She licked her lips and ran her fingers along the neckline of her tank. When I'd seen her earlier, she'd had on a leather jacket to match her leather pants. Now there was a red tank, and as her fingers dipped lower, tugging the material down, I could see she was braless. Holy fucking shit! I nearly came just from that knowledge, and when it looked like she was flicking her finger across her nipple, I started tugging on my dick again. It only took a moment before I was coming, even harder than the previous two times. She bit her lower lip and cupped her breasts.

That's it, baby. Offer them to me.

Her tank slipped a little lower and I could nearly see her nipples. Her gaze locked with mine again and a red flush crept across her cheeks. She quickly turned her back, then pulled her shirt off. The way her red hair teased across the bare skin of her back made me want to hold onto it as I fucked her from behind. She shimmied out of her leather pants and I knew the red lacy thong underneath would feature in my dreams for a while. She bent over, her ass on display. My mouth watered as I thought about tasting every inch of her.

Sarge was going to geld me if he ever found out about this. His daughter might be fully grown, but that was still his baby that I wanted to fuck. When she removed the thong and I got a glimpse of her bare pussy, I nearly fell to my knees. I'd never hungered for a woman the way I wanted this one. She reached out of view of the window and then pulled on a pair of shorts so tiny I knew her ass would hang out if she bent over again. Then came a white tank. When she was dressed again, she turned to face me.

My cock was still hanging out, though hanging might not be the word since the damn thing was hard again, and I noticed that she seemed to appreciate the sight. With a slight smile, she waved at me, then turned to cross the room. Her bedroom was plunged into darkness, and I couldn't help but wonder if she'd dream about me tonight, because she was damn sure going to be in every dream and fantasy I had for the foreseeable future.

I kept staring out the window, part of me hoping she'd turn the light back on and I'd see more of that playful side. After a while I stripped off my clothes and took a hot shower. Probably should have taken a cold one, but I doubted it would have helped much. Now that my cock seemed to be back in action, it seemed to want to remain at half-mast if not fully hard. If I didn't get myself under control before morning, Sarge wasn't going to be too happy with me. I might be an officer in this club, and he was further down the totem pole, but I was still playing with fire by lusting after the man's daughter. Of course, I could always pull the same shit Venom did. He'd claimed Ridley whether Bull liked it or not.

Ever since my brothers had started pairing off, I'd been admittedly jealous. Seeing how happy they were, it made me want that too. I'd always loved women, the feel and smell of them, how good they felt when you fucked them. But the older I got, the more I wanted just *one* woman. I wanted to fall asleep with her soft curves wrapped in my arms and wake up with her as well. I'd never trust a club slut for that type of thing, but the right woman? Someone like the goddess next door? Yeah, I could see myself keeping her.

Despite the fact I fell into bed right after my shower, sleep wouldn't come. And neither did I, for that matter. I tried to jerk off a few more times, but only ended up frustrated. After the striptease from the siren, my hand just wasn't enough. I'd never looked forward to breakfast more than I did right now.

The sun slowly crept over the horizon. More than once I heard the roar of a Harley starting up. I didn't know where my brothers were going this damn early, and I didn't much care at the moment. There was a certain tease who was weighing heavy on my mind right now. When the display on my phone read seven o'clock, I decided I'd waited long enough. If Sarge and his daughter weren't awake, they would be soon. I put on a fresh pair of boxer briefs and jeans, grabbed a navy tee and my cut. After I'd dressed, I put on my socks and boots, then headed next door. I lifted my hand to knock, but the little temptress opened the door before I had a chance. Her cheeks were pink and she looked up at me with uncertainty and a hint of desire in her eyes.

"I was just cooking," she said. "My dad's not awake yet, but you can come sit and keep me company if you want."

Oh, hell yeah, I wanted to! I nodded and stepped into the house, then quietly shut the door behind me. I followed her into the kitchen and pulled out a chair at the small square table. Her phone was on the counter with music playing at a low enough volume it wouldn't wake Sarge, but it was still loud enough that she shook her ass to the beat. I pressed down on my cock as it lengthened in my pants.

"I'm Pepper," she said. "We didn't really get a chance to officially meet last night."

"Flicker," I said, watching her ass swish side to side when the song changed over.

She picked up an egg and it slipped through her fingers, cracking on the floor at her feet. Pepper bent to pick it up, and that was as much of the torture as I could handle. Her shorts rode up, showing off the lower half of her ass cheeks, perfect globes that made me want to take a bite. I stood and pressed myself against her, placing my hands on her hips. There was only so much temptation a man could take, especially when I'd had a six-month-long dry spell.

I heard her breath hitch and she looked at me over her shoulder, that gorgeous red hair sliding across her face. She didn't seem repulsed, nor did she shove me away, and she didn't stand up, just pressed that ass back against me more. The heat of her pussy rubbed against my cock and I trailed my hands down to the hem of her shorts, then eased my fingers underneath. Her eyes dilated and her lips parted as I brushed a finger across her slit. So. Fucking. Wet.

"I think you want me as much as I want you," I said. "All this cream for me?"

She nodded, her gaze never leaving me. She remained bent over, gripping the counter in front of her, offering up that sweet pussy. I toyed with her, sliding my finger up and down her slit before rubbing her clit. She gasped and pushed back. The little bud hardened as I stroked it. Her body shuddered and I knew she was already close to coming, something that just made me even hotter. Christ! I'd never had a woman come apart so easily. I plunged my finger into her hot, tight channel and it was just enough to send her over the edge. I thrust in and out, letting her ride out her orgasm, and when she was panting and squirming in my arms, I knew that no matter how fucking pissed Sarge would get, I was going to have Pepper in my bed.

"Such a good girl," I murmured, then slid my other hand up under her shirt. Her breasts were bare and her nipple hardened against my palm. I squeezed her breast, not enough to hurt but just the right amount.

She moaned and her pussy got even hotter. I started fucking her with my finger again while I pinched and rolled her nipple. I added a second finger and my cock damn near exploded at how tight she felt. Teasing one nipple, then the other, I slid my fingers in and out of her pussy faster. In a matter of seconds, she was coming again.

"If we were in my house right now," I said, my lips near her ear and my voice low, "I'd put you on the counter and eat out this wet pussy, then I'd bend you over the table and fuck you so good and hard you'd be feeling me for hours."

I slipped my fingers out of her and trailed them up the crack of her ass, then pressed the wet digits against her tight little hole.

"And then I'd take you here. Make you beg me for it."

She was so fucking hot, and so turned on, I wondered if she was going to detonate again in my arms just from the brush of my fingers against that forbidden spot. I tugged on her nipples again while I rubbed her rosette. She trembled in my arms and I wished like hell I could strip her bare and feast on her all day and night.

"That's it, baby. You going to come for me again?" I murmured.

She squirmed and whimpered. I released her nipple and slid that hand down into her shorts, playing with her clit again. I'd barely started rubbing when she came, bucking against me and making the sweetest sounds. If Sarge weren't somewhere in the house, I'd pull her shorts down and fuck her right here and now. I knew I was playing with fire. That the man could walk in anytime. It only made the moment sweeter. I had to wonder if I wanted her so much because I couldn't have her, but then I remembered my body's immediate reaction last night before I'd even known who she was. No, it wasn't the forbidden that tempted me, but it did turn up the heat a bit.

I pulled my hands from her shorts, then pushed her against the counter, shoving her down so her breasts were against it. I glanced over my shoulder and listened intently. Not a sound in the house other than our ragged breathing. I tugged her shorts down, just needing to see her, to feel her without anything between us. Christ! She had the sweetest, roundest ass! I ran my hand over one cheek, then nudged her feet apart so I could see that gorgeous pussy.

She was glistening from how wet she was, and I couldn't resist sliding my fingers back inside of her, watching as she took them. I unfastened my jeans and pulled out my cock, knowing I couldn't have her, not right this moment, but I needed to *feel* her. I removed my fingers and ran my cock the length of her wet slit, bumping her clit with every stroke.

"You make me feel completely out of control," I told her, gripping her hips as I thrust against her. "You want this, don't you? Want my cock?"

She nodded and spread her legs a little more, but her shorts hampered the movement. If at all possible, she got hotter and wetter, and I knew I needed at least a little sample, just enough to get me through until I could really have her. My mind was in a haze of lust and need. I notched my cock at her entrance and pushed inside. The way her body tensed and her eyes went wide made me freeze. As I slid out of her, I looked down and noticed a smear of blood on my shaft. My *bare* shaft. Fuck me. I hadn't taken a woman without a condom since I'd learned how to put on a rubber.

"What the fuck?" I asked, my voice harsher than I'd intended. "You tease the hell out of me, let me finger fuck you and play with your ass, but you're a damn virgin?"

She struggled to get up, but I flattened my hand against her back, holding her still. If she moved too much, she could hurt herself more.

"Dammit, Pepper," I muttered.

Her pussy squeezed the head of my cock and I groaned, my eyes sliding shut a moment. When I opened them, I noticed that she looked a little scared, and a lot embarrassed. I didn't like that look, especially not when it was aimed at me. I'd already crossed several big fucking lines. Might as well keep going, right? I knew I should pull out and at least put on a condom, but the moment would be lost, and quite honestly, I loved the feel of her.

I slowly thrust, loving the tight clasp of her pussy.

"I'm upset that you didn't tell me and I hurt you," I said. "I'm angry that you let me pop your cherry in the middle of your dad's kitchen."

Thrust. Thrust.

"Makes me want to tie you to my bed, paddle your ass until it's red, then give you a proper fucking. Do you have any idea how much I like knowing I'm the only one to feel this incredible pussy?"

Thrust. Thrust. Thrust.

"My dick will be the *only* one you ever have," I said, the words ending with a growl.

Thrust. Thrust.

"God, baby. You feel fucking perfect."

"Flicker, please," she begged. She no longer looked scared, just turned on. "It only hurt for a second, and I…"

"You want to come with my cock inside of you?" I asked.

She nodded.

I reached around the front of her, and started rubbing her clit in fast, tight circles. I'd make her come, then I'd pull out and we'd get our clothing back the way it should be, and I'd try really damn hard not to think about being inside of her. Since she was a virgin, it wasn't likely she was carrying any sexually transmitted diseases. Little late to have that conversation anyway.

"If your daddy comes in and I'm balls-deep inside of you, he's going to lose his shit," I said.

"Don't care," she said. "Just need you. Need this."

I pinched her clit and she came, jamming her hips back against me. Her pussy squeezed me so fucking tight, I nearly blacked out from the pleasure. Without conscious thought, I fucked her hard and fast, slamming into her as she rode out her orgasm and before I could think better of it, I came inside of her. I kept thrusting until every drop of cum had left my balls, and some caveman part of me wanted to shove it deep inside of her.

"Please tell me you're on birth control," I muttered. It wasn't like me not to wear a condom, or to fuck a virgin for that matter. Even when I did wrap my dick, I'd always asked if the woman was clean, but this girl had me so worked up all reasonable thought had left me the second I'd seen her bend over in those tiny shorts.

Hell, the thought of her pregnant with my kid didn't scare me in the least. I wanted it, more than I'd wanted anything. I hadn't even known her name until this morning, but I'd never wanted a woman more than I wanted her. One way or another, she was going to be mine.

Her body locked up and I had my answer.

"I can go get the morning after pill," she muttered.

I tightened my hand on her hip and stroked in and out of her a few more times. I didn't like the thought of killing our possible child. I'd given up on the dream of a woman and kid after one after another of my brothers had fallen in love, and I'd yet to have anyone want forever with me. The way Pepper's pussy clasped me, the scent of her filling my nose, made me feel like the ground was shifting under my feet. I'd told myself for years I didn't want those things anymore, but even then I'd known I was lying, just trying to make myself feel better. The thought of Pepper leaving, of her killing our kid, made me want to do something insane, like lock her away and keep her all to myself. I could tie her to the bed, fuck her until I knew she was carrying my kid, then convince her to stay.

Now that I'd had a taste of her, I wanted more. Even though I'd just unloaded enough cum that it had filled her to the point it was gushing out around my dick, I knew I could go again. And again. And again. As long as the woman under me was Pepper. Bull had once told me that he'd known Darian was meant to be his, even though he'd tried to hold out. Now I understood exactly what he'd meant. I'd been insanely attracted to Pepper from the second I saw her, and now that I'd been balls-deep inside of her, I never wanted to let her go.

"Um, shouldn't you pull out?" she asked, looking at me over her shoulder.

I withdrew from the tight grip of her pussy and she winced a little. I wet some paper towels to clean up her and myself. She really needed to go soak in a hot bath to ease the soreness. She pulled up her shorts and I adjusted my clothes, wishing we were removing them instead.

The home phone rang and Pepper jolted in surprise, looking around. I pointed to the corner of the kitchen and a cordless phone and stand. She picked it up and answered hesitantly. I tried not to pay attention to her conversation, but she seemed familiar enough with the person on the other end that I wanted to know what fucker was calling her here. Did she have a boyfriend where she came from? I'd never been the type to go after a woman who belonged to someone, but Pepper made me want to wrap her up tight and snarl at everyone to back the hell off. It was insane! I was too damn old for this shit.

She hung up the phone and turned to face me. "So that was my dad. It seems he left the house long before you got here. Some personal emergency or something."

Had I seriously been so out of it I hadn't even noticed his bike was missing? Must have been one of the Harleys I heard start up earlier. Fuck. That didn't bode well. This tiny woman had me tied up in knots, and that thought alone made me think of tying *her* up in knots -- to my bed. And now I was fucking hard again. Perfect.

I'd never wanted a woman as much as I wanted Pepper. I had this insane urge to bare my teeth at any other guy who came near her to warn them away. To mark her, claim her. Fuck a baby into her so she'd have to stay with me.

Yep. I'd fucking lost my damn mind.

She looked around the kitchen, then her gaze locked with mine. "You have breakfast stuff at your house? I don't think I can salvage this mess."

The skillet on the stove had smoke coming from it and whatever meat she'd been cooking looked charred. Until this moment, the smell hadn't registered with me. Fuck. The house could have burned down around us and I was so focused on how good she'd felt we probably would have burned alive. What the hell was this little pixie doing to me?

"Yeah, I do."

"Just let me dump this stuff and put the dishes in the sink, then I'll come cook at your place."

I ran a hand through my hair and watched her buzz around the kitchen. Had the pixie just invited herself over? I'd had women try to get into my house before, but for the first time, I didn't mind the thought of a woman I'd fucked being under my roof. Granted, I'd mostly been with club sluts the last decade or so, and no one wanted forever with those women. But as I thought about having Pepper in my home, I hoped Sarge stayed away for a while. Maybe I could convince her to go for round two. Maybe after that, I could think logically again, have worked her out of my system enough I didn't want to do something stupid.

Pepper had me wondering if maybe the right woman just hadn't come along until now. Yeah, Sarge wasn't going to be the least bit happy. Too fucking bad. I suddenly understood exactly why Venom had pissed off Bull and taken Ridley to his house, then fucked her until she'd been carrying his kid. Because I wanted to do the same fucking thing to Pepper. Tie her to my bed and fuck a baby into her.

I was in so much fucking trouble.

Chapter Three

Pepper

What the hell was I doing? I'd saved my virginity all these years, not wanting to be like my mother. Then what happened? Some good-looking biker jerks off where I can see him and I'm suddenly craving his cock? Hell, even before that I'd wanted him. What the fuck? I'd always sworn I wasn't that type of girl, the kind to give it up to just anyone, but I'd let him do whatever he wanted while we stood in my dad's kitchen, knowing Sarge could walk in at any moment. Or at least thinking he could, since I hadn't known he wasn't home. If anything, it had given me a secret thrill that we might get caught. Maybe the apple really didn't fall far from the tree and I was my mother's daughter after all. I'd given up my V-card without a second thought, just letting Flicker take what he wanted, and I'd had to fight not to beg him for more.

I'd cleaned up my dad's kitchen, then made omelets at Flicker's house. The meal had been good, though quiet as he watched me without saying a word. Now the dishes were washed and in the drying rack, because for some reason this man didn't believe in owning a dishwasher. My stomach fluttered and I pressed a hand to my belly. It had been incredibly stupid to have unprotected sex. I had no idea if he was clean or if he fucked everything that moved. Not to mention I could be pregnant. I didn't think I was since I'd just had my period, and while I hadn't finished high school or ever taken Sex Ed, I thought I remembered reading somewhere that it was before my period that I was most fertile. I could hope anyway. If it was afterward, then I was in trouble. I doubted this guy wanted to play the part of doting daddy to a kid he hadn't planned.

Of course, my dad seemed upset that he hadn't had that chance with me. So maybe I was wrong. Flicker could be like Sarge and would be more than willing to take on the responsibility of a child. Or he could kick my ass to the curb and tell me to fuck off. Only time would tell, since he didn't seem to be in any hurry to go to a pharmacy. I'd mentioned the pill again while we ate, and he hadn't said a word. I didn't know if he was avoiding the issue and pretending we didn't have a potential problem, or what the hell was going through his mind.

Flicker moved up behind me, his body heat pressing against me and his hand settling at my waist. My breath caught and I automatically leaned into him. I didn't know what was wrong with me! I'd never been like this before, and it was scaring me a little that this man could completely own me with just a touch. I could feel the length of his hard cock pressing against me, and my clit pulsed as I remembered how it had felt to have him inside me. There was a slight twinge between my legs since he'd taken my virginity, but I hadn't lied to him earlier. It had surprised me and there'd been a quick flash of pain, but it hadn't hurt nearly as much as I'd thought it might.

"Seeing you in these shorts is making me crazy," he said. "Especially knowing what's under them. You were very naughty last night."

"Didn't see the point in changing since you've had me partially naked."

"You were wearing a thong last night until right before you shut off the lights."

I bit my lip. "I took it off because I was going to bed."

He turned me to face him, then crowded me against the counter again. "And why did you need to take it off?"

"Because I ached from wanting you, and every time I shifted, the material rubbed against me. It made me hurt for you even more," I answered honestly.

"You don't speak or act like any virgin I've ever known."

"Yeah, well, I guess having a whore for a mother will do that to a woman. I walked in on her having sex, sucking men off, being part of an orgy more times than I care to think about. Sex was never a mystery for me."

He backed up a little. "Is that why you were a virgin? Were you saving yourself for someone special?"

"I guess I was worried I'd end up like her. The boys at school always thought I'd follow that path and considered me a sure thing. I dropped out when I was sixteen, but I worked hard to get my G.E.D. and went to cooking school."

He took three more steps back and released me. I wanted to reach for him, to tell him how much I'd liked having his hands on me, but there was a warning going off in my head. *Is this how Mom started down her path?* I'd always thought she took that step out of desperation, but what if that wasn't it at all? What if she'd just enjoyed sex, liked being touched, and it had snowballed? Plenty of women had sex without becoming prostitutes, I knew that. But what if I was exactly like my mother?

"I should leave," I said, looking away. "I'll find a pharmacy so you won't have to worry about me turning up on your doorstep in a month or so demanding money or some shit."

"How old are you, Pepper?" he asked. His tone was strained, almost as if he were in pain.

I blinked at him. "Is that why you backed off? You're worried I'm underage?"

"Are you?" he demanded.

"Not hardly. I'm twenty-two. Little late if I was still under eighteen seeing as how you've already fucked me. Maybe I'm just like my mom after all."

He growled and advanced on me. Before I could run, he tossed me over his shoulder and stomped off to the back of the house. I had an excellent view of his denim-clad ass and an idea that we were heading toward his bedroom. He kicked the door shut, then slid me off his shoulder. The second he sat on the edge of the bed, he jerked me across his lap, the quick motion making me dizzy as I stared at the floor.

Flicker yanked my shorts down my legs, then pulled them all the way off. I felt the cool air caress my bare ass and pussy, then his hand came down with a hard smack. I yelped and struggled, but he placed an arm across my lower back, holding me still. He spanked me half a dozen times, my ass feeling like it was on fire.

"What the hell, Flicker?" I demanded.

His hand cracked against my ass again. "Quiet."

"But I..."

He spanked me twice more and I clamped my lips shut. He rubbed my sore ass cheek and the burn seemed to spread.

"Such a pretty red," he said. "I knew your ass would look spectacular after a few spankings."

He brought his hand down on the other cheek and I yelped again, but I'd learned that fighting was futile. If I were truly in distress, he would probably stop. While it hurt, it also was starting to make my pussy wet. I'd heard of women who got off on being spanked, but I never thought I'd be one of them. His hand cracked against my poor abused ass until both cheeks were burning. He wedged a hand between my thighs, forcing me to spread my legs.

"Mmm. Just like I thought. My naughty girl likes being spanked," he said. He teased my slit before lightly brushing his fingers against my clit. I jerked in his grasp and moaned as pleasure shot through me. My nipples hardened and chafed against the material of my tank.

He removed his arm and worked my shirt over my head, almost as if he'd heard my thoughts.

"Now that's a sight I could grow used to," he said.

I glanced at him and saw he was staring across the room. When I turned my head, I gasped. There was a large mirror on the back of his door, showing me sprawled across his lap, my breasts swinging free, my red ass under his palm.

"Arms behind your back, Pepper."

I slowly did as he said, crossing my wrists. He slid open the bedside table drawer, and then I felt him tying something around my hands. I tugged and realized I couldn't break free. Then he gathered my hair and pulled it over to the side, giving him an unhindered view in the mirror. He spanked me several more times, pausing between swats to tease my pussy.

"You came so easily at your dad's house. I bet if I used a vibrator on you that you'd explode," he said.

He reached down and I watched as he slid a plastic container from under his bed. He popped the lid and pulled out a small white box. I couldn't see what was inside, but after his words just now, I had a feeling he was about to tease the hell out of me. At least it seemed to be an unopened package. I heard him rip open the box, then he grabbed a package of batteries from the same tub. Within seconds, I heard the toy being whirring and I fought back a moan. I'd never used one before, but I'd heard they could feel amazing.

"Let's see how fast you come apart," he said.

"Wait. Why do you have brand-new vibrators under your bed?" I asked.

"Waiting for the right woman to come along so I could use them."

He parted the lips of my pussy and then placed the toy directly on my clit. I screamed and bucked from the intensity. He turned up the speed and I started coming.

"Oh, God! Flicker!"

"That's it, baby. Come for me."

I screamed and thrashed on his lap as I came, my orgasm seeming to last forever. He was relentless, rubbing the toy against my clit.

"Don't stop now, Pepper," he said.

It felt like one orgasm bled into another, until I'd come so hard and so long I felt wrung out. My clit was oversensitive and when he shut off the toy and set it aside, I wanted to weep in both joy and frustration. Despite having come so much, I still felt empty and wanted more.

He lifted me, then stood. Flicker placed me in the center of the bed, my ass in the air and my face pressed to the bedding.

"I'm going to hell," he muttered. "But what a fucking ride."

Before I could ask what he meant, he thrust deep and hard, filling me to the point of pain. I whimpered as he drove into me. On the next stroke, he seemed to hit the perfect spot and I knew I was seconds away from coming again. Could a woman die from too many orgasms? I was starting to think I might. He fucked me hard and fast, and as my pussy gushed and I screamed out my release, I felt him pounding his cum into me, the wet heat filling me up.

His cock twitched as he stilled, buried inside of me. He'd gripped my hips so tight I wondered if I'd have fingerprints there for days. The thought made me shiver, and not in a bad way. I wanted that. To be marked by him. Maybe there really was something wrong with me. I'd read a few romance novels before, mostly to see what the fuss was about, but it had seemed laughable at the time. Women like me never got a happy ever after, and yet I'd found a lot of books where the heroine had faced similar situations to my fucked-up life. I didn't know a single person from Mom's world who had ever escaped. Every single person at the trailer park was still there, those who hadn't died.

He pulled out, then unfastened my wrists. I straightened my legs and collapsed onto the bed with a groan. Flicker set the toy on the bedside table, then stretched out next to me. My hair shifted and I opened my eyes. His hand lingered near my face, and he lightly stroked my cheek.

"I shouldn't have done that," he said, "but you pissed me off."

"How did I make you mad?" I asked.

"You made it sound like you were a whore for letting me take your virginity. I shouldn't have spanked you, or tied you up, but I can't regret it. Watching you come so damn hard before I'd even gotten inside of you was a big fucking turn-on. And the way you squirted when I was balls-deep in you? Fuck! I want that every fucking time."

I smiled faintly. "You make it sound like it's going to happen again."

He leaned in closer, his gaze unblinking. "Because it is."

"You came inside me again without a condom. I really do need to head to the pharmacy. And if you're out of condoms and plan on doing this again, I should probably get a box while I'm there."

"No," he said, his voice firm.

I leaned up on an elbow, my brow furrowed. "What do you mean by no?"

He moved in closer and kissed me, his lips soft and teasing. I felt his hand sliding down my arm to my wrist. He lifted my arm slowly, inching it toward the headboard, but I gaped at him in surprise when I heard the click of handcuffs. I looked up to where he'd shackled me to his bed.

"What the actual fuck?" I asked.

"Keep sassing me and I'll spank your ass again."

"Why am I handcuffed to your bed?"

"Because I've decided to take matters into my own hands. You seem determined to get away, to kill our possible baby, and I've decided I like the idea of you being pregnant."

I blinked. Then blinked again. I must have hallucinated because he couldn't have just said what I thought he'd said. Men didn't really think that way, did they? Especially the type who looked like they had a one-night stand every day of the week.

"What?" I asked stupidly.

He placed a hand on my belly. "I think you'd look cute and sexy with your belly swollen with my kid."

"You're deranged. You know that, right? You can't just fuck me and decide to keep me. My dad is going to look for me. There are men who will..." I clamped my mouth shut, but not before he tensed and his gaze darkened and turned intensely scary.

"Men who will what?"

I shook my head, but he gripped my hair, tipping my head back. There was a hint of pain, but not enough that I was scared of him.

"You're going to finish that sentence, Pepper, or so help me God I will torture it out of you."

My heart kicked in my chest at the word torture. I hadn't thought he would hurt me, but it seemed I'd been very wrong. And now I was trapped and no one knew where I was. Oh, God. This wasn't good.

"Don't hurt me," I whispered, then wanted to wince at how pathetic I sounded.

"Hurt..." He snorted and his grip tightened on my hair even more. "Baby girl. I won't be hurting you. I will, however, make you come so much and so hard that your pussy will ache for days. I will fuck you until there isn't a drop of cum left in my balls, and you better fucking believe every bit of it is going inside you."

"I don't understand," I said.

He sighed and released me, then lay flat on his back, staring up at the ceiling. I started to think he wouldn't speak again, that I would be left wondering what the hell was going on and whether or not I was trapped with a psycho.

"What's going on?" I asked, tugging at the cuff.

"I've decided I'm keeping you," he said, refusing to look at me.

"Like a pet? Or is this one of those 'it puts the lotion on' type things? Because I'm not down for that."

He smiled faintly and turned to face me. "No, honey. Not in that kind of way. I've felt this insane connection to you from the second I saw you last night. Then that little incident when I was jerking off in here? I knew I wanted you, had to have you, no matter who it pissed off. I hadn't counted on fucking you bare, or coming inside of you. The thought of you carrying my kid? Makes me feel a little like a caveman."

"So keep me as in..." I trailed off, still not quite getting where he was going with this.

"I want you to be mine," he said softly. "My woman. It's completely insane, and I know that. Some part of me realizes this is one hundred percent nuts, but I've never wanted anyone the way I want you."

I didn't know what to say to that. I'd had plenty of guys want in my pants, thinking I was easy. But he'd gotten mad when I'd compared myself to my mother. If he didn't think I was acting like a whore, and he wanted to keep me, then... Nope, still totally confused.

"You can't just chain me to your bed, Flicker. I came to my dad for help. There are men looking for me, and they aren't the nice kind," I said.

"Your dad mentioned some trouble."

"My mom had a tendency to steal stuff. In this case, she stole twenty grand worth of drugs. She killed herself, intentional overdose, and now they want the drugs or the money from me, with interest."

He tugged on a lock of my hair. "Then it seems chaining you to my bed isn't so insane after all. If you're here, then they can't get to you."

I gaped at him, my mouth opening and shutting several times as I grasped for something -- anything -- to say to that. He didn't sound like a rational person right now, and yet I had to admit there was a small part of me that thrilled at the idea of belonging to him, of someone wanting me enough to keep me forever. Even my mother hadn't wanted me, so I'd never thought I'd have anyone in my life. Now I had my dad, and it seemed the sexy beast in bed with me didn't want to let me go.

Flicker ran a hand down his face and sighed. "Pepper, being Sarge's daughter means this club will protect you, whatever the cost. You don't have to be mine in order for that to happen, but I'm not letting you go."

I tugged on the cuffs again.

He gazed down at me, his eyes going soft and tender for a moment. "God, you're beautiful."

"Flicker…"

He shook his head. "Don't call me that. Not when we're together, alone. Especially not when we're in bed together."

"Then what do I call you?"

"My name is Daniel. My sister calls me Danny."

"You seem a little too intense to be a Danny," I said, smiling a little. "But I can see Daniel suiting you, or maybe even Dan."

"You can call me whatever you want, baby girl, as long as it's not Flicker. Unless we're around my brothers."

"So getting to use your real name is an honor of some sort?" I asked.

He nodded. "It's reserved for my blood family… and for the woman I want to keep. That would be you, in case you're confused."

"You're certifiable. You can't just take one look at a woman and decide you're going to hang onto her forever," I said. "Life doesn't work that way."

"Around here it does," he said. "We play by a different set of rules, baby. If I want you handcuffed to my bed, there isn't a damn thing anyone can do about it. Not even your daddy."

"Why?" I asked softly. "Why me?"

He rolled us so that I lay under him, his cock already hard and nudging my entrance. "I've been celibate for six months. Even though we haven't had the discussion, I'm clean. I'd never put you in jeopardy like that. Getting you pregnant is another matter. I want that, more than I've ever wanted anything. A brother once told me that he'd felt an instant connection to the woman he claimed and later married. I hadn't understood what he meant, until you. I knew I wanted you from the moment you pulled off your helmet last night and all that red hair came tumbling down. But it wasn't until I'd fucked you, saw your virgin's blood smeared on my cock, that I realized I wasn't going to let you go."

I reached up and placed my palm against his cheek. Flicker pressed closer to my hand, his eyes sliding shut a moment, and something about the gesture told me that maybe he needed someone as much as I did. Maybe I wasn't the only one who'd felt alone and unwanted all these years. He mentioned a sister, and she likely loved him, which meant he had more than I'd ever had. But it didn't mean there wasn't still a big gaping hole inside of him that he wanted to fill, and just maybe he felt I was the way to do that.

Oddly, that made me feel better about the situation, like we both had something in common after all. I'd always been the poor girl, the whore's daughter. When Flicker looked at me, I felt like a desirable woman, someone worth keeping, worth fighting for. It was a feeling I never wanted to let go.

"Maybe I want to keep you too," I said.

He grinned, then thrust deep, his cock filling me. "I think we should seal it with a kiss."

I snorted. "That's the wrong set of lips, and you don't feel like you're kissing me."

"All in good time, baby. All in good time."

Every stroke of his cock had me wanting to beg for more. He fucked me for what felt like hours, until we were both sated and breathless. At some point, he unlatched the handcuff, and I now lay curled against him, my hand over his heart. We still had to discuss the reason I'd come to the Dixie Reapers to begin with, but for now, I just wanted to savor the moment. To feel wanted. Loved.

His arm tightened around me, and I heard him whisper, "I'm keeping you."

A smile curved my lips as I closed my eyes and let sleep claim me.

Chapter Four

Flicker

It sounded like someone was trying to break down the front door and I groaned as I slid out from under Pepper. I grabbed my jeans off the floor and pulled them on, then went to see what the fucking emergency was. I ran a hand through my hair and cracked my neck before I pulled open the door, then wished I hadn't bothered.

"Where's Pepper?" Sarge demanded. "Her bike is still in my driveway, but I can't find her anywhere."

"She's safe," I said.

"How the fuck can you be sure of that?" he asked.

"Because I…"

My words froze as I felt small hands slide around my waist. I glanced behind me to see Pepper in my shirt, her hair a tangled mess. Yeah, no way her daddy wouldn't be able to tell she'd been fucked good and hard.

"Everyone's too loud," she muttered and pressed tighter to me.

"Pepper?" Sarge asked, shoving at me. I stumbled back a step, reaching behind me to wrap an arm around Pepper to keep her upright. "You asshole!"

Sarge looked beyond furious as he faced me.

"How long was I gone before you decided to take advantage of her?" he asked. "She's a kid! *My* kid!"

"She's an adult, Sarge. A woman."

"You don't know what she's been through," Sarge said. "She's vulnerable. I needed you to help me protect her."

Pepper's hands tightened on my waist a moment, then she stepped out from behind me.

"I'm sorry," she said.

"You have nothing to be sorry about," Sarge said.

"I shouldn't have come here. I wanted to meet you, and Mom thought you could help me, but I'm just causing problems."

"No," I said harshly, turning and pulling her into my arms. "Don't you dare fucking say that. This isn't your fault."

"What's going on with you two?" Sarge asked, sounding more resigned than angry at the moment.

"I'm keeping her," I said. "I don't give a fuck if you like it or not."

"Christ," Sarge muttered and stalked off only to come right back. "Really? All these years, all the woman available, and you pick my daughter?"

"I haven't been with a woman in six months," I said. "She's the only one I've wanted in all that time. And before you ask, yes, I meant it when I said I was keeping her. Pepper isn't just a quick fuck."

"And you're all right with that?" he asked Pepper.

She glanced at me, then gave her dad a nod. "I am. I think he's crazy, but I have to admit I feel the same way. Even if it's completely irrational."

I glared at Sarge. "If you were so fucking worried about her, why did you leave her alone? Where were you?"

"There was an… issue," Sarge said.

"The kind that will come back on the club?" I asked.

"No. It was personal and has nothing to do with the Dixie Reapers."

"You need to tell Torch about Pepper and what's going on. I'm sure he'll call Church. For now, I'm going to bring Pepper's things over here, including her bike, and then we're going to get cleaned up and have a bite to eat. Better yet, don't call him for another hour."

"You don't have much in your kitchen," Pepper said. "Neither do you, Dad."

Sarge snorted. "Fine. You two go shower, and I'm going to try really fucking hard not to think about you showering together, and I'll bring Pepper's bag over here. Then I'll go grab some Chinese takeout for us."

"Um." Pepper bit her lip. "I can't eat Chinese food. I love Japanese, though."

"No Chinese?" I asked.

She shook her head. "Something about the way it's cooked makes me sick. I've tried every Chinese place in the Las Vegas area and with every last one I was sick for hours after eating. I usually order Japanese hibachi steak and shrimp with rice."

"Then that's what I'll get for you," Sarge said, smiling a little. Then he glared at me. "And you'll eat whatever the fuck I bring you."

I arched a brow, but now wasn't the time to put him in his place. Sarge had a right to be angry. I'd claimed his daughter, taken her virginity, and I knew it would take him a while to be okay with that.

"Be nice, Dad," Pepper said. "It's not his fault. You make it sound like I had no part in this."

"You didn't," he said. "You're my baby, even if I didn't know about you until yesterday. No way you'd have willingly let him defile you."

She snickered and I rolled my eyes.

"What the fuck ever, Sarge. Get the hell out of here," I said.

He gave me a one-finger salute, then left, slamming the door behind him. Pepper sagged against me.

"Well, that went well," she muttered.

"Could have been worse," I said. "I can understand why he's upset. There's the age difference between us, and even if he didn't know you were a virgin, I'm sure he was telling himself you were still pure as the driven snow."

"You don't look that old," she said.

"I'm fifty-two," I said.

Her eyes went wide and her jaw dropped. "No way in hell! You don't look older than your late thirties. *Maybe* early forties, but that's pushing it."

"I'm thirty years older than you, sweetheart. That's part of what has your dad so upset. I'm older than him. But I can promise you one thing. I will protect you, care for you, and give you every part of me that I'm able to give. You being here with me? It's the greatest gift I've ever received," I said.

She blinked quickly and I realized she was close to crying.

"No one's ever said something so sweet to me before," she said. "My own mother didn't want me. I never thought anyone would."

"Come on, baby. Let's get cleaned up and we'll eat when your dad gets here with the food. I have a feeling it's going to be a long-ass day."

I herded her back to the master bedroom. I shut the door, and locked it, before leading her into the bathroom. I'd always liked my creature comforts, and I'd put a lot of time into the planning and building of my house. Including the huge bathroom with the extralarge shower. There were three showerheads in the glassed-in enclosure, and while I'd never used the jetted tub, I had a feeling Pepper would like it. The water never took long to heat, and soon steam was billowing out of the shower.

As much as I wanted to linger and take my time with Pepper, I knew that there would be other nights and mornings for us. Right now, we needed to make sure she stayed safe and out of the hands of whoever was after her. We washed quickly and I shut off the water, then handed her a towel. While she dried off, I went to the bedroom door and opened it a crack. Her bag was in the hall within arm's reach, so I grabbed it and set it down on the bed. She didn't seem to have much in there and I wondered if I should take her shopping today.

She came out of the bathroom, her hair wrapped in a towel and the rest of her completely bare. I couldn't help but stare as she came closer. She really was gorgeous, but it was more than just her looks. I'd loved the daring side I'd seen last night during her little striptease, I loved how she begged for more when I fucked her, and I'd really liked holding her in my arms. We honestly didn't know a damn thing about each other, but a lifetime together would fix that. I just knew in my gut that she was meant to be mine.

"You're staring," she said as she pulled out a thong and a bra from her bag.

I peered inside at the contents and saw she only had about three days' worth of clothes in there. I also noticed the red thong and black leather pants from yesterday were shoved inside as well.

"Do you need to wash any of this stuff?" I asked, pointing at her bag.

"You actually have a washer and dryer?"

"Why wouldn't I?" I asked.

"Well, you don't have a dishwasher."

"Because I've only ever had to cook for one. I don't exactly make a lot of dirty dishes. But I will be happy to install one for you. You'd just lose some cabinet space in the kitchen."

She paused in the middle of dressing and looked over at me. "*I'll* lose cabinet space?"

"I just meant since you'll be living here too and you seemed to know your way around the kitchen..." I waved a hand. "I wasn't trying to make a sexist comment."

"You really expect me to just move in, don't you?" she asked. "I'd thought maybe after you'd slept on it you might change your mind."

"Did you not hear me tell your dad that you were mine?"

"Well, yeah, but..." She shrugged a shoulder.

"Baby, you're mine, which means this is your home. If you want a dishwasher, I'll install one. You want the walls a different color, then I'll paint them. You hate the furniture, we'll buy new stuff. I want you to be comfortable here."

"Daniel, this is the nicest house I've ever been in, much less called home. You don't have to change anything for me."

I gripped her hip and tugged her closer. Tipping her chin up, I pressed my lips to hers in a quick kiss.

"You're important to me, Pepper. I just want you to be happy here, happy with me. Whatever you need, I don't want you to hesitate to ask for it."

She nodded and I released her so we could both dress. I grabbed my cell phone and saw a missed text from Torch.

Church in twenty.

Hell. That was nearly fifteen minutes ago. So much for Sarge giving me an hour. Probably payback for screwing his daughter. It also meant I didn't have time to stop and eat, or to make sure Pepper had food. After I finished pulling on my clothes and boots, I went to the kitchen, then came to a stop when I saw the plastic sack on the table. I pulled out the two containers and saw the fucker had gotten us the same thing, which was fine with me. I made sure there were utensils in the bag, then waited for Pepper to finish getting ready.

We walked to the clubhouse, and I made sure she had everything she needed, and let the Prospect behind the bar know that she was mine and to treat her accordingly. Diego was a good guy and I had no doubt he'd be patching in soon. Once we made him and King official brothers, we'd have to find some fresh meat to do the grunt work. Preferably guys who could actually get the job done and have a future here. I was sick of problems when it came to the Prospects.

I carried my food and a beer into Church, only getting a raised brow from Torch as I took my seat. I flipped off Sarge who only grinned. I dug into my food, admitting it was pretty fucking fantastic. I'd have to add it to the list of places I frequented more often, especially if Pepper liked this stuff.

"So, it seems Sarge and our Treasurer both have some news for us," Torch says. "Sarge, bring us up to speed."

The man nodded and cleared his throat. "A woman showed up at the gates last night. It turns out I have a kid. Well, a grown-ass adult kid at any rate. Pepper is twenty-two and I met her mom in Vegas. I found out that her mother lied to me about her age and she was a minor when we were together. She never contacted me about being pregnant or at any time during Pepper's life."

"So how did this Pepper find you?" Venom asked. "Are you sure she's your daughter?"

I snorted. "Looks too much like him, just a much prettier version."

Sarge narrowed his eyes at me. "Anyway, she's in some trouble. To give you the low-down dirty version, her mom became a prostitute and got hooked on drugs. She purposely overdosed and left a note for Pepper. The whore ripped off twenty thousand in drugs, and now those men want the drugs or the cash from Pepper. She obviously doesn't have either since it seems her mother used it to party."

"And what does any of this have to do with Flicker?" Wire asked.

"She's mine," I said. "I've claimed Pepper."

"Fucking hell," Venom muttered. "I guess we might as well throw the rule book out the window when it comes to women. None of these fuckers know how to go through the proper channels for claiming an old lady."

"Do we need to revisit the past?" Bull asked with a pointed look.

"Enough!" Torch sent a glare around the table. "Every last one of you knows how much Flicker has wanted a wife and kids. If he wants Pepper, and she's agreeable, then I don't have a problem with it."

"Where is she now?" Tank asked.

"In the clubhouse. I set her up at a table with her lunch and asked Diego to get her anything she needs while we're in here," I said.

"We need to talk to her," Torch said. "I need to know exactly who is after her and how likely it is they'll show up here."

"I'll get her," Sarge said.

"Wait. Can you give her another five or ten minutes to finish eating?" I asked. "There's not really space in here for her to sit down with her food."

"Fine," Torch said, but his lips twitched in amusement. "Ten minutes, then we'll bring her in to find out what's going on. Until then, any other business we need to discuss?"

"It's about time to patch in King and Diego. Any leads on some new prospects to take their place?" I asked.

"Just those two?" Tex asked. "Not Calder or Fenton?"

"Not sure those two have what it takes," I said, "but obviously we'd have to vote."

"There are a few guys from my old neighborhood who are looking for a way out. They've asked me before about coming to the club and seeing if this might a good fit," Saint said. "I can vouch for one of them. The other two I only know by reputation."

"Tell them to stop by next week. I'll clear my schedule Tuesday morning," Torch said. "After I get a feel for them and what they bring to the table, we can discuss letting them prospect for the club."

I finished my food and stood. Sarge glared as I left Church and went to get Pepper. She'd shoved her carton of food across the table, only half-eaten, and her jaw was tight. I glanced at Diego for some clue, and he looked ticked-off. What the fuck happened? I wasn't in Church that long.

I knelt next to Pepper's chair and reached up to tug on her hair. "Sweetheart, what's that fierce look for?"

I heard shuffling steps from the back of the clubhouse and looked in that direction. Calder was wincing with every step he took, grabbing his balls.

"Your handiwork?" I asked Pepper.

She shrugged and it was answer enough for me. I stood and faced the Prospect.

"Something you want to tell me, boy?" I asked, my voice harsh and demanding.

"I didn't know she was taken," he said.

"I told you not to fuck with her," Diego said.

"What *exactly* did you do?" I asked Calder.

"He grabbed my boob, squeezed it hard enough it still fucking hurts, and said if I was extra good he'd let me suck him off," Pepper said. It sounded like she was spitting the words through clenched teeth and I glanced at her. It looked like she'd clamped her jaw so tight her teeth might crack.

"I didn't know she was taken," Calder said again, his voice more of a whine.

"You were told to keep your hands off her," I said. "I hope she twisted your nuts hard enough you have to keep your dick in your pants for weeks. We'll discuss this more later. Get the fuck out of my sight."

Calder gave a nod and shuffled out of the clubhouse. I focused on Pepper again, reaching out to stroke her hair. If we weren't in the middle of Church, I'd have ripped his fucking arm off and beat him with it. I was pissed as fuck that he'd touched Pepper and had even hurt her. That shit didn't fly around here.

"Come here, baby," I said, tugging her to her feet. I led her down the hall and into the bathroom. I shut the door and lifted her shirt, then tried not to scare her with how fucking livid I was. She already had bruises forming in the shape of fingers, the tips peeking over the top of her bra. That fucker was dead.

"Is it going to be like this if I stay here?" she asked. "Will everyone think they can have a piece of me?"

"No! Fuck, no! I'm getting Zipper to ink you after Church is over."

"Ink me?" she asked.

"It's a property stamp. You'll be tattooed with *Property of Flicker* so no one here will dare lay a hand on you. Other clubs will realize you're important when you wear a property cut, and if they're smart, they'll protect you and keep their fucking hands off. A few of the ladies have gotten their property stamp on their backs, but most prefer their arms."

"Is this your version of peeing on me?" she asked, her eyebrow arched.

"Smartass," I muttered, but I couldn't deny she was a little bit right. "Torch, the President, wants you in Church with us. He needs to hear from you about the men in Vegas. And I'm going to tell him what Calder just pulled. You're mine, baby, and *no one* is going to fuck with you. Not unless they want me to bury their ass."

She smiled faintly. "So fierce. It's sexy hearing you say stuff like that."

I traced her nose with mine. "Then wait until you hear all the things I plan to say when we're home again."

I pulled her shirt down and led her to the double doors, pausing just outside. I felt her hand tremble a little and knew she was nervous. I gave it a squeeze and then shoved the doors open, tugging her inside behind me. Everyone stared, and Sarge rose from his seat. I wasn't about to let Pepper sit with him, not after I'd publicly claimed her. I could feel his gaze as I led her around to my seat, and then I pulled her down onto my lap.

"Everyone, this is Pepper," I said. "She doesn't really know how things work around here yet, but I'm sure the other ladies will help her get up to speed."

Venom nodded. "Once Ridley hears you've claimed someone, she'll be on your doorstep."

"As long as she doesn't have your kids in tow, I'm perfectly fine with that," I said.

"What's wrong with his kids?" Pepper whispered, but those closest heard her and snickered.

"They're little demons," I said.

"Just wait," Venom said. "You'll end up being a daddy before long, and if you have a daughter, she could end up with Dawson."

I narrowed my eyes. "That's not fucking funny."

Venom's daughters were little hellions, but his son? Holy shit! The kid looked like a sweet cherub, but there were horns hiding under all that blond hair. He was worse than the girls, and I honestly hadn't thought that was possible. He was only a year and a half, but the boy was something else. The only kid I knew of who could be worse was Havoc's daughter over at Devil's Boneyard. That little shit had even Cinder backing away.

"My name is Torch," the Pres said. "I run this club, and I consider your dad to be part of my family, which means you are too. I need to know about the men you think may be coming for you. The more you can tell me, the better prepared we'll be. Not just to keep you safe, but to ensure the women and kids here aren't in danger either."

"Are there a lot of them?" Pepper asked. "Women and kids?"

Torch looked around the room before his gaze settled on Pepper again. "Excluding you and Flicker, there are eight families inside the compound, and Cowboy lives on a ranch nearby with his wife and kids."

"I want her inked after Church," I said. "There was an issue with Calder not keeping his hands to himself, and I want to make damn sure it doesn't happen again. Pepper is mine and she will damn sure get the respect that goes with that position."

Venom grinned. "And how do you feel about that, Pepper? Getting marked as property."

The woman in my lap snorted. "I asked if he was trying to pee on me."

The table erupted in laughter and I tightened my hold on her. Good thing my brothers saw the humor in her statement. There was a time she might not have received that reaction, but the club had changed over the years. It had started when Ridley came back to us, seeking Bull when she was escaping from her mom and stepdad. Then Torch had claimed Isabella, and one by one, so many others had fallen for someone. Now the full-out parties at the clubhouse weren't the same. Women still came by on Friday and Saturday nights, and the single members and all the Prospects hung out and partied. Well, maybe not all of the single members. I hadn't been to a party in months, and I knew that Sarge hadn't either. The big draw these days were family times when we got together to celebrate birthdays or holidays. Jesus, maybe we were getting old.

"I'd be happy to ink her," Zipper said from down the table. "We can meet in my studio when we're finished."

I gave him a nod and waited for Torch to get Pepper back on track. She'd already talked to both me and Sarge about her mom and the men who wanted their money. But it almost seemed like she was hesitant to speak of it now. Her hands twisted in her lap, her gaze darted around the room, and she was too eager to not only answer questions about anything else, but then asked some in return. It was almost like she was stalling.

"The men, Pepper," Torch said. "Who are they and what do they want?"

She licked her lips and fidgeted. "My mom stole something from them. Or more accurately, from their boss. They told her they wanted their drugs back or the twenty grand the cocaine was worth, and she didn't have either."

"What the fuck did she do with twenty grand worth of coke?" Venom asked.

"Snorted it most likely," Pepper said. "She was known for buying drugs and throwing wild parties. Orgies might be a better description."

The men looked at Sarge who held up his hands.

"She wasn't into all that shit when I knew her," Sarge said. "You know I'd have never touched her."

Pepper twitched and I tightened my hold on her, trying to give her some sort of comfort and remind her that she wasn't alone. She settled against me and I felt her breathe a little easier.

"And your mom can't give them the drugs for some reason, so she sent them after you?" Tank asked. "Because I'm not tracking where this is going. How did you get involved?"

I could see the questions in Tank's eyes, and I didn't like where his mind seemed to be. No way Pepper was involved in that shit. I'd thoroughly checked out every inch of her body and she didn't have a single needle mark, no old track marks, her nose didn't show signs of cocaine abuse. Not to mention, she wasn't jittery or coming down off anything, and she didn't have drugs in her bag that I'd been able to see. The sins of the mother didn't belong to the daughter, but I refrained from calling him on it. For now.

"My mom overdosed, on purpose. Her suicide note told me about the men and told me to come find Sarge. Until then, she'd never given me a hint as to where my dad might live or who he really was," Pepper said.

Tank glanced at Sarge, his eyebrow lifted.

Sarge rubbed the back of his neck. "Pepper's mother turned to prostitution a few years after we met. She got into drugs and who knows what else. And yes, my daughter grew up around that shit, and no, I'm not fucking happy about it. Pepper got herself out of there when she was able and she's tried to keep her distance from her mom."

"Just because she's feeding us all this doesn't make it true," Tank said.

And that's when he crossed the line. I shifted Pepper, intending to stand, but Torch sent a glare in Tank's direction and another in mine. I ground my teeth together and planted my ass firmly back in the chair, but I wasn't too fucking happy. The asshole had basically called my woman a liar. A glance at Sarge showed that he wasn't faring any better. His face was flushed and his jaw was tight.

"Tank, you're out of line," Torch said. "I know those girls of yours have you in overprotective mode, but calm the fuck down."

Tank snarled, but didn't say another word.

His daughters, triplets, were beyond adorable. Everyone loved them, and I got even angrier that he thought I'd ever to do something to put them in jeopardy. Harlow, Kasen, and Westyn had every man in this club wrapped around their cute, chubby little fingers.

"Wire," Torch said. "To set Tank's mind at ease, would you please run a check on Pepper? And before Sarge and Flicker leap to her defense again, I'm not calling her a liar. I just want Tank and anyone else here with doubts to see the proof that Pepper is who she claims to be and isn't here for nefarious purposes."

Wire opened his laptop and tapped away on the computer for a moment. "Full name?"

"Pepper White. My mother was Mary Ann White. We're from Las Vegas," Pepper said.

"Anything else you want to share before I start digging?" Wire asked.

Pepper chewed her lip. "I was emancipated when I was sixteen and got my G.E.D. I graduated from cooking school. If you're asking about arrest records or something, my record is clean."

"Clean because there isn't one? Or clean because it's been wiped?" Wire asked. "Because trust me, if there's anything there, I'll find it."

Her body tensed and I saw her face drain of color. What the hell? Sarge shared a look with me, and it was enough to tell me he didn't have a clue why she reacted that way either. Was Pepper hiding something?

"What am I going to find, Pepper?" Wire asked.

"Will files from Social Services be in there?" she asked softly.

"Yes," Wire said. "Even if a record is sealed, I can still access it."

Her gaze lifted and held his. "You don't have to share everything you see, right?"

"What the fuck, Pepper?" I asked, my tone rougher than I'd intended.

Wire stared at her a moment, then started tapping away on his computer. The tension in the room grew and Pepper started to tremble. She seemed truly terrified and I didn't know why. Had she done something really wrong and was worried how we'd react? None of us were squeaky clean, but as long as she wasn't here under false pretenses, then I didn't understand why she was so damn scared.

"Oh, fuck," Wire muttered, then his gaze lifted and held Pepper's. I heard her audibly swallow. "Sweetheart, they need to know. No one will judge you."

"Please," she said softly, her lip quivering. "Don't. I'm begging you."

He shook his head. "They'll know you aren't protecting your mom. And they'll understand why you show her no love."

"I -- I don't want…" She stopped and I felt a hot tear hit my arm.

"Pepper, baby. What's he talking about?" I asked softly.

She shook her head and just let the tears fall.

"Pepper White was emancipated at the age of sixteen," Wire said. "Uncontested and pushed through rather quickly. After Social Services received a call. Mary Ann White was arrested for child endangerment and a Leon Parsons went to prison for a long-ass time. Looks like Mary Ann was released after six months for good behavior, or more likely, overcrowding."

"What the fuck does it have to do with Pepper?" Sarge asked. "What was the child endangerment charge for?"

"The reports say that Social Services arrived on scene and called the local police. Mary Ann White had accepted money from…"

"Stop," Pepper said, her voice soft and shaky. "Please. Don't say anymore."

"Baby, I know you were a virgin before you came to my bed, so what happened that day?" I asked.

"Was?" Sarge asked, his eyes narrowed at me. I waved him off because now wasn't the time for that talk.

She shook her head and refused to speak. Wire gave her a sympathetic look before letting us know what she'd suffered. I had a feeling the second he started speaking again, and I heard what she'd been through, that I was going to want to murder some fuckers. Starting with whoever the fuck that Parsons guy was, and just because he was in prison didn't put him beyond my reach.

"Her mother accepted cash to look the other way. Mr. Parsons had stripped her and tied her down. Social Services interrupted before he could do more than unfasten his pants, and the police arrested him. It seems good ol' Mr. Parsons liked them young. He was charged with multiple counts of attempted rape, rape, and molestation of minors. Once he was picked up and charged with Pepper's attempted rape, other girls came forward and spoke out. There were enough of them he'll be doing time until he's dead," Wire said.

Pepper sobbed and seemed to cave in on herself. I wrapped her tight in my arms and held her, my heart breaking for the young kid who had to have been scared shitless and wishing I could rip out Parson's spine and bring her mom back from the dead just to kill her again. My girl was so strong, or so she'd seemed. I now had to wonder if she'd grown her steel spine that night.

"Social Services paved the way for her to be emancipated," Wire said.

Pepper pulled away from me, standing and wiping the tears from her cheeks. She looked from one end of the table to the other, and I noticed that Tank wouldn't hold her gaze. Fucker better watch it. I didn't give a shit if he was my brother and the Sergeant at Arms. I was still going to beat his ass for putting Pepper through this shit.

"I shouldn't have come here," she said.

"Pepper..." I reached for her, but she danced back a step, keeping out of reach. I didn't like the haunted look in her eyes, or the pallor in her cheeks. And I sure as fuck didn't like the defeated stoop of her shoulders.

"I'm sorry," she murmured, then ran from the room.

I stood so fast my chair hit the floor. "Goddamnit! Tank, you're an asshole. If you'd left well enough alone, then Torch would have never asked Wire to dig that shit up. You pulled that same crap with Rin, and by some miracle, Wraith never knocked your teeth in. I'm not feeling quite so kind toward you right now."

"Go after her," Sarge said, rising slowly from his chair. "I'd like a few words with our Sergeant at Arms, and with Wire. Make sure Pepper knows that neither of us think any less of her."

I glared at Tank one last time and left, hoping Sarge laid the fucker out for hurting Pepper. I hurried through the clubhouse and ran outside, hoping I'd see Pepper somewhere along the road.

If she left, if by some miracle whoever was on the gate let her through, then I'd hunt her down and bring her home where she belonged, and God help anyone who laid a hand on her.

Chapter Five

Pepper

I'd never be able to face them again, especially not Flicker. How could he ever want me knowing how dirty I was? I'd worked so hard to put that night out of my mind, had stopped having nightmares after two years. I'd even felt the first hint of desire when I'd seen Flicker, something that had never happened before, and I'd craved his touch and not dreaded it. For a while, I'd been able to convince myself it was only due to my mother's lifestyle and the kids teasing me that had kept me from letting a man get close. I'd told myself I was tough, that nothing could hurt me. I couldn't live in denial anymore.

Now it was all back. Every nightmare, every horrific memory I'd banished. The way the man's hands had felt on my body, the fear that had coursed through my veins as he'd started to undress after tying me down. I could smell the stale cigarettes in the air, and feel the springs digging into my back and hips. I couldn't stop the tears. No matter how many times I dashed them away, more fell down my cheeks. It felt like I'd been sliced open and was hemorrhaging.

I was so ashamed. Social Services had sent a man to the trailer that day, or I doubt I'd have been saved in time. He'd assured me, as had the counselor I'd been assigned, that none of it was my fault, that I was a victim. It hadn't mattered. I'd scrubbed my skin that night until I'd nearly bled. I'd worked so hard to put it behind me, to live a normal life. I'd done my best to convince myself it hadn't happened, shut everything into a room in my mind and locked the door. No, I'd never dated, but it was only because no one had ever made me feel the all-consuming desire that Flicker did.

At least, I'd convinced myself of that, and in part it was true, but it was *why* I'd never felt that way that I'd managed to block entirely.

Until now, I hadn't thought about that night in over a year. And even then, it hadn't happened often. By the time I was eighteen, I'd done an adequate job of compartmentalizing what happened and becoming numb to it. Almost as if I had been an observer that night. It seemed I wasn't as numb as I'd thought. Thanks to that man's mojo on his computer, everyone in that room now knew what had happened to me, the shame I'd suffered, and I now had to battle the memories again. It was like the bandage had been ripped off and now I had an oozing sore once more. Or more like they'd cracked open my chest and left me for dead.

Flicker had left his house unlocked and I went inside to pack my things. Not that I'd really unpacked to begin with. I'd strap my pack to my bike and head out. It was a mistake to come here. Meeting my dad had been great. I'd wanted the chance to know him better, but there was no way he would ever look at me the same. I was my mother's daughter, good for nothing but letting men get off. Deep down, I knew that wasn't true, but it was how I'd been made to feel by my peers when they'd heard about the incident. Despite Vegas not exactly being small town America, when something sensationally bad happened, everyone heard one way or another. Those scars had never fully healed, and it was possible they never would.

I was carrying my bag out to my bike when a hand clamped down on my arm. I tensed and didn't move. Being inside the compound, I knew it had to be either my dad or Flicker. I was safe here, or at least I had been. What probably hurt the most was having shared such an intense moment with Flicker, finally meeting my dad, and now I had to walk away. I was losing the only two people I had in my life now.

"Where the hell are you going?" Flicker demanded, turning me to face him.

"It's fine," I said. "You don't have to pretend you still want me here. I'll go far from Alabama, and the guys from Vegas won't be a problem for you. Just forget you ever met me."

"What the fuck, Pepper?" His brow furrowed and his eyes narrowed a bit. I thought I even saw a flash of hurt, but I knew I had to be wrong. "Why are you leaving?"

"Seriously? You were just told that I'm trash, less than trash, and you want me to stick around?"

"Tr --" He growled and hauled me closer, his eyes snapping with fury. "I never, and I mean *never* want to hear you call yourself that again. You were a kid, a scared kid who should have been protected. What happened wasn't your fault, and I sure as fuck don't look down on you for surviving something like that. No one here would do that. I'm glad they found you in time, and I can assure you that I will arrange for Mr. Parsons to be tortured daily for the rest of his prison stay. If your bitch of a mother were still alive, I'd personally gut her."

My eyes went wide and my heart thundered. "Wh -- what?"

"Pepper, why would you think I wanted you to leave? Do you honestly think your dad would have let you ride out of here never to be heard from again?"

"Well... yeah."

"Why?" he asked again.

"Because… when it happened, everyone kept saying I'd asked for it, that I was just another trashy whore like my mother. I know there are pricey call girls in Vegas and other cities, women who take care of themselves and enjoy their work, but my mom wasn't like them. She was a junkie and when it came to her clients, she wasn't discriminating, if you know what I mean. As long as they could pay or give her drugs, then she'd let them do whatever they wanted. Didn't matter if they used protection or not, or whether they were clean. When she died, she'd aged beyond her years, had lost a lot of her teeth, her hair was brittle and coming out. She also had contracted more than one STD over the years."

"And you think you're anything like that?" he asked quietly. "When you look in the mirror, that's what you see?"

I hesitated.

"Sweetheart, you're beautiful and I can understand why some guys might try to tear you down and make you feel like less, especially if you shut them down and wouldn't spread your legs for them. You can't believe what other people say about you. And if you're going to listen to someone, then listen to me. You're gorgeous, fiery, and any guy would be lucky to call you his." He smirked. "Just so happens I get that honor because I'm not letting you go."

"Everyone in that room now knows what I happened," I said. "How can I look them in the eye after that?"

"Baby, no one here will think any less of you. And it's not just because you're mine, or because you're Sarge's daughter. Once they meet you, get to know you, they'll see that same fire inside that I do.

You're going to make a lot of friends here at the compound."

"Because you say so?" I asked, feeling a little snarky.

"No, because you're incredible."

I felt the tension drain from me as I looked up at him. I could tell that Flicker was sincere and really meant everything he'd just said. I gave him a faint smile.

"You're just saying that because you want to get lucky again."

He swatted my ass. "Nope. I'm speaking the truth. Of course, I plan on tying you to the bed again…" His words trailed off and his gaze shuttered.

"Don't," I said.

"I did that to you, after what you'd been through. I'm an asshole."

"You didn't know, and I promise that I never once thought about that night. I was completely focused on you and how you were making me feel." As I said the words, I realized they were one hundred percent true. All I'd thought about during that time was Flicker and all the emotions and sensation rolling through me. Not once I had thought about that night all those years ago. I'd trusted him to do those things to me, when I'd never trusted anyone before. What was it about him that called to me? That made me throw caution to the wind and take a chance? He was a stranger, a complete unknown, and yet I'd let my walls down around him and allowed him to get closer than anyone ever had.

"I won't let you leave, Pepper. If you even try to get on that bike and ride out of here, I'll spank your ass. Not to mention they won't open the gates for you.

Whether you like it or not, you're stuck here. With me."

I wrapped my arms around his waist and rested my cheek against him. "I don't mind being stuck with you, or here at the compound. I thought I was doing the right thing by leaving."

"You have to talk to me, okay? Whatever you have going on in that head of yours, let me know if you're worried or scared. Don't try to run off again because you feel like you're not worthy or some other bullshit. And that's exactly what it is, Pepper. Bullshit."

"Don't sugarcoat it or anything," I muttered.

"Impertinent wench," he said, but I could hear the affection in his voice.

"Do you have to go back to your meeting or whatever you call it?" I asked. "Do I for that matter?"

"We still need to know more about the men you think will come for you, but no. Neither of us will be going back right now. We'll take your stuff back inside, where it belongs, and then I'll call Torch and ask him to put us on speaker. I'm not going to ask you to face everyone right now, and I think Sarge will be happy to hear your voice and know that you're all right. He sent me after you, because he wanted to say a few things to Tank and Wire."

My heart warmed that my dad and Flicker wanted to protect me, cared what happened to me, and they both seemed to want me to stay. It was hard to argue, to push them away, when I couldn't think of anything I'd like more than to make a home here with them. To finally feel like I belonged somewhere, like I was part of something, had a family. My mother had never been family to me. She'd been a necessary evil if I wanted to stay out of the foster care system, but that had been it.

Flicker took my bag and then led me by the hand into the house. He kicked the door shut and didn't stop until we'd reached the bedroom, where he tossed my bag into the corner. Flicker sat on the edge of the bed and pulled me down onto his lap, his arm going around my waist as he anchored me to him. He dug his phone from his pocket and I saw Torch's name on the screen as he turned on the speaker and I heard the phone ringing as it dialed his President.

"You get her?" Torch asked.

"She's here and you're on speaker. She said she'll still talk to you, but she didn't want to go back to Church, and I wasn't going to make her."

Torch sighed and muttered something that sounded like he was berating Tank, the one who hadn't believed I wasn't here to hurt anyone. I didn't think I'd be making friends with that guy anytime soon.

"Pepper, I'm glad you're still here," Torch said. "I hate to press you right now, but the sooner we learn about the men from Vegas the quicker we can come up with a plan."

"I don't know much," I said. "I haven't met them or seen them. I know that my mother's pimp would get drugs from a guy they called Big Tony. I always found the name funny because the guy is maybe one hundred pounds and barely over five feet tall. But I think he's one of the main guys running drugs through Vegas."

"So all we have is your junkie mother's word that someone is after you, but you haven't seen even a hint that someone is coming?" Torch asked.

"Right. She did ask me for twenty grand recently, and I laughed and turned her away. I didn't know she was really in trouble."

"What if she wasn't?" someone else asked.

"What do you mean, Bats?" Flicker asked.

"What if she was just wanted to scare your girl as one last effort to torment her? She obviously wasn't winning mother of the year. Is that something she would do, Pepper? Try to scare you?"

"Um, maybe. I don't see the point since she was going to kill herself," I said.

"Wire, look into Mary Ann White and see what you can find," Torch said. "For now, we'll just handle things business as usual, but, Pepper, be extra vigilant when you're outside of the compound just in case we're wrong."

"Pepper, this is Tank," I heard a deep voice say. I tensed when I heard his name. "I just wanted to apologize. I never meant to put you through that kind of pain. It's my job to protect the club, and you're an unknown."

There were mumbled voices and Tank sighed.

"And I can be an asshole," he said, "as everyone is pointing out to me. I don't have the best track record around here for trusting women. My wife is one of the rare exceptions."

"That's because his wife is a damn saint to put up with him and smile while doing it," someone else shouted.

"Shut it, asshole," Tank said.

Flicker snickered. "That would be Grimm he's yelling at."

"When you're convinced we aren't all dicks like Tank, we'd love to have a proper meet and greet," someone else said.

"And that's Preacher. He's right," Flicker said. "When you think you can handle it, you need to meet all of them, and the women and kids. I won't push you. Just let me know when you're ready."

I nodded and stared at the phone, waiting to see if anyone else would say anything. When it was quiet, I asked a question that had been squirming inside of my brain since I showed up at the front gate.

"If you have all have normal names, like my dad and Flicker, why do you all use such strange ones every day?" I asked.

It sounded like that entire room burst into laughter. After a moment, Torch answered. "They're our road names, or club names if you will. They're earned in one way or another. It's an honor to be patched in and given a name, so that's why we don't use our birth names unless we're around our wives and kids."

"And then there's my wife," another voice said. "To this day she still calls me Venom over using my damn name."

Someone laughed and I heard Venom growl at them.

"That was Bull, Ridley's dad," Flicker whispered. "Ridley showed up and pretty much claimed Venom, much to her daddy's horror."

The more I learned about the men on the other end of the phone, the more at ease I felt. Yes, I'd been embarrassed beyond belief when Wire had shared that part of my past, but they didn't seem to care. Or rather, they didn't hold it against me or look down on me for what happened. I wouldn't say they didn't care so much as they didn't seem to think I was tainted because of what happened to me.

I heard a throat clear. "Pepper, my name's Wraith, and I'm going to tell you something that's common knowledge around here. My wife, Rin, was placed in her half-brother's care when she was a teenager. He was a local pimp and asshole of huge proportions. He whored her out and if she didn't comply, he'd beat her. Rin is accepted in this club and well-loved by everyone. So don't think for one second that what happened to you makes us see you less than any other woman here."

I looked up at Flicker and he nodded.

"If you ever want someone to talk to, another survivor," Wraith said, "then I know my Rin would be happy to listen or share her story with you. Whatever you need, she'll be there. Same goes for everyone else here that we call family. You're not alone, sweet girl. Not unless you want to be."

I felt my eyes tear and I leaned against Flicker.

"Thank you," I said.

"Pepper, it's Wire. I'm sorry for making you feel like you needed to run. They needed to know your history, and I swear to you that every man here, even the asshole at the end of the table, will protect you with our lives if it comes to that."

"I already agreed I'm an asshole," Tank said. "But don't push it, computer nerd."

"Really?" Wired asked. "That's the best you have? Don't forget I can wipe out your existence in a few keystrokes."

I heard someone sigh.

"All right, children," Torch said, sounding both tired and amused. "Everyone get the fuck out of here. Pepper, if there's anything you can think of that might help solve the mystery around your mom's death and what happened in Vegas, Flicker knows how to reach me."

I heard the line disconnect and I closed my eyes a moment.

"Told you that everyone would love you," Flicker said. "If Church is being dismissed, then I have no doubt your dad is about to show up. He'll want to make sure you're all right."

"I'm tired," I murmured, not feeling sleepy so much as emotionally drained.

"My sister always says that ice cream is the cure for everything. I always keep some in the freezer for Laken. Want some?" he asked.

"Will I ever get to meet your sister?"

"I'm actually surprised she hasn't shown up already. I can only assume her other half is holding her back. Laken isn't the type to sit around. If she wants to do something, she does it. Which is how she ended up with Ryker in the first place."

"That sounds… interesting?"

He snorted. "I wanted to punch the asshole. He fucked my baby sister in a bar, knocked her up, but I knew he was a manwhore and I wasn't about to let him anywhere near her. They ended up together anyway. Even though he's Hades Abyss and not a Dixie Reaper, they live here at the compound. His dad is the President and made up some bullshit job of ambassador between the clubs as an excuse for Ryker to stay here."

I smiled a little. "Don't you mean so your sister could stay here with her family? I think it's sweet that he was willing to do that, and that Ryker didn't demand that she go home with him."

"Only you would call either Diablo or Spider sweet."

"If he has a club name, why do you call him Ryker? Because you're family now that they're together?" I asked.

"He introduced himself to Laken as Ryker. He's never been too thrilled over being under his daddy's thumb. He's patched into Hades Abyss, but he has little to do with them unless an emergency crops up. Around here, he just goes by Ryker unless he's wearing his colors. These days, he won't wear his cut unless he's outside the compound. There's been talk about patching him into the Dixie Reapers, but I think Ryker feels it would be a slap in his dad's face, and while Spider can be a dick at times, they're still blood. Honestly, from what I've heard, Spider is more than okay with it."

"I can understand that. Mom was the only family I had, but I couldn't stand her most of the time. Didn't stop me from trying to clean her up when I found her in a puddle of her own vomit. Until…" I swallowed hard. "I just couldn't do that anymore, couldn't stay with her. It wasn't safe and I wanted out. I refused to go down that path."

"You did the right thing, sweetheart."

I heard the front door open and slam shut, then booted steps.

"Where the fuck are you?" my dad yelled out.

"Bedroom," Flicker shouted back.

"Y'all better not be naked. There's just some shit a dad should never see."

I couldn't help the laughter that bubbled up. My dad opened the door, his hand over his eyes and he was peeking through his fingers. He dropped his hand when he saw we were both fully clothed, and he dramatically sighed. I smiled, the first true smile since I left the clubhouse earlier.

"Hi… Daddy," I said.

"Hi, baby girl. You doing okay?" he asked.

I nodded, then shook my head. I ended up shrugging my shoulder. Honestly, I knew eventually I'd get back to the place where what happened didn't weigh on me, but the memories were too fresh right now.

"I told her there was ice cream in the freezer. Laken insists it cures everything," Flicker said.

"Why don't we go to the diner? We can get a slice of pie and ask them to put ice cream on top," my dad suggested. "All three of us can go."

"You don't have to treat me like I'll break," I said. "I survived what happened before, so I can damn sure deal with the memories of it."

"Doesn't mean you should have to," Flicker said.

I knew arguing with him would be pointless. I'd found that most men didn't listen unless you were saying something they wanted to hear. I doubted Flicker, or my dad, would be any different. So, I decided to go along for the ride and get pie with ice cream. If this was their way of cheering me up every time something bad happened, then I had a feeling I'd need a new wardrobe before long.

I wasn't sure how to handle people wanting to take care of me, but as Flicker tightened his hold, I had to admit that it was rather nice. As long as he didn't try to squash my independence, then I wouldn't have an issue with it. In my entire life, no one other than Louis had really given a shit about me, or made time to ensure I was all right. Even my friends had their own lives that kept them busy. I wasn't going to miss my life in Vegas even a little. I'd miss Louis, but we could always keep in touch. It was strange, being able to up and move across the country and not have a single regret, except that I didn't leave sooner.

Every day was an adventure, and I couldn't wait to see what the future with Flicker would be like.

Chapter Six

Flicker

I rubbed at my eyes and stared down at my coffee, my vision blurry from lack of sleep. It had been three days since Pepper tried to run, since Wire had reminded her of the hell she'd survived, and she had nightmares every fucking night. I'd tried wearing her out, in the best of ways, but even that didn't seem to help. Not for the entire night. Between the incredible sex and waking to her screams, I wasn't sleeping for shit, but I couldn't really complain about it. Having Pepper in my bed, knowing she was mine, made the exhaustion more than worth it. I only wished I knew how to stop her from reliving the worst night of her life.

Wire had called too fucking early, before the sun was even up, and now I was sitting at the damn kitchen table waiting for him. I didn't know what he needed to discuss that couldn't be said over the fucking phone, or at a decent hour. When the front door opened and I heard more than one set of steps coming toward the kitchen, I eyed the doorway. Wire came into the room first, then Torch, Venom, and Tank followed. Fuck my life. The visit didn't bode well for my morning.

The fact all the club officers, plus Wire, were now in my kitchen wasn't comforting. If this was a club matter, Torch would have called Church. Meeting here meant it was personal. Which meant it most likely had to do with Pepper.

"I'd ask if you were hung over, but I'm guessing your woman is keeping you up all night," Torch said with a smile.

"Lucky fucker," Wire muttered.

"Yeah, she is, but not necessarily in the greatest of ways. Ever since Wire told everyone what happened to her, all those memories came back, and she's been having nightmares."

Wire winced and I could see the shame and remorse in his eyes. He hadn't thought for a second what hearing that would do to Pepper, or even just reminding her of that night, and as much as I wanted to punch him, I could understand why he'd done it. Didn't mean I liked it, nor approved of his methods. He could have asked Pepper to leave the fucking room before he started spewing that shit. It was hard enough for me to hear about it, but Pepper had fucking lived through it. The last thing she needed was to have all that dredged up and thrown in her face.

"We're here because Wire found something about your girl," Venom said.

"Like what?" I asked.

"Carmine Galetti has put out the word that Pepper is a person of interest to him. It's a capture order, with a price for anyone who brings her in unharmed. So, the good news is they don't want her dead," Wire said.

"And the bad news?" I asked. If he'd made sure I knew that was the good part, that meant there was definitely something bad to be added to the statement.

"They've contacted every criminal family and every one percent club within three hundred miles of Las Vegas, and word is spreading. I don't think they believed she'd travel so far when she left Vegas, and they likely aren't even one hundred percent certain she isn't still there somewhere. But the way the news is spreading means it will reach the East Coast before long," Torch said. "I don't think they're aware of her connection to this club, or they would have widened their search."

"And how did Wire find this information?" I asked, looking at the club hacker.

"Reckless Kings got wind of it in one of their chapters out that way. I contacted our allies about Pepper, wondering if anyone out west had heard something," Wire said. "I did a search on the computer and didn't find anything new since Church the other day. Got a hit on her mom, though. Mary Ann White's body has been found, and her death was ruled an accidental overdose. I guess since Pepper took the suicide note with her, they don't realize the bitch did it on purpose."

"Are the Kings going to keep their eyes and ears open?" Tank asked. "If anyone gets word that Pepper is here and someone is coming for her, we need to know. I don't have the panic room ready yet."

I rubbed my beard and sighed. After Jacey had been snatched inside our own damn compound, Tank had decided enough was enough. A building went up about six yards from the clubhouse. Tank had installed a small armory in there, and was working on adding a panic room, which would actually be a sub-level under the structure. The men he'd hired were making it fireproof, bombproof, and completely safe for the women and kids. Since our families were growing rapidly, it almost meant we needed a large space and at least two small bathrooms down there. Just a pedestal sink, small shower, and toilet in each, but if shit went sideways fast and the Reapers were badly hobbled, they could be stuck down there for a while. A kitchen area was part of the plans as well.

Torch had already ordered at least a dozen bunk beds and half a dozen couches. His wife, Isabella, had suggested a cabinet of some sort to hold board games or other toys and books to keep the kids occupied, and another selection of reading material for the ladies. The space had been divided into six areas to give it a homier feel, if such a thing was possible for that type of shelter. It was our hope that damn thing would never be used, but our women did love to get themselves into trouble. Or more accurately, they showed up with trouble hot on their heels, much the way Pepper had.

"No one in this town would receive that type of message except us," I said. "Not since we took care of Rin's brother and the crooked politicians in town. I'm not going to put Pepper on lockdown, but I think it would be safer if she had someone with her whenever she left the compound. A brother and not just one of the old ladies."

"Agreed," Venom said.

"I wouldn't say anything to Pepper just yet," Torch said. "Unless she asks. Even then, try not to add to her stress levels right now. I'm sorry to hear she's having nightmares. If you think she needs to speak to someone, I can call Doc Myron and ask if his partner would be willing to stop by."

"Appreciate it," I said. "I'll mention it to Pepper, but I don't know how she'd feel about speaking to a counselor. She prides herself on not needing anyone. Even the night she came here, she was full of sass."

"I'm sorry for what I said in Church," Tank said. "Even though I was worried about my family, all our families, it was out of line. I could have handled it better."

"We're all responsible for Pepper's current situation," Torch said. "I gave the order for Wire to dig up shit on her. The only one who tried to protect

Pepper was you, Flicker. Well, and her daddy. We've already spoken to Sarge and smoothed things over."

"I understand the club takes priority," I said. "But I was officially claiming her, which makes her part of the Dixie Reapers. As an officer, I shouldn't have had my woman questioned like she was a common criminal. Even if I didn't know much about her, my word should have been good enough. You didn't object even a little when I said I was claiming her, until that shit was brought up. Other than Bull, none of us had seen Ridley since she was a kid, but when she showed up no one questioned her or made her feel like she'd done something wrong. Yet Sarge's daughter comes to us, and you make her feel like she's trash."

Tank shifted in his seat, and I held the gaze of every man at my table. I'd done a lot for this club, bled for them, broken the law countless times, and when I'd needed them to back me up, they'd nearly driven away the woman I wanted to keep. It wasn't something I would forget anytime soon. They were my brothers, and I would die for them, but I was pissed as fucking hell. No amount of apologizing would make Pepper's pain go away.

Speaking of my sexy woman, she padded into the kitchen, her hair mussed and her eyes still shut. I smiled, not having a clue how she hadn't walked into a wall by now. She yawned and rubbed a hand down her face, then continued across to the room to the coffeepot. I watched her fumble with the cabinet door and reach in for a mug before pouring coffee into it. She took a large swallow, then sighed, her body slumping against the counter.

"Baby girl, you should probably go put on pants," I said, just grateful she hadn't wandered in here completely naked. My shirt did an adequate job of covering everything important, and Wire was the only single guy here. I noticed he kept his eyes averted.

She mumbled something and drank more coffee.

"Pepper." I barked her name in a sharp tone that had her lifting a hand and giving me the finger.

Torch coughed to cover a laugh and I saw Venom's shoulders shaking with silent merriment. I flipped them off before looking at my woman again.

She tipped her head back and drained the cup before pouring more. When she turned, her eyes narrowed and her lips in a snarl, she froze as she noticed the other men in the room. Her eyes went wide and she gave a cute squeak.

"Like I said, you should probably go put on pants," I said.

"You could have fucking said we had company!" She stomped out of the room, her coffee sloshing over the rim of the cup and splashing onto the floor. The bedroom door slammed and both Torch and Venom burst out laughing, apparently unable to contain themselves a moment longer.

"You're going to have your hands full," Torch said.

"Glad my sweet Emmie isn't like that," Tank said.

"Speaking of Emmie," Wire said, "what's the latest on that she-devil sister of hers?"

"Lupita isn't a devil. She had some issues to work through, but she's doing better. I think. We haven't seen her since the day she left here to go detox down at the beach," Tank said.

"Think she'll come back?" Wire asked.

Tank snorted. "Why? You want to try and take her on? I'm pretty sure she'd eat you alive."

"No, not even a little bit. Not my type. I just wondered if we'd see her around sometime since your woman is related to her. How can she stay away from those adorable nieces she has?" Wire asked.

"Whatever demons Lupita is fighting, I'd rather she not do it here," Torch said.

"I second that." Venom tapped the table. "There's a difference in our women being *in* trouble and actually *being* trouble. And Lupita is trouble with a capital T. I know she saved Wraith's ass, and we'll always be grateful, but that shit she pulled later isn't something I want to deal with again."

"Anyone else wonder if Sarge knocked up another woman? I mean, if he had Pepper and didn't know about it, isn't it possible she could have a brother or sister out there? Maybe even more than one? Preferably a sister. Just wondering if we should expect more to show up," Wire said. "It would be hard as fuck to trace unless he was on their birth certificates."

"Preferably a sister." I snorted, seeing exactly where he was going with that one. And if she did have a sister, no way I'd let any of the fuckers who hurt Pepper anywhere near them.

"Most states require the father's signature," Torch said.

"I know you're pissed at us," Tank said, "and you have a right to be. Just know that if anyone comes for Pepper, we'll have your back, and hers. No one is going to take her from you."

"Wire, did you look into Leon Parsons some more?" I asked, changing the subject.

Wire nodded. "He's at the High Desert State Prison. I checked into their correctional officers and anyone else higher up the chain of command. They're all squeaky clean, so if you're wanting something to happen to dear Mr. Parsons, no one who works there is going to help or look the other way."

Just fucking great. Of all the places for that asshole to be sent, it would have to be one of the prisons that wasn't corrupt. It wasn't going to make it easy to get to him, but I'd find a way. One way or another, that man would pay for what he did to Pepper and those other girls. His prison sentence wasn't anywhere near good enough. I wanted him to suffer, to hurt, to live in constant fear for however long he remained breathing.

Pepper wandered back into the room, this time wearing a pair of leggings and a tank. It wasn't perfect, but at least she was fully clothed. I didn't like that anyone would be able to see down her shirt if she leaned over, and I could damn well see that she wasn't wearing a bra. As she sank onto my lap and I gripped her hip, I realized she wasn't wearing panties either. Fucking hell. I closed my eyes and tried to count backward from one hundred. Anything to stop my cock from getting harder than it already had. Not that it took much. Pepper could just be in my general vicinity and I wanted her.

"Morning, Pepper," Torch said. "I hope we didn't wake you."

She shook her head and leaned against me.

"We were just discussing some business," I said, "but they're on their way out. Aren't you, brothers?"

Tank nodded and stood, the others following his lead. When the front door had closed behind them, I could feel the tension drain from Pepper. I hated that she didn't feel at ease around them, but they only had themselves to blame. After everything she'd been through, it wouldn't be easy for them to win her trust.

"I should spank your ass," I said.

She jolted and looked over her shoulder at me. "Why?"

"Because you came in here practically naked, then came back not wearing a bra or panties. You think I didn't notice?" I asked, sliding my hand across her hip and reaching up to cup her breast. "I'm intimately familiar with this body, baby."

"I..."

I swatted her thigh. "Up. Stand up, Pepper."

She stood and turned to face me.

"Strip."

She audibly swallowed and slowly removed her shirt and leggings. When she was bare and her nipples were pebbling in the cool air, I spread my legs and motioned to my lap.

"Face down, baby girl."

Heat flared in her eyes as she settled across my legs, her ass in the air. I felt her wrap a hand around my leg as she anchored herself. The little tease spread her thighs a bit, letting me see her pretty pussy. I brought my hand down on her ass, the loud *crack* making my cock jerk. There was a pink handprint on her ass cheek, and I smiled, knowing it would be a lot redder before I was finished. I landed blow after blow on her pale skin, feeling the heat coming off her. Pepper started squirming, and fuck if she wasn't getting wetter by the second. I paddled her ass until I knew she'd think long and hard about this moment every time she sat down for the rest of the day.

She wiggled again and I realized she was trying to get some relief. Naughty little girl. Not on my watch! I pushed her thighs wider apart and there was a hitch in her breathing. I lightly smacked her pussy, making her jerk. When I did it again, she moaned, just like I thought she'd would. Oh yeah, she liked it. I swatted her harder, not enough to really hurt, more of a stinging sensation, but it was definitely turning her on.

I spread her pussy wide and saw how hard her clit had gotten while I'd spanked her ass. I pinched down on it and Pepper thrashed on my lap as she started to come. I backed off, and smoothed my hand over her thighs.

"Don't come until I give you permission," I said. "If you come before you're allowed, then I'll have to punish you."

"Flicker, please," she begged.

I swatted her ass. Hard. "Who am I when it's just us?"

"Daniel," she said, then squirmed some more. "I need you. Please!"

I rubbed her clit, light strokes that nearly made her detonate the second I touched her. I grinned as she came, a loud keening sound coming from her, and earning her more spankings -- something I enjoyed giving her. My jeans were soaked from her release, but I didn't fucking care. She whimpered and cried as my hand cracked against her ass several more times.

"What did I say? You didn't have permission to come, did you?"

She shook her head frantically. "No."

"I should leave you like this, all needy and aching for my cock."

"Daniel, please don't. I want you so much."

"Then show me."

She practically fell off my lap she tried to get up so quickly, then she dropped to her knees between my legs. Pepper quickly unfastened my pants and pulled out my cock. I reached out and fisted her hair, making sure she looked me in the eye. I could see the desperation in her gaze, and fucking loved that only I could do that to her.

"I'm going to fuck your mouth, Pepper. You're going to give me complete control, understood?"

"Yes," she said, her voice breathy as she squirmed some more.

"Open."

Her lips parted and I painted them with pre-cum before shoving my dick into her mouth. I nearly groaned with how good it felt. She sucked as I fucked her with long, deep strokes.

"That's it, baby. Take all of it," I murmured, loving the way her lips stretched around me.

I saw her hand slid between her legs and I abruptly pulled from her mouth.

"No touching, Pepper! You don't come unless I say you can. If you can't follow the rules, I'll tie you up and do what I want with you."

Her eyes dilated and she panted. Fuck! After hearing what had happened to her, I'd felt like a sick bastard, an asshole for having tied her to the bed our first night together. But I was quickly learning that she needed to be bound, craved it as much as I craved her submission. She trusted me, knew I wouldn't hurt her, and that was the biggest fucking high I'd ever felt.

"Do you want to be tied up, Pepper?" I asked softly.

"Please, Daniel."

I let her hair go and tipped her chin up. I caressed her lips and softened my voice, "Do you need it, sweetheart? Do you need me to be on control, to take away your options and use you how I see fit?"

She nodded. There was a flash of shame in her eyes and I leaned down to kiss her, hard, tasting both of us in the process.

"Nothing we do together is wrong, Pepper. I will always give you whatever you need. If it's a spanking, you'll get it. If it's being tied up and fucked hard, then I'll gladly do it. Never feel ashamed of what happens when we're together. Understood?"

She nodded again.

"Is that what my woman needs? To be bound and fucked?" I asked.

"Yes, Daniel. It makes me feel…" She bit her lip.

"You can tell me, sweetheart. Whatever it is, I won't judge you."

"Free," she said softly. "It makes me feel free. I don't have to worry about what I'm doing. I can just focus on everything you do to me, and knowing it's you tying me up makes me feel… protected, I guess. It's hard to explain. Maybe I'm just crazy."

"Go to the bedroom, Pepper, then kneel on the bed with your hands behind your back."

She shot to her feet and took off to the bedroom. When I'd wanted to keep her, I never thought for a second she'd let me do any of these things to her. At least not on a regular basis, but she seemed to crave it as much as I did. I'd always been careful with the club whores, just giving them a quick fuck to blow off steam. It had been a while since I'd been able to bind someone. No one knew about my needs, not here at the club anyway. I wasn't ashamed by any means, and had heard rumors that Zipper took things even further than I ever did. It was just something private that I'd never felt the need to share.

I stood and made sure the doors and windows were locked before I went to the bedroom. Pepper was kneeling in the center of the bed, wrists crossed at the center of her back. I'd only bound her hands before, tying them behind her or to the bed. I wondered if she needed more than that. She'd mentioned the ropes made her feel protected. I eyed the closet and decided to find out how far she'd go before she freaked out.

I pulled a bag off the top shelf and removed the long length of silk rope. I'd bought it years ago, but never had a chance to use it. Some part of me had hoped I'd find the perfect woman and get to use it on her, but that woman hadn't shown up until now. I smoothed my hand down her hair and pressed a kiss to her temple.

"Do you know what a safe word is, Pepper?" I asked, my heart pounding in anticipation.

"Y-yes." She glanced at me.

"I need a safe word, Pepper. A word you can say when you want me to stop, and I will cease what I'm doing immediately. There's a bit of discomfort at times, but I don't want to do anything that scares you or hurts you."

"You don't secretly have a dungeon hidden in this house, do you?" she asked.

"No, baby. I have plenty of new sex toys I'd like to use on you, lots of rope, but that's it. I'm not going to hit you with a paddle, shove a ball-gag in your mouth, and I don't have a special room. I'd much rather spank that ass with my hand."

She seemed to relax a bit. "Red. My safe word is red."

I ran the rope through my hand and contemplated her from every angle before deciding for certain what I would do. It was too soon for anything overly complex. I needed to go slow with her, ease her into things. She'd been a fucking virgin and here I was wanting to tie her up in knots, the kind that would take hours. I shifted her body so that her back was straight and I could pull her arms farther behind her. I positioned her exactly the way I needed her, then I started at her upper arms, wrapping and knotting until I'd reached her wrists.

I ran my hand down the center of the knotwork and smiled. Looking over at the mirror on the door, I admired how fucking beautiful she was. Her eyes were closed, her lips parted, and there was a look of complete serenity on her face. I pressed in behind her and wrapped my arms around her waist. I kissed her temple, then her cheek, and her neck. Her pulse fluttered against my lips.

I slid my hands up her torso until I cupped her breasts. Her nipples were already hard little points and I pinched down on them, tugging until she made the sweetest sounds. I worked those pretty pink tips, wondering if I could make her come like this. Her body trembled and I rubbed my cock against her ass. Pepper thrust her breasts harder into my hands. I pulled, pinched, twisted, and tugged on the sensitive peaks until she was screaming my name.

Smiling at how beautifully she'd come apart, I decided to give her a reward.

"What do you want most, Pepper?" I asked.

"I want you to take what you need from me," she said, her voice soft and slurring a bit, as if she'd gotten high off the pleasure I'd given her. "Fuck me, Daniel. Give me your cock however and wherever you want."

I chuckled darkly. "Probably shouldn't offer me things like that."

"Why?" she asked.

I thrust against her ass, wedging my cock between her cheeks. "Because I'd really like to fuck you here. Hard and deep. Ever since you bent over in that little striptease, I've wanted to pound this ass, give it a thorough fucking."

She shook harder in my arms and fuck me if it didn't seem that she liked what I was saying. Maybe my dirty girl wanted that as much as I did.

"Do you want my cock in your ass, Pepper?"

"Please, Daniel."

I reached into the bedside table drawer and pulled out the lube. I coated my fingers liberally before I started to prep her. Ideally, I'd have preferred if she'd worn a plug for at least a few hours. I wasn't a small man, and the last thing I wanted was to hurt her. Her body resisted, just as I'd known it would. Fuck me. Virgin ass. Virgin pussy. Virgin mouth. And it was all mine. I'd gotten to claim two of the three so far, and today I'd take the last of her innocence.

I worked my fingers into her, scissoring them, pumping them in and out. Her breathing was choppy and sweat coated her skin. She never said the safe word so I kept going. When I felt I'd prepped her as much as I could, I slicked my cock and spread her cheeks wide. My dick twitched as I started to push inside, and I knew I would remember the way she looked, accepting me into that tight little hole, for as long as I lived.

"Fuck, baby. So God damn beautiful. And so fucking tight!"

Once I'd sunk all the way inside of her, I shifted our bodies, adjusting so that I'd have better control and be able to take her deeper. I wrapped my arms around her torso and stroked in and out of her. Slowly at first, hoping like hell I wasn't hurting her. Pepper didn't sound distressed, so I kept going. She'd say the word if she needed to.

"Gonna fuck you harder, sweetheart. You ready?" I asked.

She murmured her consent and I let go, no longer hold back as I drove into her. Soon, I was slamming hard and deep with every thrust. As incredible as Pepper felt, I didn't want to come without her. I reached between her legs and rubbed her clit. My hips jerked, my movements not as coordinated, and I knew I was about to blow. I pinched and tugged on her clit, growling out the order for her to come right fucking now. She screamed her release, her ass clenching on my dick. I didn't stop until every drop of cum had been wrung from my balls. Even then, I was still hard and wanted more.

Fucking Christ! What the hell was she doing to me? I felt like a sex-crazy man when I was around Pepper. I could probably fuck her until my dick fell off and some part of me still wouldn't be satisfied, would still crave her.

"Jesus, woman," I muttered, then trailed kisses down her neck. "Am I hurting you?"

"Only in the best of ways," she murmured. "Do it again."

I chuckled, but hell if my cock didn't like that idea. I felt it jerk and twitch inside of her. I fucked her again, slower this time, and less frantic. I made her come twice before I filled her ass with my cum again. I knew she'd be sore as fuck since it had been her first time, but she'd given me a precious gift. Her body sagged in my arms and I knew she was spent, both physically and emotionally. I untied her, then ran my hands over her body in soothing strokes. After pressing a kiss to her cheek, I went to run a hot bath, then carried her into the bathroom. Stepping into the tub, I sank until the water threatened to overflow, Pepper cuddled against my chest.

"Relax, sweet girl. I've got you," I told her, lightly rubbing her arms, stomach, thighs… anywhere I could touch. The way she lay so trusting in my arms made my heart feel strange. There was a warmth that spread through me, and I wondered if this was what it felt like to fall for someone. I'd never been in love, but if anyone could knock me over that ledge, it would be Pepper.

Chapter Seven

Pepper

A week had passed since I'd found my dad and moved in with Flicker. A week, that despite what had driven me here, had been one of the best of my life. The things I experienced with Flicker were beyond amazing. I'd never thought I'd crave the things he did to me, but I found that I couldn't get enough. Every time we were together, I wanted more. Not just the sex, but all of it. I loved it when he tied me up, when he used the toys on me, and I especially liked it when he spanked me. I wanted to explore more with him, fantasies I hadn't realized I needed to make reality, but I didn't know how to ask for it. What if he thought I was a complete freak and asked me to leave?

I craved him beyond the bedroom -- not that we confined ourselves to the bedroom for those activities -- but I also loved just cuddling with him on the couch, or enjoying a cup of coffee with him at the kitchen table. The way he looked at me, always watching, made me feel wanted. No one had wanted me. Ever. Not my mother, and none of the guys I'd met. Oh, they wanted in my pants for a one-shot thing, just to say they'd fucked me, but they didn't want to keep me. I felt protected, desired, even needed. Coming here was the best thing I'd ever done.

My cell phone had died sometime during my stay, and I'd discovered my charger didn't work. Flicker's wouldn't fit my phone, so I'd finally asked one of the Prospects to pick one up for me in town. When my phone lit up, I saw over forty missed calls, more than a dozen voicemails, and at least fifty texts… all from Marcus. My heart was pounding as I listened to one message after another before reading over the texts, and a feeling of dread hit me. It felt like an ice cold rock had landed in my stomach and my hands shook as I quickly called Marcus. The cloud of bliss I'd been in suddenly evaporated.

"Where the fuck have you been?" he asked, sounding damn near frantic, just like he had in his messages.

"I'm not in Nevada and my phone died. I just plugged it in this morning. Marcus... did you find Louis?" I asked.

"Yes and no. I know where he is now, but I can't get to him," Marcus said.

"What does that mean?"

He snorted. "You know damn fucking well what it means, Pepper. You brought this shit to our door. You're the reason Louis isn't safe in our apartment. Because of you and that stupid whore you call a mother, my boyfriend has been taken and they won't release him unless I turn you over."

My mouth ran dry and I stared out the bedroom window. I could see my dad's house, see the room I'd slept in that first night. The life I'd started to build for myself was unraveling before my eyes. If I went back to Las Vegas, if they got their hands on me and realized I couldn't give them what they wanted, I'd likely end up buried somewhere in the desert. And that was the best-case scenario. I didn't want to think about what they would do to me before putting a bullet through me. If I couldn't give them their drugs or money, they'd want something else. I knew how those men worked. I'd be made an example, probably stuffed in a brothel somewhere to work off the debt before they slit my throat or shot me.

"I don't have what they want," I said softly, "but I'll come. I'll get Louis back for you, Marcus. It's the least I can do. I never meant to drag the two of you into this."

"I know you didn't, Pepper, but I can't lose him. You have to fix this shit."

"I know. I will."

I disconnected the call and let the phone drop to the floor. Looking around the room, I knew that Flicker would never understand, and neither would Sarge. They'd find a way to keep me here, lock me away until it was too late. I couldn't let anything happen to Louis, not because of something my mother did. She'd ruined enough lives already. After all I'd been through, it seemed I couldn't escape her even when she was dead. It looked like I'd have to clean up her mess one final time, and I could only hope the two men I loved -- the man I wanted to spend eternity with, and the dad I'd never known -- would one day understand.

I shoved a few clothes into my bag, not bothering to take the new things Flicker had purchased. I stared at the leather outfit I'd worn here and it seemed fitting that I would put it back on to leave for what would probably be the last time. I fisted my keys and stared at them, wishing someone had thought to hide them from me. I knew it was weak, that even if I didn't have my bike, I'd have found a way to save Louis. He'd stood by me and now it was my turn.

I changed my clothes and shouldered my bag. I started out of the bedroom, pausing one more time. I glanced at the mussed sheets and shut my eyes. Images of the nights and days with Flicker filled me with a sense of peace. Even if it hadn't lasted long, he'd given me the best week of my life. It was the happiest I could remember ever being. I knew I couldn't leave without any explanation whatsoever. Before I left, I stopped in the kitchen and pulled a sheet of paper and a pen out of one of the drawers. I hastily scribbled an excuse for my abrupt departure, and made sure he knew that he'd made my life better, worth living. And I promised that if it was at all possible, I'd return to him. A drop of water hit the page and I blinked, realizing it wasn't water. I was crying.

Dashing the tears from my cheeks, I set the pen and paper in the center of the kitchen table and went out to my bike. He'd insisted I keep it under the carport next to his. Flicker had taken off earlier, so it was just my Indian under the covering right now. Something about club business and he'd be back later. I only hoped he didn't hate me when he got home and found my note.

The engine purred as I started my bike. I put on my helmet and took my time reaching the front gate. If I seemed like I was in a hurry, they'd be even more suspicious. Bad enough I had my bag with me. As I came to a halt at the gate, I felt my stomach drop. Shit. Diego. I hadn't interacted with him much, but I'd heard Flicker discussing the Prospects a few times. Diego and King were their best two, and I knew neither of them would let me leave without a fight. Not if they thought I didn't have permission.

He crossed his arms and stared down his nose at me. Yeah, this wasn't going to go well. I pulled off my helmet and held his gaze. I wondered if I looked as scared as I felt. He took a few steps toward me, reaching out to shut off my bike and pocket the keys.

"What the fuck, Diego?" I asked.

"Can't let you leave, Pepper. Not when I can't promise Flicker and Sarge that you're coming back."

"Are you a fucking mind reader now?" I demanded.

"Your hands are shaking, your eyes are nearly black from how fucking terrified you are, and you packed your shit. Since no one is with you, I'm going to guess this is an unauthorized trip."

"Fuck you. Give me my damn keys."

He shook his head, then pulled his phone out and sent a text.

"Who are you messaging?" I asked, my throat going dry.

"I'd suggest you go home, Pepper. You don't want to be at this gate in the next few minutes."

What the hell? Was he threatening me?

"I can't go home if you don't give my keys back," I reasoned and wondered if there was a back way into the compound. There had to be a way out other than just this gate, right?

He arched a brow and didn't budge. "You have two legs. Walk."

Fucker. I flipped him off, but he only smiled. "Motherfucker," I muttered.

"Nope, not my style. Unless she's a MILF."

Ew. I gagged, which only made him laugh. More than I needed to know about the Prospect. Before I could decide what to do, I heard the crunch of boots across gravel and turned. My eyes went wide when I saw not one, not two, but four bikers heading my way. What the fuck? Had he used the biker equivalent of a bat signal when he sent that text?

"Four men for little bitty me?" I asked, turning to face Diego again. "Am I that dangerous?"

"You're Sarge's kid. I'm not taking any chances," he said.

I narrowed my eyes before glancing at the others again. I'd met them briefly, but didn't know them well enough to know how this would play out. I needed to leave or Louis could die. I could only imagine what those sick bastards had done to him so far. My life was too harsh for someone like Louis. He'd grown up in a middle-class home with loving parents, and every creature comfort he could want or need. Even if they didn't agree with him having a boyfriend, he hadn't exactly had a tough life. If ever there was a place where someone could be openly gay, it was Vegas.

"Pepper, get your ass off that bike," Preacher said.

"Aren't you a man of God?" I asked. "Shouldn't you try *not* to cuss?"

He pointed to his cut. "Do I look like a fucking priest? Just because I'm an ordained minister doesn't mean I'm an angel. Don't make me repeat myself, little girl. Get your ass off that bike."

I tensed my jaw and glared at him.

"Don't be difficult, Pepper," Savior said. "Flicker would have a damn fit if he came home and you were gone."

"Sarge won't be too happy either," Bats said.

"You don't understand. I need to leave. If I don't, someone could die," I said, hoping to reason with them.

"So you want us to let you leave so *you* can die instead?" Saint snorted. "Ain't happening, sweetheart. Like it or not, you're one of us. Family. We don't send family off on suicide missions, especially a woman."

"Well, that's the most sexist thing I think you've said around me," I muttered. "I might not have a dick, but I can hold my own."

"Who's in charge?" Preacher asked. "I know all the officers are gone, as well as a few members like Wire and Cowboy."

"Bull," Saint said. "He's the most senior brother with the others gone."

Preacher snickered. "I'm telling him you called him a senior."

Saint flipped him off. "Asshole. You know what I fucking meant."

Preacher pulled out his phone and made a call, speaking to someone I could only assume was Bull. He nodded a few times and when he hung up, he stared at me, then the others. "Church. And he said to bring Pepper."

Before I could do anything, Saint hauled me off the bike and carried me toward the clubhouse, tucked under his fucking arm like I was a Goddamned football. As I stared at the ground, I ground my teeth and plotted my revenge. I'd find a way to get back at him for this. Make all his shit pink, put itching powder in his underwear, add blue dye to his shampoo. Something to embarrass him as much as it embarrassed the fuck out of me to be carried like this.

When we entered Church, he dropped me to my feet and pointed to a chair that I knew was Flicker's. "Sit."

I sat with a huff and folded my arms, staring at them like a petulant child.

Bull came into the room, with several other brothers on his heels. They all sat in what I assumed were their regular spots, despite the fact the other chairs were vacant. I guessed it was a respect thing, and I'd likely been given Flicker's chair since I was his. I didn't have a property cut yet, even though Flicker said he'd requested one, but Zipper had inked me not too long ago. I'd just wanted a simple *Property of Flicker* in black ink on my forearm. No frills or extras.

"I'm too tired for this shit," Bull said. "Just tell me what's going on and we'll go from there."

"Pepper was leaving," Saint said. "Said someone was going to die if she didn't."

Bull stared at me. Hard enough I squirmed under his gaze. It felt a little like being sent to the principal's office.

"You already know my mom stole drugs from some bad people. Since they couldn't find me, they took my best friend. If I don't go back to Las Vegas, then Louis could die. They've already had him several days," I said.

"Not happening," Bull said.

"You can't keep me here," I snapped. "I'm not your fucking prisoner."

"No, you're Flicker's old lady, and club property. It makes you one of the most prized possessions around here, Pepper. He's the last of the officers to claim someone, and he would totally lose his shit if you took off and we stood back and let it happen. Not to mention Sarge would tear the fucking place apart." Bull ran a hand through his long hair. "Look. I get it. You feel responsible for your friend and you want to save him. Running off without a plan isn't the way to do it."

"They aren't going to release him just because you show up," Savior said. "He knows too much, has probably seen things he shouldn't, or heard things. He's a liability to them now."

"So I just leave him there to die?" I asked. "I'm sorry but I'm not that fucking heartless."

The men studied me in silence. I had to make them understand. Louis was the only true friend I'd ever had, and even though we weren't constantly up each other's butts and shoving our noses where they didn't belong, it didn't mean we weren't close. Probably as close as I'd ever gotten to someone before coming here. We'd lived our lives and met once a week for coffee or dinner. But he'd been all I had, and I wouldn't abandon him now.

"What clubs do we know out that way?" Saint asked.

"Reckless Kings has a compound outside Vegas. Savage Knights aren't too far away from there either," Grimm said.

"Lords of the Void are in Northern California. Wouldn't take them long to reach that area," Coyote said. "I have some connections with that chapter."

"I don't know about clubs, but I have some ex-military buddies out that way," Rocky said. "I'm sure they're up for a bit of excitement."

I eyed the man, not sure what he meant by excitement, or who the hell would think going up against gangsters would be a good time. There were times I felt like I'd fallen down a rabbit hole, even these guys were kind of tame compared to the people my mom had hung around in Vegas. Or so I'd thought. If going after criminals was their idea of a good time, I might have been mistaken. I knew they weren't fluffy bunnies, but they'd seemed like good men.

Bull tugged on his beard and nodded. "Okay. Pepper, you're officially on lockdown. You're going to keep your ass at Flicker's house, and I'll assign two men to make sure you don't leave. In the meantime, Coyote, reach out to the Lords of the Void and see if they'll help. Saint, contact Reckless Kings. Tempest, you know someone with Savage Knights, don't you?"

Tempest nodded, but his lips thinned into a hard line and I had a feeling he didn't want to be the one to reach out to them.

"Rocky, reach out to your contacts and see who can help. We'll need reconnaissance for certain, find out where exactly they're holding her friend and our best options for extraction. Bats and Gears, you take first shift watching over Pepper. I'll send someone to relieve you in a few hours. Four-hour shifts until Flicker gets home. Then he can decide what to do with her." Bull stood up. "Get the fuck out and handle this shit. I'm going home and going the fuck to sleep."

Coyote snickered. "Darian wearing you out, old man?"

Bull growled at him. "She wants another kid. The other two are more than enough, but every time I blink, she's crawling into my lap and begging me for a baby."

"And there's something wrong with that?" Tex asked. "If Kalani could still have kids, I'd gladly give her more. Stop bitching and be grateful."

Tex looked a little pissed, and if he wanted more kids and couldn't have them, I understood his frustration over Bull's whining. I didn't know much about their situation, or Kalani, but if his wife wanted more kids and couldn't have them, then it must be painful for both of them. I'd noticed early on that women who wanted kids often had trouble conceiving, then the ones who made shit parents seemed to pop them out like fucking rabbits. I'd always thought it was unfair.

Bull shrugged. "I know. I don't exactly have a rough life with Darian and the kids, but I'm getting too damn old for midnight feedings and diaper changes. I'm sixty for fuck's sake! I'll be dead before the baby would even graduate from high school."

I blinked at Bull. "Sixty? But…"

"But what?" he asked.

"You don't look that old. Shouldn't your hair be all silver like Torch's if you're sixty?"

Tex coughed to cover a laugh and I heard a few snickers around the table. Bull rolled his eyes toward the ceiling and muttered something that sounded like *save her if Torch hears that shit*. He walked out without another word and I was left looking around the table wondering what just happened.

"Did I say something wrong?" I asked.

"Nope. Unless you say that shit in front of Torch," Savior said. "He's a little touchy about how old he looks considering his wife is so young. Most of the time it doesn't bother him, but he recently had a birthday, so he's been a bit growly about his age."

"Doesn't help that Bull is older than him by a few years," Grimm said. "The man ages too fucking well if you ask me. Hardly seems fair. By the time I'm sixty, I'll probably be fat and bald."

Tempest laughed. "Yeah, right. I think you work out more than anyone here. Even with all the shit you eat, you still have a fucking eight-pack. Fat and bald. I'll believe it when I see it."

"All right. We've been given our orders," Tex said as he stood. "Get Pepper home. I'll have one of the Prospects deliver her bike."

I looked around as the men all got up. Not a single one looked in my direction. It pissed me off a little bit. Were women so far beneath them that we were just decorations? Didn't they have anyone who could kick ass if the need arose? I knew I wasn't the toughest chick around, but if someone tried to take me down, I'd fight like hell to break free. And I sure as shit didn't like them talking over me, or about me like I was some little kid.

"It's like I'm not even here," I said.

"Oh, we know you're here," Bats said. "And you'd damn well better still be at the compound when Flicker gets home. I'm not about to have my balls cut off because you decided to be a hero. That man is completely crazy about you. Anything happens on our watch, and he'll massacre every last one of us. Brothers or not."

I thought that was a bit extreme and highly unlikely, but I kept my mouth shut and followed the men out of the room. My babysitters took me home, staring at the door as I shut and locked it. I went straight to the kitchen and balled up the note I'd left Flicker, tossing it into the trash. I sent Marcus a message that I was under house arrest, but help would be coming. It would have to do for now, and I hoped like hell I wasn't lying to him. If the guys didn't come through, and soon, then I'd have to find a way out of here. I wasn't letting Louis die, not if I could do something about it.

From my place on the couch, I could see Bats pacing in front of the house. I sighed, hating the feelings of helplessness that swamped me. I'd always prided myself on being strong, taking charge of my life, and getting shit done. Sitting on my ass while everyone else was off trying to solve my problems felt all kinds of wrong. I needed to help Louis, and yet I couldn't leave the compound. I'd tried to do the right thing, but it didn't count for much if my friend lost his life. If I lived through this crap, I needed to sit down and have a conversation with Flicker. It was bullshit that I was confined to the house, like some weak little woman who couldn't do shit. If he thought he was getting laid after this, he'd better think again. I was going on strike.

Chapter Eight

Flicker

I'd been away for two days. Two. And the compound seemed to be in utter chaos. I looked at Torch, Venom, and Tank before looking back at the massive line of bikes in front of the clubhouse, and what looked like a dozen men patrolling the damn fence with AR-15s. What the fuck had happened while we were gone, and why hadn't we gotten a phone call about this shit? Part of me wanted to go straight to the house and check on Pepper, but if something had happened to her, I didn't think the club would have kept silent about it.

Fox and Slider, from Hades Abyss, both came out of the clubhouse and headed toward us. I saw Cobra and Wolf from Devil's Fury standing on the porch, along with a few members from Devil's Boneyard. Another look at the other officers with me showed they were just as confused, and not quite holding onto their tempers. Torch looked about ready to fucking blow, and Venom's jaw was clenched so fucking tight I worried his teeth might crack. Tank seemed cool, but his eyes told another story.

"What. The. Fuck?" Torch shouted.

Everyone halted in their steps, except Fox and Slider. They stopped a few feet away, holding eye contact with Torch. The Pres was starting to look a little flushed, and I wondered if we would be short a few members by end of the day. He looked ready to tear of some heads.

"Got a call yesterday," Fox said. "Your women sure are a fuck ton of trouble."

"Pepper?" I asked, my gut clenching.

Fox shrugged. "She tried to leave. Diego stopped her and your boys took over, confining her to your house. She's not the most pleasant of women when she's caged."

Slider rubbed at claw marks on his neck.

"Pepper did that?" I asked, motioning to the four red slashes.

He nodded. "She didn't like it when I hauled her ass back to the house. She gave your boys the slip and was trying to climb the fucking fence."

"It has razor wire on top," Tank said, looking dumbfounded.

"Didn't seem to deter her," Slider muttered. "Batshit crazy bitch."

"That's my woman you're talking about," I reminded him. "Who the hell are all the men here, and why are they patrolling the perimeter?"

"Well, your woman is one reason," Fox said. "The other is to make sure no one comes after her. You don't have a great track record of crazy people staying on the correct side of the fence. No offense."

"He's not wrong," Venom muttered. "Told you we needed to beef up security around here. Get more Prospects and make sure we don't have any weak points of entry. There's too much for us to lose now."

"We'll definitely need more after we patch in Diego and King. It will happen soon. Hell, they've been with us a little over three years. They've paid their dues and proven themselves," Torch said.

"Not too sure about Calder and Fenton," I said. "At first, it was just Fenton fucking shit up, but Calder is about on my last damn nerve too. In three years, they've screwed up more than most and been given too many damn chances."

Venom and Torch nodded.

"Only reason they're still here," Tank said, "is because we're low on Prospects. We need fresh blood, and we need more than a few at a time. I like Cinder's idea of only accepting ex-military with high security clearance, then having Wire dig through their lives to make sure they aren't hiding shit."

"I can do that," Wire said. "Give me some names and whatever info you've got. I'll tell you everything down to what they had for breakfast that morning."

"As much as I hate to let Calder and Fenton hang on, giving them false hope, I don't know about cutting them loose until after Pepper is safe," Torch said. "I don't think they'd turn traitor, but if they get pissed-off who knows what shit they'll pull."

"Agreed," Venom said.

I looked around, noticing most of the men patrolling didn't seem to be wearing a cut, which meant they weren't part of a club. So where the fuck did they come from? And who had authorized all these people to be here inside the damn gates with my woman?

Fox noticed the direction of my gaze and smiled a little. "You can thank Rocky for the extra hands. He called in favors with his military pals. We had twenty show up. Can you believe that shit? They've been patrolling in shifts, and they're apparently down for whatever the fuck you might need."

"Noted," I said.

As much as I didn't like the strangers on our turf, I was glad that Rocky had called them in, and thankful to whoever had called in the other clubs. If Rocky trusted these men, then that was good enough for me. For now. If they wanted to stay, I liked the idea of Wire digging into their lives to make sure they weren't rotten. We needed help if things had gone sideways with Pepper while I was gone. I hadn't wanted to leave her, but it couldn't be avoided. Casper VanHorne had called a meeting, something he'd claimed couldn't wait. He'd asked for all officers and Wire to attend, as well as Spider from Hades Abyss and Grizzly from Devil's Fury, which had left our compound vulnerable. I didn't doubt my brothers could handle shit, and they apparently had, but it felt wrong for all of us to be gone at once.

My mind was still reeling over what VanHorne had asked of us. It wasn't completely out of the question, but fucking hell. I was trying to extract Pepper from the Mafia, not join forces with another branch of the bastards. After Devil's Boneyard had taken out Silva, another monster had taken his place, one of his henchmen. Mateo Gomez. The difference was that Gomez wanted insurance, a way to guarantee he didn't run into complications for his business in the US. The fucker was clever, but not clever enough. No matter what deal was made, it wouldn't stop any of us from putting a bullet between his eyes if we thought he needed it.

I knew he hadn't just made a deal with our club. No, he'd gotten VanHorne to get an agreement with Hades Abyss, Devil's Fury, and Reckless Kings as well. He wanted muscle stateside to back him up, and we were the lucky fuckers selected. I couldn't deal with that shit right now, though. It hadn't gone quite the way Gomez had wanted, but Torch had worked something out. I only hoped Saint would forgive him in this lifetime.

"Pepper's at home on lockdown?" I asked to clarify where I'd find my woman.

"Unless she's escaped again," Slider said.

"Then I guess I'm going home," I said.

"Church in an hour." Torch looked around at our little group. "We need to be caught up to speed, and I want to know what's been set in motion while I was gone. I know I put Bull in charge, but fucking hell. A phone call would have been nice."

I couldn't have agreed more. I turned my bike down the road that would lead me home. When I pulled into the carport, I noticed Pepper's bike was there, and I couldn't help but laugh when I saw they'd found a way to keep her off it. A rubber-coated chain had been strung through the front tire, then down the frame of the bike and through the rear tire, with at least two locks keeping it in place. Whoever had set it up, had made sure it wouldn't scratch the frame or the chrome, which I knew Pepper would appreciate, even if she didn't like having her wheels on lockdown just like her.

I was curious exactly what she'd done to the men while I was gone. It seemed a bit extreme to put her on house arrest and chain her bike. Had she really tried to climb the fence, razor wire and all? It seemed insane, but I knew Pepper could be determined when she put her mind to something. I didn't know what had happened, but something had set her off, made her feel like she needed to run, and I'd damn sure find out what it was, then handle that shit. My woman wasn't going anywhere, not unless I was with her.

Gears was standing at the front door, his tense expression relaxing when he gave me a nod. "Thank fuck you're here. See if you can reason with her."

My curiosity was growing as I entered the house. I heard the TV going in the living room and peered inside. Pepper was on the couch, a pillow wrapped in her arms and her feet on the coffee table. Her jaw was tight, her eyes rimmed in red, but it was the scratches and bruises on the parts of her body that weren't covered that pissed me the fuck off.

"Who touched you?" I asked, my voice harsher than I'd intended.

She jerked and looked at me, her eyes going wide for a moment. I could see the pulse pounding in her throat from across the room.

"Pepper, who did that to you?" I asked again.

She glanced at her arms and exposed legs, just shrugging her shoulder.

"Oh, no, sweet girl. I need more than that from you. I want to know who laid their hands on you and left marks behind."

"A few bruises are from Slider when he pulled me off the fence."

I nodded, already knowing he'd done that. I just hadn't realized he'd marked her in the process.

"The scratches are from the bushes about a mile down the fence line," she said.

Did I want to know why she'd gotten scratched by those bushes? The look in her eyes told me that no, I most certainly didn't. Probably another one of her escape attempts.

"The bruises on my wrists are from Saint, who has apologized profusely and said he feels like shit. He was trying to restrain me when I attacked King," she said.

"Why did you attack King?" I asked, almost dreading the answer. Where was the sweetheart I'd left in my bed? Jesus. It was like my woman had been replaced with a fucking rabid honey badger.

"He called me a bitch, said I needed to keep my bony ass at home where it belonged, and let the men handle shit. Then he shoved me."

"He shoved you?" I asked slowly, thinking there was probably more to it than that. I'd never seen King lay a hand on a woman, unless she was begging for it.

"I may have gotten up in his face and cussed him out," she admitted.

"Fucking hell, Pepper. What's going on? When I left, you seemed fine. Happy even. What changed?"

"Louis is in trouble. He's my best friend and because of me, he's been taken. If I don't show up and turn myself in, then Galetti will give the order to kill Louis. It's why I need to leave, Daniel. I don't want to go. I never wanted to leave you, or my dad, but I can't let Louis die because of me."

"Where's Sarge?" I asked. "He should have been here watching over you, and talking some fucking sense into you."

Her lips turned down and her brow furrowed. "He wasn't with you?"

"No." I reached for my phone and called Sarge. It went straight to voicemail. "When's the last time you saw your dad?"

"The night before you left. His bike was gone when I went outside the next day. I just thought he was with you on club business."

"Christ. So we need to rescue your friend, keep you out of Galetti's hands, and find Sarge. He keeps disappearing and it's starting to piss me off. I hope like hell he didn't go after that man on his own." I sent a text to Wire, asking him to use Sarge's GPS on his phone to get a location. No need to alert Torch or Venom until we knew whether or not the man was actually MIA or just off having fun. Fuck of a time to do it, though.

Wire immediately messaged back. *On it.*

"Wire is going to find your dad," I told her. "But for now, come here."

She got off the couch and approached me, slowly. Almost as if she were afraid I would be angry or try to hurt her. I'd never given her cause to fear me -- except for that one time she'd mistook my words -- and as I studied the marks on her skin again, I realized my brothers had done this to her. Made her afraid. Yes, they'd been trying to restrain her so she wouldn't run off and get killed, but they'd been too rough. Something I'd be discussing during Church in a bit.

When Pepper stopped in front of me, I wrapped her in my arms and pulled her tight against my chest. I'd missed the hell out of her while I'd been gone. I fisted her hair and breathed in her sweet scent. After a moment, she melted against me, her body relaxing and all the tension draining away.

"Please don't leave me again," she said.

"I'm not going anywhere. Not right now. There will be times I need to go out on club business, but I'm sticking by your side until all this mess is over. You're safe, Pepper, and I'll make sure Louis is safe too. Whatever Galetti wants, we'll find a way to give it to him."

"Money. He'll want money," she murmured. "Since I can't give him the drugs, he'll want their value plus interest. And that's if he's willing to take that. Who knows how long he was after Mom to give it to him, and it's been over a week since I found her dead."

"We'll handle it, sweetheart."

I tipped her chin up and noticed the dark smudges under her eyes. She hadn't been sleeping, probably for fear her friend would die. I kissed her softly, then led her to the bedroom. We didn't have time for me to strip her bare and kiss every inch of her, but that wouldn't stop me from holding her for a bit. I removed my cut and my boots, then lay on the bed, tugging her down. I held her close and rubbed her back.

"I have to go to Church in a bit," I told her. "I'm not leaving the compound, Pepper. You need me, you come to clubhouse. Someone will get me."

"All right," she said, her voice sounding small and defeated. I hated that. I wanted that fire I'd seen in her from the very beginning.

"Everything else was fine while I was gone, right? You aren't feeling sick? No one hurt you intentionally? Or threatened you?" I asked.

"They were trying to keep me locked up in the house to wait for you. They didn't mean to hurt me, Flicker. I know that. And I feel fine. Just tired."

"Sleep, baby girl. I've got you."

She nodded and yawned. It didn't take long before she was snoring softly, and I pressed a kiss to her forehead. She'd exhausted herself, worrying over her friend, and likely stressing over my absence. Torch wouldn't like it, but I wasn't leaving the compound for the next few months unless either Pepper was with me, or I would be gone less than a day. She needed time to adjust to this way of life, to being cared about, and having people who wanted to keep her safe.

When it was time to leave, I kissed her cheek and eased out of bed, careful not to wake her. I put my boots and cut back on, then walked to the clubhouse. I could have taken my bike, but if she woke up and looked outside, I wanted her to see it in the carport, to know I hadn't left the compound. I was the last to arrive, and I noticed none of the other clubs had joined us.

Torch called everyone to order, then waited for quiet to descend in the room.

"How's Pepper?" he asked me.

"Bruised and scratched all to hell," I said. His eyebrows lifted. "It seems our brothers got a little rough when trying to physically restrain her. I didn't get a chance to look her over as well as I'd have liked, but I saw marks on her arms, legs, and a few were peeking out of the neckline of her shirt."

Torch glared at the members who had been left behind and had dealt with Pepper during her frantic attempts to reach her friend.

"What. The Fuck? Since when do we hurt women?" he asked. "Who the fuck laid hands on Flicker's old lady?"

Saint looked a little green. "Some are from me, but I swear I didn't mean to grab her that hard. She was struggling and I was worried she'd get hurt if I let go."

A few more hands went up around the room. Saint was the only one who looked truly remorseful for his actions, and I knew Torch would probably let him off with just a few harsh words. He had a soft spot for the kid, and I had to admit that Saint wasn't the type to ever hurt a woman or child. It had surprised the hell out of us when he'd disappeared for a while, only to return home with a daughter. The kid had always been almost too fucking perfect.

"Everyone who hurt Pepper will stay after Church. We're going to have a little talk," Torch said.

Tank cracked his knuckles and I wondered if he'd be helping. I had a feeling his words would come across with his fists. Even though he hadn't trusted Pepper at first, I knew that had changed and he would protect her just like he would the other ladies in the club.

"What do we know about Pepper's situation?" Torch asked.

"Her friend, Louis, has been taken," I said. "They want to exchange her friend for her. Pepper says they'll either want their drugs, or the cash value plus interest."

"I'll contact Galetti when this is over. I'd planned to handle it, then Casper called that fucking meeting. Maybe we can make the man see reason. If all he wants is money, then we'll give him what he wants. If he wants Pepper, we'll fucking gut him," Torch said.

Worked for me. I knew it would be too easy, just throwing cash at Galetti. Pepper had a point. As long as he'd waited, he would need to make an example of her. Letting her go, even if she paid him a huge sum, would make him look weak. Men like Galetti couldn't let something like that happen. Weakness meant he'd be taken down, killed, and his territory would be gobbled up by someone else.

"I have some friends in Vegas. They've checked out Galetti's place. I have confirmation that Pepper's friend is there, and he's in rough shape but still breathing. Extraction is possible, but we'll need one hell of a distraction," Rocky said.

"What's the setup?" Tex asked.

"Six-story building outside the city. Galetti has Louis on the top floor, under guard. The building can only be accessed with a code, and there seems to be some sort of scanner set up in the elevator, possibly retinal. Only authorized persons can get to the top floor," Rocky said.

"Manpower?" Coyote asked.

"Four guards in the room with him, two more on the floor near the elevator, and several scattered throughout the building. Only two in the lobby. All armed with nine-millimeter handguns. My buddies didn't see any AR-15s or anything heavier than a Glock. Doesn't mean they don't have access to them, but they don't seem to carry them," Rocky said. "I'm willing to bet they have an armory or something set up inside."

"Why not call Galetti now?" I asked. "If he's not willing to take the cash, then better to find out while we're all here so we can come up with a plan. No fucking way I'm letting Pepper go in there. We'll have to get Louis back some other way."

Torch nodded and pulled out his phone, then looked across the table at Wire. "Number?"

Wire tapped on his computer and spit out a string of numbers. Torch tapped them into his phone, then put it speaker.

"Who the fuck is this?" a man asked when the ringing stopped.

"Galetti, I presume?" Torch asked.

"Depends on who wants to know. How did you get this number?"

"Don't worry about that. My name is Torch and I'm the President of the Dixie Reapers. I understand you want Pepper White."

"You know where Miss White is hiding?" Galetti asked.

"I do, but I have a counteroffer. Pepper doesn't have your drugs. She didn't even know about them until after her mother overdosed. But I'm willing to pay you for your trouble, if you agree to leave Pepper alone and to release her friend, Louis."

The line was quiet except for the man's breathing.

"Your Pepper has put me in a precarious situation. Even though she didn't steal my drugs, she's liable for them. If I let her go with just a slap on the wrist, it won't look good. I have an image to uphold," Galetti said.

"I understand that, Mr. Galetti. What if I sweeten the pot a little? I know you deal in harder drugs, but I'm willing to make a deal. I'll give you thirty grand in cash, and another five grand worth of premium pot. I understand that you've already roughed up Louis a bit, you can make sure people have witnessed your... lesson to Pepper, and you'll be getting more compensation than what your brick of coke was worth," Torch said.

"It's an interesting proposition," Galetti said. "Why would you offer so much to secure Miss White's debt?"

"Pepper is the daughter of a Dixie Reaper," Torch said. "And she's the old lady to one of my officers. If you hurt Pepper, then I'll have no choice but to start an all-out war with you, Mr. Galetti. And it won't just be my club coming for you. We have family connections with several others who would be more than willing to give aid in taking down you and your organization."

"I see." Galetti got quiet again. "I will think over what you've said and call back in forty-eight hours."

The line went dead and I stared at Torch. "You think he's really going to consider it?"

"No," Torch said. "Make sure the perimeter is secure at all times. Now that I've told him where Pepper is located, he'll send someone for her. It's partially Casper's fault this shit has gone on this long.

If he hadn't insisted we meet immediately, then tied us up for several days, then we could have dealt with Pepper's issue sooner. His ass can come lend a hand."

Venom snickered. "I'm sure he'll just love you demanding his presence."

Torch flipped him off, then dialed Casper, putting it on speaker again.

"You're not going back on our deal," Casper said when he picked up.

"Not trying to, but I need you here."

"I'm not at your beck and call," Casper said, sounding amused and slightly annoyed at the same time.

"Someone named Galetti is coming for one of the old ladies. Since I couldn't handle this shit because of your meeting, you're going to come help us keep Pepper safe. Because if Galetti's men get inside, it's not just Pepper in trouble."

Casper growled. "That fucker better not harm one hair on my daughter's head."

"So you'll come?" Torch asked.

"I'll be there in a few hours. And I'm calling that fat bastard on my way there."

Wait. What?

"You know Galetti?" I asked.

"In a matter of speaking. We aren't friends or associates, but I've had dealings with him and his organization in the past. I'll make sure he knows if he goes against the Reapers that I will consider it a personal attack."

Right. And no one in their fucking mind would go after Casper VanHorne. Some had tried, had even targeted Isabella to get to him, but it never worked in their favor. They usually ended up dead for their efforts. If Galetti sent someone for Pepper, knowing that she was protected by VanHorne, then the man was batshit fucking crazy. Casper was the most notorious assassin in the country, and for good reason.

"I'll have the guestroom ready when you get here," Torch said, then ended the call.

"Now what?" I asked.

"Now, we wait. Go spend time with your woman and let her know trouble could be coming. Better for her to be prepared than kept in the dark. When Casper gets here, we'll come up with a game plan for taking out Galetti." Torch waved a hand. "Everyone out. Go do what the fuck ever."

I stood but hesitated. After everyone had left, I approached Torch. He looked tired, and I knew he just wanted to go home to his wife and kids. There was just something I needed to say first.

"Thank you," I said.

"For what?" he asked.

"Protecting Pepper. For calling in Casper, and offering Galetti a deal. If he accepts, you can take the money from my share of our profits."

Torch snorted. "That girl is family, even if she weren't yours. The club will cover the cost, but I don't think Galetti is going to accept. Too fucking easy. And let's face it. When it comes to our women, nothing is ever easy. They're worth the trouble, but it would be nice if we ever got one without having to kill someone along the way."

"Good luck with that," I said. "When are you going to tell Saint?"

"That he'll be housing a nineteen-year-old woman in his house?" he asked, his eyebrows raised.

"No, that you offered him up as a husband to one of Gomez's daughters. You know how he feels about accepting a woman into his life, especially now that he has a kid. He's not going to let just anyone near his daughter."

"I'll deal with it later, but Saint will do as he's told. Always has and always will. That kid hasn't caused much trouble since coming here. He's protected my family and given blood and sweat to keep this club safe. If I explain the situation, he'll do what's needed."

"I hope you're right."

I tapped the table, then headed out. Saint would be Torch's problem. I didn't think the kid was going to accept a wife as easily as Torch believed. Only time would tell.

Chapter Nine

Pepper

While Flicker was at his meeting, or Church, my phone kept buzzing with incoming texts. I was scared to look, but eventually I couldn't help myself. A few were from Marcus, asking why the hell I wasn't helping Louis. It was the ones from a blocked number that made me rush to the bathroom and throw up. I sobbed as I hugged the toilet. It seemed that my time had run out.

Flicker found me lying on the floor in the bathroom, my throat sore from crying so damn hard. He knelt beside me and smoothed my hair back.

"Pepper, what's wrong?"

"Louis." I took a shuddering breath. "He killed him. He…"

"How do you know, baby girl?" he asked.

"Phone. Someone sent pictures."

Flicker stood and rushed into the bedroom. He must have found my phone because he started cursing and it sounded like he'd punched the wall. More than once. When he came back, he knelt in front of me again and pulled me into his arms.

"I'm so fucking sorry, Pepper. I thought it was handled. I don't know what game Galetti is playing now."

"He's not going to stop, is he?" I asked. "He'll come for me, or kill everyone I care about until I turn myself over to him. He's a monster and we won't be able to reason with him, will we?"

"It's his answer to Torch's offer," Flicker said softly. "Torch offered to pay him, even offered some weed as well, and it seems Galetti is turning down that offer and sending a message."

"Marcus will never forgive me," I said, feeling broken inside. Louis and his boyfriend were the only people to stand beside me, until now. We might not have had the perfect friendship, but it was more than I'd ever had before. And I'd failed them when it counted most and Louis had lost his life.

"This isn't your fault, Pepper. If anyone is to blame, it's your mother. She got you into this mess and took the easy way out. If she'd faced them and not killed herself, then they never would have come for you. I can understand where Galetti is coming from. Doesn't make it right, but the man can't hold his territory if people think he's weak," Flicker said.

"I should have turned myself in to him," I said. "Then Louis would be alive. He didn't deserve to die like that."

The images had been brutal. While I didn't have any desire to die, it tore me apart knowing that should have been me and not Louis, my sweet friend who had never hurt anyone in his life. He'd been a gentle soul and it was my fault he was gone, regardless of what Flicker said. Yes, my mother had put me in this position, but I could have saved Louis.

I let Flicker hold me. I knew he wanted to help, to make me feel better, but nothing could do that. Well, maybe one thing. I wanted Galetti to pay for what he'd done. Monsters like him should be removed from the world. I knew that wasn't realistic, that evil people had been around since the beginning of time, but if there was a way to wipe them out, I'd do it. I'd never understand how someone could brutally murder another person, especially just to make a point. What kind of person did that?

"We'll stop Galetti," Flicker said. "I promise, Pepper. Your friend will be avenged, and we'll make sure Galetti never harms another person."

"I want to help," I said.

"I know you do. You're as fierce as you are beautiful, but I need you to stay here where it's safe. If you're out there where Galetti can reach you, then I'll be distracted. Promise you'll stay here, behind the gates," he said. "I mean it, Pepper. I need to know he can't get to you."

I gave a slight nod, but I wasn't about to verbally agree. It wasn't technically a lie if I didn't voice my answer, right? Because if I had half a chance to make sure Galetti never drew another breath, never harmed another person, then I'd do it. I knew that Flicker wanted to keep me safe, and I appreciated it, but I'd never had anyone to fight my battles for me, and I didn't know that I wanted to start that crap now.

"I need to show those pictures to Torch and Casper. I'm going to forward them to my phone, then delete them from yours," he said. "You don't need to see that shit again."

"Who's Casper?" I asked. I knew there were still members of the club I hadn't officially met, but this was the first time I'd heard that name.

"Torch's father-in-law, which is funny as shit because the man is younger than Torch. Casper made a deal to protect his daughter, Isabella. Torch claimed her as his old lady, never thinking he'd actually love her, but the two of them are crazy about each other."

"Guess all of you go for younger women, huh?" I asked, smiling a little. It reminded me of the woman at the diner. My dad claimed she was too young for him, but I had to wonder if there was something there, a connection he was trying to deny. I couldn't wait to see how that played out. Speaking of… "Where's my dad?"

"Shit. Someone was supposed to check on him. Let me see if Wire got a hit on his GPS. He wasn't in Church and no one's seen him since the morning the officers left. He wasn't with us, so we don't know where the fuck he went."

My stomach churned. "He wouldn't go after Galetti alone, would he? I know he's ex-military, but he's not invincible."

"I don't know, but I wouldn't put it past him. Honestly, when I found out Sarge was missing, that was my first thought. You're his daughter, Pepper. He'll want to protect you, even if it costs him his life. Can't blame the guy."

"Find him, please. And if he did leave and go after Galetti, send someone to bring him back. I can't lose him, Daniel. I just can't."

He cupped my cheek and pressed a kiss to my forehead. "We'll keep your daddy safe, Pepper. You have my word."

I nodded and let him help me off the floor. I splashed some water on my face and brushed my teeth. My heart still ached over the loss of Louis, but I felt better. At least, a little bit better. I knew it would take time to heal. Even though I'd never lost anyone but my mother, a woman I'd stopped caring about long ago, I'd been around plenty of people who lost loved ones.

I heard him in the other room talking to someone on the phone. Staring at my reflection, I wasn't too sure I liked what I saw. I'd run from my problems before, but then it had been smart. Leaving Louis with that madman had been the wrong thing to do. I'd known it, and I'd done my best to reach him, but my best hadn't been good enough. Not blaming myself was going to be difficult. The only thing that could have saved Louis was me turning myself in, and I'd been willing to do it even if it meant I died. Be willing to do something and actually doing it were different. I'd failed.

My stomach lurched and I ran to the toilet, throwing up again until there wasn't anything left and I was just dry heaving. Flicker found me on my knees, hugging the porcelain bowl again. He helped me get cleaned up, then he carried me outside. I didn't know where the hell we were going or why, but there was a truck idling in the driveway.

"Where did that come from?" I asked.

"When I heard you getting sick again, I called one of the Prospects to bring a truck over. You're going to the doctor, Pepper, and don't fucking argue with me. I'll make sure you're well-guarded. As much as I want to keep you here at the compound, I need the doc to make sure you're okay."

"He can't come here?" I asked.

"Well, he has in the past, but since he hasn't treated you before he may want to run tests and that would be easier at his clinic."

Seemed reasonable enough. Flicker buckled me into the back seat, then climbed into the passenger side. I recognized King in the driver's seat, and when we approached the gates, I saw three men on bikes waiting for us. One pulled in front and the other two fell in line behind the truck. It seemed a bit much just to go see the doctor, but I wouldn't argue. This time. If Flicker thought I'd go for something like this every time I wanted to leave in the future, he was dead wrong. I could understand the need for extra security right now, but I hoped it wasn't going to be an everyday type of thing. I'd feel smothered in no time.

I hadn't paid much attention to the little town I would now call home. When I'd arrived, I'd been too nervous and focused on meeting my dad for the first time. I hadn't really had a chance to get out and explore, or get a good look at the place during the daytime. It was cute. Nowhere near as big as Vegas, but it seemed like a great place to raise kids. I wondered if Flicker and I would ever have a family. I hadn't thought about it too much in the past, not knowing who would ever want to marry someone like me. Not that Flicker had asked me to marry him, just move in with him. It was still more than anyone had ever offered before.

As we passed the diner, I smacked my hand against the window. "There! It's my dad's bike! Isn't it?"

The truck came to a halt and Flicker looked in the direction I pointed. "Yeah, that's Sarge's Harley. I'll call it in and have someone track him down."

"I need to see him, Flicker. I need to know he's okay."

Before anyone could stop me, I'd unbuckled and leapt from the truck. I went running for the diner, but as I hurried inside, I didn't see my dad anywhere. I scanned the place twice before a waitress came over.

"Can I help you, hon?" she asked.

"I was looking for my dad. His bike is out front."

"Sarge?" she asked.

I nodded.

"Go down the alley. There's a glass door, but you won't be able to see through it. There's a buzzer next to it. He's with Lily up in her apartment."

Lily? I thought that was the name of the waitress who had been checking him out, the one who had the ass he hadn't been able to stop staring at when we'd come here that first night. I nearly knocked Flicker over as I rushed back outside and down the alley. I heard him calling me, but I wasn't about to stop and explain. If my dad was with Lily, then he was likely all right, but I needed to see for myself. What if everyone just thought they were together but he'd really been snatched by Galetti or someone else?

I pushed the buzzer and waited. I felt Flicker grip my arm and knew he'd yell at me first chance he had, but I didn't much care.

"Can I help you?" a voice asked through the intercom.

"I'm looking for Sarge," I said.

The intercom went silent and I waited for what felt like forever before my dad opened the door. He looked tired and almost defeated. What the hell was going on? If I'd known this Lily person wasn't going to be good for him, I'd have never suggested he hook up with her.

"Dad, what's going on?" I asked. "You just disappeared."

"Sorry, baby girl." He pulled me against his chest and gave me a hug. "I've been dealing with some stuff. We'll talk about it soon, okay? I'm still figuring shit out. I'm sorry if I worried you."

"Have you not looked at your phone?" Flicker asked.

Sarge shrugged, then pulled it out and stared at it. "Dead. Must have forgotten to charge it."

"There's a crime boss after your daughter and you didn't think to fucking check in?" Flicker demanded.

"I figured she was safe here. Look, I'm dealing with some shit and it's got my head all fucked up." Sarge sighed. "Pepper means the world to me. Finding out I have a daughter is amazing, but there are things that were put in motion before she arrived and I'm trying to handle the fallout."

"Louis is dead, Dad," I said. "Galetti took him. I was supposed to go turn myself in and he would let Louis go, but I was put on lockdown at the compound. Galetti, he..."

Flicker ran a hand down my hair. "It was brutal. Pepper's been sick all morning so I'm taking her to see Doctor Myron. She saw your bike and jumped out of the damn truck."

My dad tipped my chin up. "Listen to Flicker, honey. And the others. They'll keep you safe. I'm damn sorry about your friend, but if I had to choose between that boy and you, I'd pick you every time. Stay alive, whatever it takes."

"Are you coming home?" I asked.

"Soon. Might bring Lily with me, if I can get her to listen to a fucking thing I say. Stubborn-ass woman."

I smiled up at him. "If she's stubborn, then that's a good thing. She'd need to be in order to handle you."

"You might be right." My dad tugged on a lock of my hair. "I'll be home soon. Stay out of trouble."

Flicker snorted but didn't comment. I glared at him, but he just winked at me. I gave my dad another hug, and then Flicker led me back to the truck. The doctor's clinic wasn't much farther. I hadn't expected all of them to come inside with me, but they did. King and Flicker stayed by my side, and the other three -- Bats, Grimm, and Savior -- stayed near the door.

A few women in the waiting room gave them looks, clearly uncomfortable with the bikers lurking. Well, except one. The way she was eyeing Savior, she looked like she'd be more than willing to climb him like a tree and hold on. It amused me, seeing the way the public reacted to them. To me, they were just men -- some of whom could be really damn annoying -- but a few of the women in the waiting room looked downright scared.

"What's that grin for?" King asked, looking around, as if trying to see what was so funny.

"Just observing the other people waiting to see the doctor," I said.

He looked around again, his brow furrowed. "What about them?"

"You don't see how you make some of them nervous? Except the one lady who looks ready to lick Savior from head to toe."

Flicker snickered and put his arm around me. "You get used to it."

"Yeah, well, someone looks at you like you're a lollipop and we're going to have words. Possibly with fists," I said.

He brushed a kiss to the top of my head. "You're the only woman I want, baby girl."

"The two of you are rather nauseating," King muttered.

Flicker flipped him off, making one of the ladies gasp. She shot up off her chair and rushed to the front desk. I was assuming she'd changed her appointment since a moment later she practically ran from the clinic. If that offended her, then I felt sorry for her husband or boyfriend. She'd looked like the type who didn't know how to have a good time. But then, there were plenty of men like that too, so maybe she was with her perfect match.

I wasn't very good at waiting.

"Hey, we didn't even sign in," I said, starting to stand, but Flicker pulled me back down.

"Don't need to. King set up your appointment when he brought the truck over. They're expecting you," Flicker said.

Well, that was different. I was starting to see that being with the club would take a bit of adjustment. Things didn't seem to work for them like it did for regular people. I only hoped that meant if they did tangle with Galetti that no one would get into trouble over it.

A nurse stepped out of a doorway that led to a long hall. "Pepper White."

I stood and Flicker did as well. King stood up and I glared at him. He promptly sat his ass back down. No way in hell they were both going back there with me. Flicker was mine, but King didn't have any business hearing whatever the doctor had to say. I didn't care if he did feel like he needed to protect me. I didn't think anyone would attack me in here, and if they did, I had Flicker with me. And it wasn't like I couldn't hold my own if the need arose. At least, I assumed I could. After the night that had changed my life, I'd taken some self-defense classes. In theory, I could protect myself if I needed to even though I'd never tested it.

I was shown to a room and climbed onto the padded table while Flicker placed himself between me and the door. I thought it was sweet, but unnecessary. We were at the doctor, not in a war zone.

Famous last words, or thoughts in this case. An unassuming blonde woman in scrubs came in, flashed me what to be the evilest smile I'd ever seen, injected something into Flicker and my guy fell straight to the floor.

"What the fuck?" I jumped off the table, but I had nowhere to go.

The bitch pulled another syringe out of her pocket and uncapped it. When she came toward me, I kicked out at her, my toe colliding with her elbow. It knocked the needle from her hand, but it didn't slow her down. She reached for me, her hands going around my throat. I slapped and punched at her, doing my best to break free. Her grip tightened and spots danced across my vision. My knee landed hard against her ribs and she grunted in pain, but didn't let go. After a moment, everything started going dark. My last thoughts were that I hoped Flicker would forgive me when he woke up.

Chapter Ten

Flicker

"Son of a bitch!" I roared in fury at anyone within hearing distance. How the fuck had Pepper been taken? I'd only faced Pepper for a moment, and I'd heard the door open, but before I'd even turned around, someone had injected me with something. Whatever the hell it was, it had knocked me out for hours. Fucking hours! Who the hell knew where Pepper was by now, or if she was even still alive.

"Where the fuck were you?" I demanded of King and the others who had been with us. "How did she get past you?"

"Back entrance," King said. "None of us thought someone on Doc Myron's staff would hurt her. We left the building and your woman vulnerable."

"Doc had some cameras installed out back after a break-in last year. A blonde woman in scrubs and a big ass guy in a suit put your Pepper into a black SUV. We pulled a plate number, but Wire ran it and it's been stolen off a damn Prius," Grimm said.

"You know who has her," Torch said. "We were only waiting for you to wake up before we acted. Whatever the fuck they gave you knocked you out for a few hours. Plenty of time for Galetti's people to put her on a jet and fly her to Vegas. Rocky's contacts confirmed a woman matching Pepper's description went into Galetti's building. She appeared unconscious."

"And they didn't fucking do anything?" I demanded.

"They didn't want to risk harming Pepper further," Torch said.

"We can figure shit out when we get there. I'm going to Vegas and I'm getting Pepper back. Who the fuck is going with me?" I asked.

Casper VanHorne stepped from the shadows of the room. I'd known he was at the compound, but I hadn't even realized he was in fucking Church with us. Damn ghost! But if the scary son of a bitch was on our side, I didn't care how fucking creepy he could be.

"My jet can be fueled and ready to leave within the hour," Casper said. "It can't hold everyone, though. Including me, eight men can go."

"Sarge and I are going," I said, knowing Pepper's dad wasn't going to sit this one out. The man gave me a nod where he lounged in his seat, looking too relaxed. I knew that was the furthest thing from true though. He had that look in his eyes, the *someone fucked with my daughter and I'll slaughter them all* look.

"I'll go," Rocky said. "The guys in Vegas will be happy to get their hands dirty."

"I'll go too," Tempest said. "Savage Knights offered some men. I'll help coordinate when we get there. I may not always like the fuckers, but at least I'm familiar to them."

"That leaves room for three," Casper said.

"I'm in," said Tank. "I owe Pepper."

I gave him a nod. Yeah, he did fucking owe her, and I was grateful he was going.

"Me too," said Tex.

The doors slammed open and I grinned when I saw who was walking into Church unannounced. Motherfucker. I hadn't even realized he was getting out.

"Can anyone join this party?" Hammer asked.

"When the fuck did you get out?" Cowboy asked.

"This morning," Hammer said. "Thought I'd surprise you fuckers. What are we discussing?"

"Flicker's woman was kidnapped and taken to Vegas by a boss named Galetti," Venom said. "We're organizing a team to go after her. Only room for one more, and as much as I'm sure you'd like to get back in the game, I'm not letting you get mixed up in this shit the day you get out of prison."

Hammer flipped him off and Venom responded in kind.

"We can introduce everyone later," Torch said. "Hammer has been with this club a long-ass time, but he's been serving time for drug trafficking. Lots of new faces since you went away, brother. Now isn't the time for a reunion, though. The man who has Pepper already killed her best friend in an effort to draw her out."

"What the hell kind of name is Pepper?" Hammer asked, giving me a smirk.

"Ask her daddy," I said, pointing to Sarge.

Hammer's jaw dropped. "No shit? I didn't know you had a kid."

"Neither did I," Sarge said. "Pepper was a surprise, but there's no doubt she's mine."

"Fuck. All right. Well, tell me what you need and I'll do it," Hammer said. "Even if you're confining me to the compound, or at least the town, there has to be something I can do to help. I may not know Pepper, but if she's Sarge's kid, then she's a Reaper by blood."

"Rides an Indian like Flicker too," Grimm said. "Should have seen her when she showed up that first night. Dressed head to toe in black leather, riding that damn bike like she was part of it. No wonder this fucker fell hard and fast."

"You're just jealous," I said.

Grimm shook his head, but he was smiling. No one knew his story when it came to the fairer sex, but there was definitely something in his past he didn't want to discuss. I'd always thought it had to do with a woman. He had a good time like anyone else, but he never let the women get too close. Except the old ladies. I always figured it was because they were taken and safe. Anyone unattached he kept at arm's reach until he needed a quick release.

"One more," Casper reminded everyone. "Who's going?"

Torch lifted a hand, but Venom was shaking his head.

"What the fuck do you mean by that shit?" Torch demanded of the VP.

"Talk to your wife," he muttered.

Torch narrowed his eyes and looked around the room. Tex looked a little uncomfortable, and so did Zipper. It seemed Isabella had been keeping something from Torch. I had a feeling he was going to be a daddy again. His daughter, Portia, was a year and a half now, and his eldest daughter, Lyssa, was nearly six and a half years old now.

"Fuck me," he muttered. "She's pregnant, isn't she?"

Tex cleared his throat and looked the other way. Yep. Torch was going to be a daddy again. Lucky fucker.

"Mara's pregnant too, but I'm still going," Rocky said. "She's only six weeks along so she should be fine. If she needs something, I know Ridley will help her."

"You didn't notice your wife was getting a bit… plumper?" Tex asked.

"Just how fucking long has she kept this from me?" Torch asked.

"About three months," Venom said. "Ridley asked her to tell you. My woman went with her to the doctor to verify the pregnancy. And if Ridley knows something then…"

"Then all the women know, which means the rest of you fuckers know." Torch sighed and leaned back in his seat. He looked both annoyed and happy at the same time. It seemed the Reapers family was growing again. With some luck, Pepper and I would have a kid in the near future.

"I'll go," said a voice from the doorway. King stood just inside. "I know I'm not a patched member, but Pepper was taken on my watch. It's only right that I help get her back."

"Fine," Torch said. "And we'll discuss you listening in at doors when you get back."

King nodded, but his jaw was set and I knew that if he had to do it over again, he'd have still listened at the door. He was a good kid, would make a great addition to the club, and I knew Torch would be patching him in soon. Regardless of him breaking into Church, he'd proven himself countless times. Helping get Pepper back just solidified his place here.

"I'll make the arrangements," Casper said. "I'll also secure lodgings for a few days. If she's in rough shape, she won't be able to come home right away. You should prepare yourself. Galetti might be small compared to some of the men you've faced, but he's a sadistic bastard."

I'd already seen the proof of that. Poor Louis had hardly been recognizable, and there hadn't been much left of him. Torch dismissed everyone and I went to pack a bag, not just shoving my clothes in the duffel but some things for Pepper as well. When I packed her bathroom shit and saw the unopened box of tampons on the counter, I stopped. Other than the days I'd been gone, we'd had sex frequently, and I knew for damn sure she hadn't been bleeding any of those times. I picked up the bathroom trashcan and shifted it to see the contents, in case that was her second box. Nothing in there either except dental floss and tissue.

I looked at the box again and a feeling of dread hit me. If Pepper had those, then she'd been expecting her period, and she obviously hadn't used any of them yet. So either she was late and was carrying my kid already, while in the hands of a madman, or it wasn't quite time yet. Fuck me. As much as I wanted a baby with her, I really fucking hoped that she wasn't pregnant. It was bad enough that Galetti had her, but if he had my unborn kid too, nothing would stop me from tearing him apart.

Taking down another bag from the top of the closet, I filled it with my guns and ammo, as well as my favorite knives. I knew it was going to get bloody. There was no way Galetti would let Pepper go without a fight, and I wasn't leaving Vegas until that asshole was dead. Whatever it took, I'd make sure he wasn't breathing when this was all over.

I carried my bags outside and walked to the clubhouse. Two trucks were already running so I tossed the duffels into the back of one and climbed inside. King was driving with Tex in the front next to him. Casper was in the back seat with me. When the other truck was loaded, we drove to the airstrip and boarded Casper's private jet. There were exactly eight seats and I wondered where they planned for Pepper to sit when we rescued her. Casper must have known what I was thinking and he pointed to the back of the plane.

"Bathroom and bedroom are back there. The bedroom is small, but your woman can lie down if she needs to while we're in the air," Casper said.

"Thanks. Let's go get her."

He nodded and told the pilot to take off. It was the longest fucking flight of my life, but I was thankful someone had thought about transportation when we reached our destination. Several SUVs were waiting. I didn't know where the command center was located, but I wanted to get there quickly and figure out how I was getting Pepper back.

There were pictures pinned to the hotel room walls. I didn't know who was paying for all this shit and didn't care. They could take it from my account, as long as Pepper was safe, that's all that mattered. I saw the surveillance pictures from when Galetti had taken Louis, and the new ones showed my sweet Pepper tied to a chair. Her face was bloody and there were more bruises on her arms than had been there previously. I hadn't even realized I'd fisted my hands at my sides until my knuckles cracked.

Rocky made the introductions, but I barely heard their names. I didn't give a shit what their names were, as long as they would save my Pepper. Every last fucker in this room was expendable, including me, if it meant she would go home. I needed to tell them my fear that she was pregnant, but the words were stuck in my throat.

I tried to focus long enough to hear the plan and remember my part. My gaze kept straying to those pictures and my heart ached. Galetti was going to die. I'd make certain of it. I didn't give a shit who took his place, but anyone who came after my family was going to pay in blood. Pepper was my old lady, and I'd damn sure marry her one day. Assuming I lived long enough. Nothing was guaranteed in life, especially in my life. Flirting with the darkness, doing illegal shit, always came with a price. I'd been willing to pay it thus far, but I had a family to think about now. I'd always had my brothers, and they were family even if they weren't blood, but now I had a woman and possibly a kid to think about.

"I think Pepper's pregnant," I said, the words coming out soft, but they almost seemed to echo in the quietness of the room.

"That asshole has my daughter *and* my grandkid?" Sarge asked.

"Yep. Think so. Don't know for certain, but…" I shrugged. I wasn't about to tell the entire room that I thought she'd missed her period. Pepper would have my balls if I embarrassed her like that.

"Shit," Rocky muttered. "All right. Let's move the fuck out. Get Pepper out of the building at all cost, and do it gently. Once she's clear, we're taking down every last one of the fuckers."

One of Rocky's friends and one of the Savage Knights both dropped bags onto the bed. They unzipped them and started passing out guns. I'd packed my own and retrieved them, noticing that Tex had brought his as well, and so had Sarge. I rolled my shoulders and cracked my neck. It was time to get my woman back.

Galetti's building was only a few miles from the command center. It was in a secluded area, which meant we didn't have to worry about civilian casualties. Small blessing, but I'd take it. Tex, Sarge, and I waited while Rocky and his men took care of the perimeter. When they gave the all clear, we approached the building, our guns gripped and ready to fire.

Using one of the dead men's keycards, Rocky opened the doors and we crept inside. Two men were within our sights and went down quickly, each receiving a fatal headshot from the men at my sides. When we got to the elevator, I remembered what Rocky had said before. I checked for a scanner and saw it required a handprint. I dragged one of the bodies inside and used the asshole's print to gain access, then pressed the button for the top floor.

Before the doors shut, the others joined me, including Casper. The Savage Knights accessed another elevator and piled inside. When we reached Galetti's floor, he was ready for us, a gun pressed to Pepper's head. One of her eyes was swollen shut, and her cheek was turning black. She was holding her mouth funny and I hoped like hell he hadn't broken her jaw.

"I knew you'd come," Galetti said. "One more step, and your precious Pepper will have her brains splattered everywhere."

I focused on my woman, knowing the others were watching Galetti.

"Baby girl, look at me," I said.

She lifted her chin, but I could tell she was having trouble focusing. My poor baby had been beaten to hell. My throat grew tight as I looked at her.

"Pepper, you're getting out of here. You hear me?"

She nodded.

Galetti laughed, but he wasn't laughing for long. Casper had done that shit where he hid in the darkness and he'd crept around behind the man. He nailed Galetti in the head with the butt of his rifle. The asshole fell to the floor with a groan, but he was still awake. Casper nodded for me to get Pepper. I rushed to her side and unfastened her. She collapsed into my arms, unable to hold herself upright anymore.

"I've got you, sweetheart. We're getting out of here, okay?"

I pressed a kiss to her temple and walked straight to the elevator. Sarge gave me a look that let me know he'd handle Galetti personally. Tex rode down with me, along with two of the Savage Knights.

"Your club ever needs anything, I'm there," I said.

"We don't tolerate the abuse of women," the one called Seeker said. "He'd have killed her."

"And your kid," the other said, the name *Doc* stitched on his cut.

Pepper made a gurgling sound and I looked down at her. Her breath rattled and a trickle of blood slid from the corner of her mouth.

"Shit," Doc muttered. "She's worse off than I thought."

He pulled a phone from his pocket and made a call. I didn't pay much attention, too busy watching Pepper, and making sure she was still breathing. I heard sirens when we exited the building and tensed, but Doc placed a hand on my shoulder.

"Easy. No one's going to prison. I have some connections around here. Called a bus for your girl."

"Bus?" I asked.

"Ambulance," he clarified. "The ER doctor is a friend. He'll take care of her. If any questions are asked, he knows how to make this shit disappear. You'll be in good hands."

The ambulance pulled up and the paramedics took Pepper from me. I rode along with her, not wanting to leave her side for a second. I didn't give a shit what happened to Galetti and any men he had left.

I knew my brothers and the other men would take care of the problem. No one was leaving that building alive unless they were on our side. Right now, Pepper was my main focus.

Everything happened in a blur when we got the hospital. The doctor let me stay with her. I tried to pay attention to what he was saying, but I was holding onto Pepper's hand and willing her to stay with me. When they cut her clothes from her, the bruises lining her body made me want to scream and beat the hell out of someone.

"Broken rib," the doc said. "Maybe two of them."

"Your friend, Doc, said she was pregnant," I said, worried that the hospital wouldn't check and might harm the baby. "I don't know how he knew. I'd said she might be, but he sounded one hundred percent certain."

"We'll do a test before we order any X-rays or anything that could harm the baby. But knowing Doc, he's probably right. He has an uncanny ability to look at someone and know something is wrong, and if he tells you that you have a certain ailment, you likely do. Never seen anything like it."

I nodded.

It felt like days passed, but the clock showed it had only been hours. They confirmed Pepper was pregnant. She also had two broken ribs, two missing teeth, her jaw was bruised and swollen but thankfully not broken, a black eye, more bruises on her body than I wanted to count, and two of her fingers had been broken. The ER staff patched her up and made her comfortable. When Sarge walked in, I knew that Galetti had been handled.

I relayed everything I'd learned about Pepper's condition, and left to get some coffee while Sarge sat with his daughter. I knew he needed a moment with her, and I honestly needed to clear my head a bit. After getting the shittiest coffee I'd ever had, I stepped outside and breathed in the fresh air. Or as fresh as it got in Vegas.

"They're all dead," Rocky confirmed, coming to stand next to me. "Savage Knights said they'd handle the cleanup. Once your girl is cleared, we can go home."

"She's pregnant. They confirmed it," I said. "I damn near lost her and my kid today."

"But you didn't." Rocky slapped me on the back. "Whatever Pepper needs, we're here. She's one of us, Flicker, and you know we'd all die to protect her. Mara has already called to see if she's okay. The ladies will be more than happy to help care for her when we get home."

"Thanks."

He gave a nod and went back inside. I finished the sludge the hospital called coffee, then went back to Pepper. They were going to move her to a room when one was available, and wanted to keep her for at least a day or two for observation. I knew they wouldn't hold onto her too long since everything was being swept under the rug, so to speak, but I also knew they wanted to make sure she'd be all right when she left. I was so damn thankful to everyone who had helped not only retrieve her, but those at the hospital who were making sure she healed. That she lived.

Without Pepper, I was nothing. If anything happened to her, they'd have to bury me right next to her. I might not have known her long, but she was my entire fucking world.

Epilogue

Pepper
Six months later

I watched Flicker outside the window, pacing and smoking a cigarette. He'd promised to quit, but I noticed when he was stressed he couldn't seem to resist. My ribs were still tender, but the rest of me had healed nicely, and I was starting to look like I'd swallowed a basketball. The kid inside of me was fucking huge, and I was getting worried our son was going to split me in half when he was born. We hadn't decided on a name yet, but there was still time.

"If he's this bad now, wait until you go into labor," Ridley said.

"No kidding." I smiled as Flicker paced by the window again. He hadn't wanted to leave my side for a second since he'd found me in Vegas. Even though Ridley, Mara, and Darian were visiting, and he'd given us space, he hadn't been able to walk away from the house. It was starting to drive his brothers crazy, and they'd been giving him shit over it.

"Any word from Sarge about his mystery lady?" Mara asked.

"You mean Lily?" I asked. "He won't talk about her. I'm not really sure what happened between them, but it's obvious something did. He's constantly pissed-off these days, and while he still goes to the diner, he sits in another section, then just stares at her."

"Not creepy at all," Darian said, then laughed. "He's going to chase her off for sure."

"How are you feeling?" Ridley asked.

"Swollen. Achy. But it's all from the pregnancy. Everything else is fine. My ribs still hurt a little, but

Doctor Myron said those would take some time to heal completely."

"I think we're about to be evicted," Mara muttered.

Sure enough, the front door opened and slammed shut. Flicker stood in the living room doorway, folded his arms over his chest, and glared at my guests. He was so damn adorable. Not that I'd dare tell him that.

"Out," he said, jerking his head toward the front door.

Mara and Darian patted his arm as they passed, but Ridley stopped in front of him.

"She might put up with your surliness, but I won't. Treat her right or I'll kick your ass." Ridley flipped him off and followed the others outside.

Flicker narrowed his eyes in the direction of the women, then turned to face me.

"She's a menace," he said.

"You love her and you know it."

He knelt in front of me, placing his hand on my belly. "I love *you* and our son. The others are tolerable."

"What about Laken?" I asked.

"She's a menace too."

I couldn't help but laugh. The day we'd come home from Vegas, Laken had already been in the house. She'd made a few dinners and stuffed them into the freezer so Flicker only had to reheat them. She'd also cleaned the house, changed the bed linens, and had some balloons for me. I hadn't had a chance to spend much time with her because Flicker was always running her off, but she seemed sweet. I hoped once he calmed down that I could be friends with her. Even though I was healed, and would be delivering our son in the next few months, he still didn't tolerate anyone in our home for more than fifteen to twenty minutes.

It would be cute if it weren't so damn annoying.

"You feeling okay?" he asked.

"Never better." Well, that was mostly true. Even though he constantly hovered, he hardly ever touched me intimately. It was almost like he was afraid I'd break. I'd put up with it so far, knowing that finding me so badly beaten had left him shaken. "Although, there is one spot I hurt a little."

He tensed. "Where?"

I slowly slid my knit dress up my thighs and spread my legs. "Here," I said, pointing to my pussy.

His heated gaze locked with mine, and that was all the warning I had. Whatever had held him back before didn't seem to be an issue now. Flicker ripped my panties off, then gripped me tightly. He pulled my legs over his shoulders before his lips fastened on my clit. I nearly screamed from the intensity, it had been so long since he'd touched me like this. I was panting in minutes and ready to explode. He licked, sucked, and teased until I was ready to beg him to let me come.

"Please, Daniel. I feel so empty."

"Come for me, sweetheart. Give me your cream, and then you can have my dick."

"Daniel." I gripped his hair, and then I was coming, so fucking hard. I screamed out my release, my body going tight as pleasure zinged through me from head to toe. He licked me until the last tremor shook me.

He quickly stood, shoving his pants down his thighs, then he was over me and filling me. He drove in hard and deep, just the way I liked it. I gripped his shoulders and wrapped my legs around his waist. It felt like forever since he'd taken me, given me all of him.

"I missed you, missed this," he said, thrusting harder and deeper.

"I missed it too. Don't make me wait ever again," I said.

"I won't. Christ! Pepper, you're so damn tight. So fucking wet. I can't last."

He shifted so that he brushed my clit with every stroke and soon I was coming again. It seemed to be all he was waiting for. His grip tightened and he drove into me, fucking me like a man possessed. He roared as his cum shot into me, and still he kept fucking me. His cock didn't even soften after his release, and Daniel didn't slow down even a little.

He made me come twice more, and I was boneless with mind-numbing pleasure. I stroked his shoulders, his arms, murmuring nonsensical things as he continued to thrust into me. When he came a second time, I felt his cock jerk and twitch inside me. He was panting so hard it sounded like he'd run a marathon. Without separating our bodies, he lifted me and carried me down the hall. In the bedroom, he kicked the door shut, then somehow managed to get out of his boots and pants without dropping me. I helped him remove his shirt, then pulled my dress over my head and popped my bra clasp. Naked and sweaty, he carefully laid us down on the bed, grinding his pelvis against me.

"You sore?" he asked.

"No, and if I were, I wouldn't tell you. I expect at least five more orgasms before morning. You owe me after keeping your distance." I smiled and kissed his jaw. "Think you're up for it?"

"I was giving you time. You were so badly injured, and pregnant. I was worried I'd hurt you."

"Daniel, I'm fine. More than fine."

The words had no sooner left my mouth than I felt him growing hard again. I couldn't help but laugh and cling to him.

"I love you, Daniel. So fucking much."

"Love you too, baby girl. More than anything in this world."

"Then show me."

He winked and did exactly that, all night long. Best. Night. Ever.

Spider (Hades Abyss MC 1)
Harley Wylde

Luciana -- All I've known is pain and suffering at the hands of men -- even from my father, a man who was supposed to love and protect me. When I'm dropped off with a club of bikers, I figure it's more of the same. It never occurred to me the President of Hades Abyss would be my salvation, or that I would fall in love with him. I never knew men could be honorable and kind. He's all gruff and domineering, but under that rough exterior I can see the heart of gold he tries to hide.

Spider -- Assassin Casper VanHorne, Picasso of wet work and pain in my ass, has asked my club to take in two Colombian princesses. Well, he didn't use the term *princesses*, but I have no doubt they'll be spoiled little bitches. The first time I see Luciana and her sister, I think I've got them pegged just right -- until I look in Luciana's eyes and see the fear she's trying to hide.

I didn't want to fall in love, didn't want a woman in my life... but sometimes the Fates know better than a mere mortal man, and Luciana is exactly what I need. When her father demands her return, I vow to keep her safe. No fucking way I'll let the sick bastards who hurt her get their hands on her again. Now that she's mine, I'll march into hell if need be in order to keep her by my side.

Chapter One

Spider

I had shit to do, business to handle for the club, and where the fuck was I? At the airstrip outside of town, waiting on Casper Fucking VanHorne and the little Colombian bitches I'd agreed to take in -- temporarily. I'd left out that last part, but no way were some rich little princesses going to stick around my club for long. I'd do everything in my power to run their asses out of there. I understood Casper's reasoning behind the major favor he'd asked of my club, but it didn't mean I had to like it.

The jet touched down and moved down the runway. When it came to a stop, I folded my arms over my chest and waited. Rocket and Fangs were with me, along with a Prospect who'd brought the SUV to transport the little divas. It seemed to take forever before they were on the ground and heading toward us. The younger one appeared terrified, her eyes wide and her hands clutched in front of her, almost as if she worried someone would jump out at her. The eldest held her shoulders back, her chin lifted at a defiant angle, but her lips were pressed tightly together. Neither appeared to be the overly confident young ladies I'd expected. Despite the bravado of the eldest, they both seemed a few seconds away from running in the opposite direction.

What the hell had I gotten myself and my club into this time? Rocket had agreed to house the younger one. We didn't exactly have a bunch of women running around to help care for them, nor was I going to leave them unattended. Since his younger sister had lived with him until she'd passed, he'd seemed like the best choice. At least he knew how to handle a teenage girl. Rocket pushed off his bike and walked toward them, stopping in front of the youngest.

"Violeta, right?" he asked.

She nodded, her lip quivering.

"I'm Rocket. You'll be staying with me. Do you speak English?"

"Yes." Her voice was soft and slightly accented. "I will be good to you."

Rocket frowned and looked at me, but I didn't know what the fuck she was talking about. Maybe her English wasn't as great as she thought. I just shrugged and waited on the older one to reach me.

"Luciana, I'm Spider," I said.

"I know who you are. I've been informed I'll be living in your house."

"Yes. I have a room set up for you. Where's your shit?" She stared at me blankly. "Your clothes? Shoes? Jewelry or whatever the fuck else women pack when they move?"

She shrugged a shoulder. "Our father didn't deem it necessary to send us with more than an overnight bag. We each have two changes of clothes."

"Casper," I said, a bit of growl to my voice as I stared at the man responsible for this shitstorm. "What the fuck?"

"I'll provide each of them with a shopping allowance to buy the necessities. After that, they're your problem." Casper arched a brow, as if daring me to utter a word of complaint. "Once my jet is refueled, I have someplace to be."

There was a flash of fear in Luciana's eyes, but I tried to dismiss it -- and the tightening in my gut. There was something incredibly wrong, but I couldn't quite figure it out. I would in time, but right this moment, I needed to get these two home and settled.

Rocket curved his arm around the smaller of the two and led her over to the SUV, leaning down to speak to her.

If Luciana needed coddling, she'd have to get it elsewhere. I waved my hand and she started to follow Rocket and her sister. The Prospect grabbed their small bags and loaded them into the SUV.

Fangs folded his arms and watched them. "Something's off. Like really fucking off."

I completely agreed, and I didn't like it. Casper hadn't made it a secret that he had plans for Mateo Gomez, the girls father, and was merely playing nice for now. Didn't mean I wanted my club mixed up in this shit, but with the promise of a favor from the notorious assassin, I couldn't exactly say no. With some of the shit my club dealt with, having a guy like Casper VanHorne at your back could mean the difference in coming back home on your own two legs or in a body bag. But as I watched the two young women get into the SUV, saw the haunted look in their eyes, I had to wonder just what the fuck was going on.

The Prospect climbed into the SUV once the women were secure, and he waited while the rest of us mounted our bikes. I took point with Fangs, and Rocket pulled up at the rear. I didn't expect trouble, and yet I was always cautious, even in my own damn town. The compound was just outside the city limits, a few minutes down a two-lane highway. This part of Missouri didn't get a lot of traffic, but after my son was in an accident along with a Dixie Reaper and the Reaper's woman, I'd learned not to trust even those who lived near the compound. Anyone could be bought for the right price, except my officers. I'd trust them with my life, along with the other patched members of my club.

As we approached the gates to the compound, our newest Prospect, a kid who was quickly proving himself, let us in with a wave. Teller Reed was a good kid once you got through the tough skin he'd grown in order to survive. I had high hopes for him, and since he'd asked to prospect I'd seen a lot of improvement. We'd make a man of him, eventually.

The Hades Abyss compound had changed a bit over the years. After seeing the setup at the Dixie Reapers and Devil's Boneyard, I'd decided to improve a few things. Most of the homes had been small before, but now all officers had large houses. We'd also added a pool and picnic area, even though none of us had families. I'd seen the look in a few of the men's eyes and knew they'd settle down if they found the right woman. We'd all been hardcore bachelors long enough. Not to mention the family-oriented area was nice when my son visited with my grandson.

Fangs went straight to the clubhouse, but the rest of us continued farther into the compound. We took the winding road toward my home and I pulled into the carport. I shut off my bike and waited as Luciana got out of the SUV. The Prospect, Marcus, grabbed her bag and waited for instructions. He'd only been with us about eight months, but he showed promise.

"Put her bag in the guest room," I said with a nudge of my chin toward the front porch. Marcus hastened to obey while I studied Luciana.

Her hair was pulled up on top of her head in a messy knot, and she didn't have so much as a speck of makeup on her face. She was young. Really damn young, even though I'd been assured she was twenty-one. That made her forty years younger than me. I was old enough to be her fucking grandfather. It was complete insanity to have agreed to this nonsense.

"Go on inside, girl. One of the club girls picked up some bedding she thought would be appropriate. Just look for the purple room and that one's yours."

She gave a slight nod and hurried inside.

When Marcus came back outside, I held up a hand to stop him. He watched me, but his gaze flicked to the SUV a few times. I knew he was curious about the girls and wondered why they were here. While every patched member of the club knew the score, the Prospects only knew the girls would be staying here for a bit.

"They say anything on the way here?" I asked.

"No. The younger one cried a lot. I've never questioned the club, or you, Pres, but this doesn't feel right."

"Something is strange with this deal for sure, but I don't know what just yet. In the meantime, treat the girls like guests. Not like club whores. Spread the word to the other Prospects too. These two aren't a damn thing like what I'd expected."

He gave a quick nod, then rushed over to the SUV. Rocket led the way, and I sighed as I looked at my house. It had been a nice quiet sanctuary, and now there was a woman inside. A stranger. A girl I'd thought would be entitled and spoiled, but who seemed more scared than anything else. It made me wonder exactly what their father had told them. Or Casper for that matter. Did they have any idea why they were here?

I made my way inside and went straight to the kitchen. I shook my head as I looked at the damn fancy coffeemaker Laken had insisted on giving me this past Christmas. It had taken me weeks to figure the fucking thing out. If I hadn't been worried about hurting her feelings, I'd have stashed it and just used my simple one with an on/off switch. Who needed all the bells and whistles on a coffeemaker? AlthoughI had to admit being able to set a timer was nice when I had a set schedule in the morning. I liked walking downstairs to a fresh pot of coffee.

I brewed a pot, then sat at the table to enjoy it. I had a feeling I might need something a lot stronger if I was going to tackle the issue of Luciana and Violeta. Had the third girl arrived at the Dixie Reapers' compound yet? I wondered what Torch thought of all this. I could call and ask, or I could wait for Luciana and ask her myself what the fuck was going on. As fearful as Violeta seemed, and given her odd comment, it made me think things were about to go sideways with this deal.

I finished my cup and poured another. As I reclaimed my seat, Luciana came downstairs, her tread soft on the staircase. She froze in the kitchen doorway when she saw me. I waited, wondering if she'd run the other way or be brave enough to come closer. I had my answer a moment later when she came farther into the room and looked at the coffeepot with longing.

"You can have a cup. They're in the cupboard over the coffeemaker. I don't keep creamer, but there's regular sugar in the canister on the counter and some milk in the fridge."

She wordlessly walked to the coffeepot and got down a mug. She filled it, then opened the fridge and pulled out the milk, staring at it a moment. Her questioning gaze met mine. Had the kid never seen milk before? Or maybe it was the fact I had to use the watered-down shit.

"I'm an old man, darlin'. I can't stomach whole milk anymore. Even the two percent is too rough, so I only stock one percent. If you'll give me a list of things you need, I'll have someone pick up a few groceries."

She added the milk to her coffee and put the carton back in the fridge. After looking around the kitchen with confusion etched on her face, I pointed to the drawer next to the stove. She walked over and slid it open, pulling out a spoon. Luciana sat next to me and stirred her coffee.

"Guess it's a little stressful and weird to leave your home and go somewhere new," I said.

She just stared at her cup and didn't say anything, but I noticed her lower lip trembled a bit.

"Your dad probably has a big mansion in Colombia. I know this place isn't a palace, but hopefully you'll be comfortable."

I honestly hadn't given a shit. Until now. The more I watched her, the more certain I became things weren't as they seemed. That fucker! Casper hadn't made a deal with Gomez for his own merit. He'd been trying to get these girls out of Colombia. I just didn't know why, but I would. And soon. If shit was heading my way, I wanted to be ready.

Luciana sipped her at her coffee and still didn't say a word. I noticed her body was tense, and her hand shook a little. The girl was scared. Was it because of being somewhere new? Leaving her only home? Or was it something else, something that would likely piss me the fuck off? I shouldn't have offered to keep her here. Anyone else would have been a better option. Hell, the girls could have shared a room at Rocket's place, or Luciana could have stayed with Shooter or Knox. Both were a fucking lot younger than me. Maybe she worried I'd try to take advantage? She'd likely be disgusted if I made a move on her, not that I planned on it.

"Luciana, I don't know what you think of me, and I honestly don't give a shit. But I can assure you that I don't take unwilling women, so if you're worried I'll force myself on you while you're here, you'd be wrong."

She audibly swallowed, and the coffee sloshed over the rim of the mug and onto the table. "You won't have to force me. I know my place and what's expected of me."

What. The. Absolute. Fuck. "Come again?" I asked.

She finally met my gaze and held it for longer than a few seconds. "I'll do as you ask. Do you want me here?"

She stood and started to unfasten her pants, and it felt like my heart was about to stop. A picture was forming in my mind, and it wasn't pretty. I reached and placed my hand over hers, halting her movement. Not fast enough that she hadn't already started to shove her pants down her legs, and not before I saw the marks.

With a growl, I stood fast enough my chair fell over. Fury filled me as I stared at her lower belly, right above the delicate lace trim on her panties. Slowly, I reached for her and lifted the hem of her shirt a little. Enough to see not only more marks, but to notice there was a slight roundness that was too firm to be fat. I worked her jeans down her thighs and took in the roadmap of pain that was etched into her skin.

"Who did this to you? And whose kid is in your belly?" I asked my voice harsher than I'd intended.

"My father's men made the marks. The baby…" She licked her lips. "I don't know."

"Your father's men?" I asked, my gaze lifting to hers.

"When I disobeyed, I was given to his lieutenants for punishment. They were permitted to do anything they wanted, as long as it didn't kill me."

"And they raped you?"

"Sometimes," she said. "Usually they just hurt me and whored me out for a night as a reminder that I wasn't in control of my life. That I was nothing and inconsequential."

I closed my eyes and focused on breathing before I did something I would regret. I heard the rustle of clothes and when I looked again, Luciana was completely bare. Bile rose in my throat when I realized what she thought. Poor girl thought she'd been sent here as punishment, to be tortured and raped. And she thought I was enough of a monster to do something like that. Not that she knew a damn thing about me. I could understand, considering what she'd been through and the types of men she'd been around.

"Put your clothes on, Luciana."

"You don't want me?" she asked softly. "You're going to send me back?"

"No, honey. I'm not sending you back. Never. But you're not here to be fucked. I took you into my home because a powerful man asked for a favor. Until this moment, I didn't understand his reasoning. I don't think Casper wanted a fucking favor. He just wanted to make sure you and your sisters were safe." I ran a hand down my face and turned away from her. "Put your clothes on, Luciana. Next time you're with a man, it will be because you chose him and asked for his cock. Not because some asshole is taking what isn't offered."

"I don't have to service you or the others here?" she asked, sounding confused and a little fearful.

"No, you don't."

"Then what am I supposed to do?"

"Whatever you'd like, Luciana. I can get you some books, you can watch TV, go for walks. If you leave the compound, you have to have someone with you. Preferably more than one. But you're not a captive, and you're damn sure not a whore. No one here will hurt you. Especially not me."

She didn't make a move to get dressed, and fuck me if I didn't want to look. I was sick with myself over the temptation, but I was a guy who hadn't fucked anyone in months and I had a beautiful naked woman in my kitchen. My dick didn't seem to care that she wasn't here willingly. I hoped like hell she didn't notice I was getting hard. Despite the marks on her body, she was still stunning, with soft curves. I'd always been a breast man, and it was hard not to notice that hers were a perfect handful.

"Luciana. Please get dressed," I said, hoping my tone didn't sound as strained to her as it did to me.

"You do want me," she said and moved closer, but I held up a hand.

"Stop. I told you. No one here will force you, and you aren't a damn whore. Just get dressed and give me some space."

"You're going to protect me, yes?" she asked.

"Of course. I'm not a complete asshole."

"And if my father comes? If he decides he wants me returned?"

"Then I'll tell him to fuck off." Did she honestly think I'd just hand her over to that monster?

She came even closer and I groaned as she pressed her breast against my palm. I tried to jerk my hand away, but she wrapped her fingers around my wrist.

"But if I'm yours, then he couldn't take me, couldn't force me to go with him," she said. "I could be yours. *Only* yours."

"Luciana." Fuck, was that my voice? The woman was killing me. "I'm too Goddamn old for his shit. I'm probably your grandpa's age. Let me go... and put your clothes on. I mean it, girl. There are plenty of younger men in this club if you want to convince someone to make you their old lady."

"Old lady?" she asked, and yet she still didn't release my fucking hand. I could have jerked it away, but I didn't want to accidentally hurt her. And all right, so I *was* an asshole because I liked the feel of her breast in my hand. Satan was holding a special seat for me.

"It's what we call the women we patch, ink, and claim. Except my club only has one, and she lives with the Dixie Reapers."

"She's with another group of men?" Luciana asked.

"Yes." Damn. My voice sounded strangled even to my own ears. "My son, Ryker, lives there with her. She's his wife. His old lady. And they have a kid together. My grandson. So see, I'm too fucking old for you, Luciana. Let me go, girl."

She pressed my hand tighter to her breast. "Do I feel like a girl to you?"

Jesus Christ. Was she trying to kill me? I gave up my battle and turned to face her. Instead of drawing away, I pulled her against my body and ground my cock against her, letting her feel how hard I was.

"Is this what you want? You want to feel how hard I am because a naked woman is in my damn kitchen pressing herself against me? You want to hear that I think you're beautiful, sexy, and that my dick would love to be inside you?"

She gasped and her eyes darkened, but it wasn't with fear. Fucking hell. She seemed turned on by my words.

"I'm an old man, Luciana. I'm sixty-one years old. Forty years your senior. I have a grown-ass son who's older than you, and a grandkid. And I got snipped so I can't have more kids. I don't even fuck more than once every few months. One pussy is as good as another, right? So why let some bitch think she has control over me just for the sake of sex? I'm not a nice guy. I've done bad shit, used women without a single thought for their feelings. I'm not the kind of man you want in your bed. I'm hard. I like control. And I take what I fucking want."

She licked her lips and blinked up at me.

"Do you understand? Just because I won't torture you or rape you like your father's men, it doesn't make me a good guy. I'm still an asshole, and I'm going straight to hell when I die. I'm not the man you need."

"Maybe you're exactly the man I need," she said softly. There was a bit of hope blazing in her eyes. "If the President of the Hades Abyss claims me, then my father can't take me away. Not without starting a war."

"Is that what you want? My patch? My name inked on your skin to keep you safe?" I asked.

She nodded.

"You don't have to spread your legs for that. Hell, I probably won't live much longer anyway. I'm surprised a bullet hasn't taken me out already. You want to be my old lady, fine. But it's in name only. You don't have to offer up your pussy in exchange."

"If I'm yours, but you fuck someone else, your men will know. And they'll laugh at me. They won't respect me and will think you don't want me."

"Sweetheart, you can pretend all you want, but there's no way you want an old guy between your legs. My balls are silver-haired and wrinkled. While I still have a head of hair, the muscles I used to have diminished over time."

She didn't look convinced, and I knew I was damning myself for what I was about to do, but she needed to see. I needed to prove to her that she really didn't want me. I didn't delude myself. The young whores who spread their legs for me at the clubhouse did it because they wanted to be with the President of the club, wanted bragging rights and maybe some security. They weren't the least bit turned on by my body. If Luciana wanted security, I'd give it to her. But she didn't have to fuck me for it.

I stepped away and pulled off my cut, laying in the kitchen table, then jerked my shirt over my head. She stared and reached out, brushing her fingers across the silver hairs on my chest. I still had some muscle, but I wasn't ripped like the younger guys, not like I'd been once upon a time. Just the last three or four years, I'd noticed that it was a hell of a lot harder to maintain any sort of definition. My six-pack wasn't hard as granite anymore and had nearly vanished. I was fit, but I wasn't as bulky as the other guys.

She trailed her fingers down my arm, pausing to trace my tattoos. When she reached for my belt, I didn't stop her. I'd let her look. No way she'd desire me, not a pretty young thing like her. She worked my belt loose, and then unfastened my pants. Luciana pushed them down my hips, then tugged my boxers down. My dick was hard and upright, the head angry and red, but I wasn't going to make a move on her.

She studied me, reaching out to cup my balls. My eyes slammed shut as I tried to control myself. Fuck but that felt good. She rolled them, squeezed a little, then wrapped her fingers around my shaft. I opened my eyes and looked down at her. Age had taken me from over six feet to more like six feet even, but she was so damn tiny I was still about a foot taller than her.

"Do you know what I see?" she asked.

"An old, randy bastard who needs to keep his dick to himself?" I asked with an arched eyebrow.

"I see a man who has given much to his club, a man who has protected not only those who serve him but also his blood family. I see a man who didn't take me when he could have, a man who tried to push me away and do the right thing. I don't care if you claim to have done bad things. Spider, you're an honorable man when it counts."

"You see all that, huh?" I asked with a bit of amusement, and a smidge of embarrassment. No one had ever said shit like that to me before.

"I see a man strong enough to stand up to others, a man who commands the respect of others. And this cock?" she asked, looking down as she stroked me. "It's thick and long. Beautiful. This cock? It doesn't scare me."

I didn't know what the fuck to say to that. But if she kept stroking me, I was going to come all over her hand. It had been too fucking long since I'd been with a woman. When she dropped to her knees, my heart stalled and I reached for her, intent on stopping her, but my hand froze and my body locked from shock as her lips closed over the head of my dick.

Holy. Fucking. Shit.

Chapter Two

Luciana

I'd never had a man push me away and not take what I offered. What I'd been *told* to offer. Not once had I ever been tempted to be with a man just because I wanted him. I'd never felt desire, not since my father's lieutenants punished me the first time. I'd been fifteen and a virgin. After that night, I learned what sorts of monsters lived in this world, and that my father was one of them. He'd watched as they violated me, listened to me scream and cry for help, and had done nothing but stare at me with a cold gaze.

I shoved those memories aside as I stared at Spider's cock. I'd been terrified when I stepped off the jet, worried that my life would be just as bad here, if not worse. I didn't know this man, had never heard of him until Mr. VanHorne had said I would live with Spider. I'd done exactly as I'd been told, and I'd offered myself to him. Even stripped off my clothes and prepared to do whatever he wanted. And he'd rejected me. Not because he didn't find me pretty, but because he had honor and hadn't wanted to force himself on me.

I licked my lips and leaned forward, taking his cock into my mouth. He was salty with a hint of musk, but I decided I rather liked it. I heard him mutter a few curses and his body was so damn tight, but he didn't pull away. Placing my hand on his hip, I drew him closer as I swallowed his cock, urging him to fuck my mouth. At first, I'd only wanted his name as protection. But now that I'd seen the horror in his gaze over what had been done to me, and his adamant refusal to touch me, I knew that he was a good man. Honest. Decent. And I needed that. If I were ever to completely belong to someone, I wanted it to be a man like Spider.

I licked and sucked, and it wasn't long before I felt his fingers loosen my bun and sift through my hair as it tumbled down my back. Spider groaned and I chanced peering up at him. His gaze burned bright with lust and wonder as he stared at me, watched as I took his cock as far as I could.

"Luciana."

The way he said my name gave me goose bumps. It was almost reverent, and I wanted to hear him say it again. I pressed on his hip, urging him to take what he wanted, but he seemed content to let me do the work. I didn't know if he worried he would scare me, but the man in front of me no longer made me fear for my future. It was insane that I could trust him so fast, but I'd stared evil in the face every day of my life. And this man wasn't evil. Controlled. Definitely an alpha. But he had a good heart.

Spider was a protector, the type of man I'd dreamed about, yet thought didn't truly exist.

His cock swelled and he groaned again. "Gonna come, pretty girl. Better pull off."

I glared up at him in defiance and sucked harder, hollowing my cheeks, and was rewarded a moment later with the hot splash of his cum. He thrust a few times, filling my mouth and throat with his essence, and I swallowed it down. A shudder raked his body as he pressed deep, his silver hair brushing my lips as his cock twitched and softened. I gave him a few more sucks before releasing him.

He might not have the body of a twenty-year old boy, but things like a chiseled abdomen would fade over time. The scars I noticed along his torso spoke of a man strong enough to survive. Like me. I'd survived, but now I wanted to live, and I wanted him to show me how.

"You didn't have to do that," he said.

I rose to my feet and hesitated, but he opened his arms and I went to him willingly. I placed my cheek against his chest, over his heart, and felt it thumping hard. No one had ever held me, not since I was a little girl. Not in tenderness anyway. It had been so long since anyone other than my sisters had hugged me, since anyone had shown true affection. My eyes misted with tears and I held on tighter.

My sisters. If Spider was a good man, then it meant Violeta and Sofia were likely with honorable men, too. We were safe. For now.

"I mean it, Luciana. Sex isn't part of the agreement. I'll claim you, but I don't expect you to be in my bed. You can keep your room, live your life. I only ask that if you decide to sleep with another man that you're discreet and don't get knocked-up. It's no secret I've been snipped so any baby other than the one you carry now, the men would know you'd been with someone else."

My body tensed and I pulled back to look at him. "Why? I get a free pass to fuck anyone so you can do that same? Was I so terrible at sucking your cock?"

He shut his eyes a moment and when he opened them again, I saw a hint of tenderness, something I doubted he showed many people. The man I'd first seen at the airstrip, the tough alpha, the stoic guy who looked hard and tough, was likely the side he showed the world. But this man, the one looking down at me now, it almost felt like this side of him was just for me.

"No. That's not why, and you know damn well I liked that. I won't make you feel like a whore, Luciana. I don't want you to feel obligated to --"

I pressed my fingers to his lips and swallowed hard. I reached down and gripped his hand, then placed it between my thighs. His eyes darkened as he stroked my pussy.

"I don't get wet for men I don't desire." I hesitated only a moment. "In fact, I've never gotten wet for a man before. Only for you, Spider."

And it was the truth. Whenever I'd been ordered to offer myself to a man, I'd made sure to use lube before meeting him. None of the men in my father's world cared if a woman enjoyed herself or was a willing participant. If they'd hurt me, it would have only turned them on more. Maybe it was insane to be wet and needy right now, after all the horrors I'd faced, but his tender touch, his adamant refusal to do anything he thought might harm me, was the biggest turn-on.

"Luciana, you've been horribly abused, physically and sexually. I'm not sure that... I don't know that sex is a good idea. At least, not right now. You need time to heal, to process everything that's happened. I'm not saying never. You know I want you. I couldn't hide the fact I was hard, and I just came in your damn mouth."

My lips twisted a little. "I never have."

He blinked once. Twice. "Never have what?"

"Come. I've never had an orgasm."

A slow smile spread across his face. "Well, I guess I can't let that stand, now can I? Doesn't mean I'm putting my cock inside you, though."

"Then what..." I squealed as he gripped my waist and lifted me onto the table. I placed my hands on his shoulders to steady myself. Spider pulled the chair over and sank onto it.

"Too fucking old to kneel on this damn wood floor," he muttered.

Gently, he kissed the scars that marked my belly, hips, and thighs. His beard tickled, but what he was doing, the way he touched me, brought tears to my eyes and made my throat tight.

Other than my eyebrows and the hair on my head, the rest had been removed permanently. I'd always hated it, hated the way it felt to be bare down there. Exposed. Until now. Spider traced his tongue along my slit, and I gasped as I leaned back and spread my thighs wider, giving him better access. No one had ever put their mouth on me before, except for the man who'd bitten me and not in a fun, sexy way. I still bore the scar on my inner thigh. They'd always shoved their cocks into me and that was it. They'd get off and be done with me.

For the first time since my body had been marked, I wasn't ashamed of the scars. I didn't feel ugly or degraded. Spider made me feel beautiful and desirable. He wasn't using my body as a way to punish me, wasn't taking what he wanted whether I liked it or not. He was giving me an incredible gift, and proving yet again that he was different from the other men I'd known.

He held me open and sucked on my clit. I could feel something building, a warm buzz settling under my skin, and a tingling where he'd placed his mouth. My nipples hardened and my pussy clenched, feeling empty. Too empty. I needed more. He circled my clit with his tongue before lightly biting down, and it was enough to make me see stars. The strangled cry that left my lips turned into a wail as he worked the sensitive nub, making my orgasm go on and on. I was trembling and breathless, my thighs shaking as I felt moisture gather under me. My cheeks warmed when I realized it was coming from me.

Spider wasn't finished with me yet, though, and he didn't stop until I'd come twice more. He'd given me pleasure unlike anything I'd ever experienced, and yet I still ached, felt like something was missing. He pushed his chair back, his chest rising and falling with his labored breaths, and I realized he was just as turned-on as I was -- still needed more, just like me.

I eyed his cock, biting my lip when I saw he was hard again. I eased off the table and straddled him. Spider's gaze locked on mine and he slowly shook his head, warning me not to do it, but I'd never been good at listening. In Colombia, I might have hesitated. With Spider, I knew I wasn't in any danger. I placed my hands on his shoulders and lowered myself onto his cock, taking him all the way inside me.

"Luciana." His tone held a hint of warning, but I ignored it.

"I'm clean, if that's your concern."

"I am too, but that doesn't make this a good idea," he said.

I wanted this, wanted him. If he didn't want to touch me after this, then I would have at least experienced how incredible sex could be once in my life. Even though he'd spoken of other men in his club, younger ones, I knew I didn't want them. It was younger men who had hurt me. I understood that not all men were like that, or at least I did now, but I didn't think I'd ever trust someone my father's age or younger, not enough to get naked with them.

"Please," I said softly. "Make me forget. Give me something good to dream about to keep the nightmares away."

His gaze softened a fraction. "You don't play fair, girl."

"As they say, all's fair in love and war, right?"

"And which do you think this is? Because I've never loved a woman in my life, and I'm not offering that now." He didn't speak harshly or coldly. Merely stated the facts.

His words hurt, but I tried not to take it personally. If our roles were reversed, I'd likely feel the same way. If a man like Spider ever did love someone, I knew he'd give his whole heart to her, and she'd be damn lucky. But we were strangers and hadn't exactly gotten off on the right foot.

"I've been fighting a war my entire life." He might not see it that way, but it was how I felt. "Maybe for once, I just want something nice to hold onto for a bit."

He glanced down at where we were joined. "Do you want to be in charge? Will that make this easier for you?"

"Are you worried I'll have a flashback?"

"It's not an unreasonable concern. If we do this, I don't want you back in Colombia. I want your mind here, with me, and knowing that it's my cock inside you."

I reached up and ran my fingers through his beard. "I know it's you."

He stared at me, not so much as blinking. I worried that he'd send me to my room or make me leave the compound entirely. Had I pushed things too far? Mr. VanHorne hadn't said a word to us except to tell us where we were going and who we would stay with when we arrived. My sisters and I had thought he was a broker of sorts for our father, sealing a deal and using us as currency, but I knew now that he'd been trying to find a place to keep us safe and out of our father's hands.

I wasn't ready to leave my safe haven. I'd barely even arrived.

"Get up," he said.

My breath hitched as I stood, his cock slipping free of my body. I curled my shoulders, prepared for the lecture, his anger, and being banished from the Hades Abyss compound. Spider stood and pointed to the table.

"Turn around and lean across it. Ass in the air."

My eyes widened and I hastily obeyed. My heart pounded, feeling like it might crash right through my chest, as I heard the rustle of his jeans hitting the floor. He gripped my hips and nudged my feet apart, grabbing a fistful of my hair and tipping my head back.

"You panic at any moment, get scared, or just want me to stop for any reason, you fucking tell me. Understood?" he asked.

"Yes, Spider."

"Good girl."

I felt his cock brush against my slit, and then he was pressing inside. He went deeper than he had when I was sitting on his lap and I moaned at how good it felt. With one hand in my hair and one on my hip, he started stroking in and out of me. I'd never imagined that sex could feel like this. It made me feel closer to him, like we were sharing something special. I knew it didn't mean anything to him, but it did to me. Being the President, he had his pick of women, and like he'd said before, one pussy was as good as another. Didn't stop me from closing my eyes and dreaming that it meant more.

He released my hair and cupped my breast. As his fingers pinched and rolled my nipple, I could feel that sensation building again, the one I'd experienced right before my first orgasm. He growled and his hips jerked harder against me, his thrusts getting rougher. It was the perfect combination, and soon I was screaming out my release. I felt his warmth splash inside me and his cock twitched as he buried himself deep.

"I never knew," I murmured.

"Hold on," he said and wrapped an arm around me. He sat, pulling me down with him so that we remained connected. I leaned back against his chest and smiled when he gave my breasts a gentle squeeze before playing with my nipples again.

"No bad thoughts?" he asked, his voice a deep, gruff rumble in my ear.

"None," I said, floating on a cloud of bliss.

"Still want me to claim you? Think you need that extra layer of protection? Because you don't. No one is taking you from this compound if you don't want to go."

"Can we negotiate?" I asked.

"Negotiate?" Humor laced his voice.

"Mm-hm. You claim me, and in exchange I get to suck your cock whenever I want, and you give me more orgasms. Now that I know what they feel like, I want more. Lots more."

He chuckled and pinched my nipples until I squealed from the sting of pain.

"Greedy wench."

I bit my lip and relaxed against him even more. "I'm being serious, Spider. If you claim me, I don't want it just to be in name only. I know you think you're too old for me, or that I don't really know what I want. I'm not some stupid child."

"Never said you were," he said. "Just think you haven't been given many options in life, and I don't want you to settle on an old bastard like me and discover later that there's someone better out there. I'm not going to be able to give you kids, Luciana. You'll want a family one day, aside from the one in your belly already. A kid that's formed between you and the man you love. That man isn't going to be me. I got snipped and won't be having kids ever again."

I placed a hand over my belly. I'd been terrified since I discovered I was pregnant. Not just terrified about how the child was conceived and that I didn't know who the father was, but scared that the poor kid would have a shitty life like I had. I'd worried that they'd be born a boy and turned into a monster, or worse, born a girl and abused the way I'd been.

His hand covered mine and he placed a kiss on my shoulder. "I know you're scared. You have every right to be. This baby isn't going to suffer, Luciana. If you want to keep it, then I'll help you any way I can. Get you a place of your own, make sure any men who come around are the good sort. The kid will need a daddy, and not just some jackass who doesn't give a shit. If you decide you can't handle seeing the kid every day, then I'll help you place the baby in a good home. No one will force you to do anything you don't want."

"You already are. Forcing me."

His body went taut and he immediately pulled me off his cock and stood. "Knew I shouldn't have done that. It was stupid. I'm sorry, Luciana. It won't happen again."

He grabbed his clothes and started to walk off as I gaped at him, not knowing what the hell had bitten him on the ass.

"Spider, what are you talking about?"

"Forcing myself on you. Knew better than to take you the way I did."

That's what he thought? Men were so stupid at times. "*Idiota.*"

He froze and turned to face me. "Excuse me?"

"No, you're not excused. Not even a little. I was talking about you forcing me to stay away from you, to pick someone younger because you seem to think it makes them better. You're wrong. Being with a younger man will only trigger my fear."

He took a deep breath before approaching me. "Trigger your fear."

I nodded.

"Because only younger men hurt you?"

"Some were close to my father's age, but yes. Most were younger. Some still young enough to be considered boys, but already being groomed to turn into soulless brutes like their fathers."

We stared at each other for a few minutes before something flashed in his eyes.

"Violeta. Has she suffered like you?" he asked.

I nodded slowly. Spider cursed and dug into the clothing in his arms. He pulled out a phone and dropped his clothing, tossing the leather vest onto the table again, before pacing in the kitchen.

"Rocket, be extra careful with Violeta. Things aren't as they seem, and nothing we've been told is the truth. She's damaged and I can't predict what she may be thinking or feeling right now. Whatever you do, treat her kindly and speak softly to her. I'm calling Church. Be there in an hour."

I didn't hear what the other man said, but Spider mentioned something about Prospects watching us. I remembered the man who brought us here wearing a patch that said *Prospect* on it. He'd been young. Close to my age if I had to guess, which had terrified Violeta and kept me on guard as well.

"Spider," I said softly.

He glanced at me, stopping in the middle of his conversation.

"If the men you're leaving with us are like the one who drove us here, then it will terrify Violeta."

He pinched the bridge of his nose. "Rocket, bring her to the clubhouse. I'm going to call Fox and make sure the place is cleared before we take the girls there."

Spider disconnected the call and made another, to Fox I presumed, and I heard him tell the man to make sure the whores were gone. Whores? Ice filled my veins.

"You keep whores here?" I asked, taking a step back.

"What?" His eyes narrowed, then he smiled a little. "Not the way you're thinking. We call the easy club pussy 'whores'. The women are there voluntarily and get off on being used by a lot of men. I know you probably can't understand that after everything you've been through, but there are women who like jumping from one dick to another. Or sometimes more than one at the same time. None of the women are abused or forced."

I tried to calm my racing heart, processing what he'd said.

"There's a bathroom across from your bedroom. You should get cleaned up and change before we have to go." He turned and walked away, leaving his clothes in the middle of the floor and his vest on the table. I picked them up and followed him to the back of the house, pausing in the doorway of what had to be his bedroom.

I heard a shower running and saw his bathroom was just an open archway, but the shower was designed so that I couldn't see him. Just a tiled wall. I moved farther into the room and found his laundry hamper, placing his dirty things inside. Except the leather vest with all his patches and his title. That I draped over the foot of the bed. I didn't think he'd even realized he'd left it, but I'd noticed he treated it with care.

There were a few other rumpled clothing items on the floor, so I picked them up and shoved them into the hamper too. I straightened his bed and then went back to the kitchen to pick up my things. I walked upstairs and went into the bathroom. Whoever had picked out the bedding must have stocked the bathroom too. He'd called her a club girl. Had he meant one of the whores he'd spoken about on the phone? Or someone else?

The vanilla-scented soap was a little much for me and made me sneeze, but I used it since there wasn't anything else. The shampoo was a plain, unscented generic one that I knew would leave my hair snarled and rough. He'd mentioned making a list of things I needed, and I hoped he'd let me pick out new bathroom items as well as my favorite foods. Although I wasn't certain I could get the ingredients for my favorite meals here. I had to remember I wasn't in Colombia anymore.

I wrapped a towel around me, purple like the bedding, and went back into the room he'd given me. I pulled out the leggings and shirt I'd stuffed inside, as well as a clean bra and panties. Once I was dressed and had pulled my hair up again, I made my way downstairs. I didn't know what to expect. Would Spider acknowledge what happened between us? Or would he be gruff and standoffish again? I could tell he hadn't wanted me here, maybe still didn't.

I thought about Violeta. She'd been terrified of what her life here would be like. She was only seventeen, but that hadn't mattered to our father or his men. Her innocence hadn't spared her from his form of punishment. My heart ached that I hadn't been able to save her or Sofia. At least Violeta was close enough I could comfort her, but Sofia had gone to another club. I'd heard the President speak to Casper VanHorne about a marriage. I hoped that meant Sofia would be cherished and loved. Surely Mr. VanHorne wouldn't have placed her in the care of some unfeeling man, not after he'd done his best to get me and Violeta into the Hades Abyss. I just hadn't realized at the time it would be a safe location, a place where we didn't have to live in fear.

Spider was at the front door, his hands shoved into his pockets. He'd put the leather vest back on over a sleeveless black shirt that showed off the tattoos on his arms. He might claim to be old and out of shape, but his arms were still muscular, and I hadn't detected an ounce of fat on him when he'd been naked in the kitchen. Despite the age differences between us I found him to be attractive, and now that I'd had a taste of the pleasure he could give me, I wanted more.

I only wished the baby I carried was his and not some random stranger's. Although, my worst fear was the baby hadn't been fathered by a stranger, but by a soulless man in my father's employ. I'd kept my pregnancy hidden, and it had surprised me that Spider had noticed. If my father knew of the child in my womb, he wouldn't have let me go. Not until the baby was born, so he could do with it as he pleased.

Whatever it took, I needed to protect my child. The baby might not have been planned, or conceived out of love, but this little one was innocent and deserved a chance at a good life.

Chapter Three

Spider

I stared at the men around the table, knowing I could trust them to keep Luciana and Violeta safe. They were good men, even if they didn't always walk on the right side of the law. Then again, neither did I. As their President, I got my hands dirty long before they did. I never asked anything of them that I wasn't willing to do myself.

I had Casper VanHorne and Torch on speaker, my phone in the center of the table so everyone could hear.

"All right, Casper. I know you aren't really trying to keep peace with Mateo Gomez, so what the fuck is going on?" I asked. "Because Luciana came here thinking she was going whore for me and the club, and her sister was scared shitless thinking she would be raped by my men."

"I have a man inside Gomez' circle who was watching him. When he was offered Violeta, he started digging deeper. The news he gave me wasn't good, and I knew I needed to act. I can't work on dethroning Gomez with his daughters present, so I got them out of Colombia and put them somewhere safe. With two of the four clubs I trust."

"Why not Devil's Fury or Devil's Boneyard?" I asked. "Why put two of them here?"

"Devil's Boneyard has already dealt with more than their fair share of victims from the Colombian cartel. Devil's Fury took in some of those women as well. Torch, I asked you to place Sofia with Saint for a reason. I'm not ready to explain just yet, but know that she suffered more than the other two," Casper said.

I started cursing because after hearing, and seeing, what had been done to Luciana I couldn't fathom Sofia's fate being even worse. I glanced at Rocket and saw that he looked both sick and furious. The way he'd gently handled Violeta, and the tenderness I'd seen in his eyes, told me that he already felt a connection to her. She was likely a reminder of the sister he'd lost, and I had no doubt he'd protect her with his life.

"So you're trying to take down Gomez," Torch said. "What do you need from us?"

"For now?" Casper asked. "Just keep the girls safe. If I need assistance with Gomez, I'll ask."

"Does Saint need to be concerned about Sofia?" Torch asked.

"She won't hurt his daughter if that's what you mean," Casper said. "It's part of why I requested she be placed with you. Sofia loves children and responds well to them. Animals too. It's adults she has an issue with, and for good reason. Anything unusual happen with the girls yet?"

"You mean aside from Luciana stripping off her clothes and telling me I could do whatever I wanted to her?" I snorted. "Or the fact she's covered in scars and told me a story that might give me nightmares for a while?"

"I know," Casper said. "My guy was there one of the days Luciana was tortured. It sickened him to see what they did, but if he'd interfered he'd have died and those girls would still be trapped. When they'd strapped Violeta down, he'd been expected to participate and he couldn't do it. Thankfully, he gave them an excuse they accepted and they don't seem suspicious just yet. He's on borrowed time before they figure out he's not a heartless creature like them."

Fangs, Bear, and Fox were eyeing me closely.

"What, motherfuckers?" I snapped.

Fox arched a brow. Being my VP, not much fazed him, not even my temper.

"Something we need to know, Pres?" Fox asked.

"What the fuck are you talking about?"

Bear smirked. "You had a taste of the little Colombian princess, didn't you?"

Casper growled over the phone. "Spider, I swear to Christ. Did you fuck that girl already? I thought you had more damn sense and decency than that."

"I didn't fucking rape her, assholes." I speared them all with a glare, even the damn phone, though I knew Casper couldn't see me. "If I had consensual sex with her, it's no one else's fucking business, you cocksucking motherfuckers."

Marauder lifted a brow. "Wow. That's a lot of fucks even for you. And for the record, I'd rather eat pussy than suck a dick, but maybe the others are into that."

I flipped him off, my silent *fuck you* making Shooter and Knox chuckle.

Surge tipped his head and gave Marauder a contemplative look. "Don't knock it 'til you've tried it."

I hadn't seen that one coming. I stared at Surge for a moment, but he just grinned. Guess his door swung both ways, since I'd seen him balls-deep in club pussy more often than I'd have preferred. Not that I gave a shit where he put his dick, as long as it didn't blow back on the club in a bad way, but that could happen with bitches just as easily as with another man.

Slider gave him a wink, and I decided I wasn't even going down that rabbit hole. Not right now anyway. If the guys wanted to fuck each other, I wasn't going to stand in their way. I preferred a hot, wet pussy over some dude's hairy ass, but to each his own.

"Can none of you be serious for two seconds?" Casper asked. "How are the girls? Spider, don't toy with Luciana. You have enough club pussy around there to occupy you. Leave the girl alone unless you're serious."

I stared at the table a moment, tracing the woodgrain with my finger. I needed to reel Casper in, remind him who he was fucking talking to, but he'd given me the perfect opportunity. Luciana's words still played in my mind. I wanted her to feel safe, to be secure in the knowledge she didn't have to return to Colombia.

"Luciana asked me to claim her." I looked at my men, watching for their reaction. "I told her she should think it over and not make a rash decision. She doesn't have just herself to consider. She's pregnant."

"You're considering it?" Fox asked, his brow furrowed. "You always said you'd never settle down. After the shit with Ryker's mom, you said bitches were only good for fucking and not keeping."

"I'm considering it," I admitted. "I just think she's making a mistake that she'll come to regret, and once I ink her, that's it until I draw my last breath. Even after I'm gone, I'd expect you fuckers to take care of her and treat her like a damn queen."

No one said a word about my demise, but they knew better than most that I walked a fine line when it came to staying alive. Some of the shit I handled could easily end with my body being tossed into a shallow grave. It was a risk I was willing to take, and I knew every man at this table felt the same. Torch's club might be a bit more law-abiding these days, not getting their hands quite as dirty, but then most seemed to be settling down and starting families. The majority of my club were still bachelors, and I didn't see that changing anytime soon.

"And the kid she's carrying?" Bear asked. "You didn't want kids after Ryker. That's why you got snipped."

"That ball's in her court. If she wants to keep it, then I'll do what I need to. If she decides to give it up, I'll help her with that too. Even if we aren't together, I'm not going to leave her defenseless. I'm an asshole but not a total bastard."

"If Luciana trusted you enough to *ask* for sex, then maybe you really should claim her," Casper said. "She acts braver than her sisters but deep down she's terrified of men. Showing you a different side? That's a huge step for her. If she's letting you in and giving you a glimpse of how vulnerable she is, then she's dead serious about being yours."

I was afraid he'd say something like that. I didn't like it. Luciana seemed sweet, and I was furious over what she'd been through, but I wasn't the settling-down type. Ryker's mom had lived with me, so that my boy could be under my roof without a fight, but I'd never really made her mine. I hadn't patched her or inked her, hadn't married her, and I damn sure hadn't let her put any sort of claim on me other than being the father of her son. Ryker had been a mistake when I was seventeen, but he was the best damn one I'd ever made. His mom had resented me for all I'd withheld from her and the club pussy I'd screwed even while she lived with me. She'd cursed me when she'd died. Women were too much damn trouble.

But there was something about Luciana that gave me pause. She wasn't like the other women I'd been with, and I'd seen the pain in her eyes when she'd thought about me claiming her but fucking other women. When Ryker's mom had pulled that shit, it hadn't bothered me. But the idea of making Luciana cry or doubt herself? That shit fucking hurt. Only under my roof for two hours and already she had me by the balls. Maybe I was getting too old for this shit.

The doors to Church cracked open and Luciana peered inside, her wide gaze skirting around the room before landing on me. I should reprimand her, but there was something in the way she gripped the door that made me pause. Her knuckles were white, and there was tension bracketing her mouth.

"What's wrong, Luciana?" I asked.

"I… Violeta and I were wondering if you'd be finished soon?"

"Do you interrupt your father's meetings?" Fox asked her, his tone sounding almost bored.

Luciana paled and slowly shook her head before lowering her gaze, no doubt remembering exactly what happened when she disobeyed Mateo Gomez.

I growled at Fox, but he winked at me. What the fuck was he up to now?

"Think you should come apologize to your man for breaking the rules?" Fox asked. "Beg his forgiveness and hope he lets you stay?"

"My…" Her head jerked up. "My man?"

"You wanted him to claim you, right?" Fox asked.

She slowly nodded, then looked at me again. I crooked a finger, beckoning her closer. Luciana took a step into the room, the door closing behind her. As it clicked shut, she flinched but kept moving toward me. She stopped within arm's reach and glanced at the men around the table again. Her gaze locked on mine and she licked her lips, making me notice the lower one trembled.

"I'm sorry," she said.

"Sorry for what?" I asked.

"I interrupted your meeting. I understand that I need to be punished." She reached for the hem of her shirt and I quickly closed my fingers around her wrist and pulled her toward me. Her startled gaze flew up and the pulse pounded in her neck.

"Do you remember the talk we had before coming here?" I asked.

She hesitated a moment, then nodded.

"And did I not tell you that you were no longer a whore? That you wouldn't be tortured?" I asked.

"Yes," she said, her accent getting thicker with her fear.

"So why were you about to undress in front of my men?" I asked.

I felt a tremor run through her and I tugged on her again, not stopping until she landed in my lap. She cast a furtive look at my men before turning to me again.

"Luciana, I'm not Mateo Gomez. I don't run this club the way he runs his organization. My men aren't going to hurt you, they won't rape you, and they sure as fuck aren't going to accept money for anyone else to fuck you. Any one of them so much as looks at your naked body, and I'll have to beat them."

The tension in the room intensified and I felt the anger coming off everyone around the table. I knew without a doubt they'd protect her, even if I wasn't able to anymore.

"I'm safe," she murmured. "With you."

"Yes, you're safe. Even if I weren't here, you'd still be safe."

"Because you're going to claim me?" she asked, her lips twisting a little as if she were almost afraid to hope for such a thing.

I reached up to cup her cheek and she pressed against my hand, her eyes sliding shut a moment. Peace rolled across her features, only to disappear the moment she moved away from my touch.

Fox leaned closer and Luciana pressed as far back as she could without falling on the floor. I gave my VP a glare that would scare most men, but not Fox. He just smirked before focusing on Luciana again. He gave her the smile that melted the panties off most women, but I could almost smell the fear coming from Luciana.

"You know, maybe instead of letting this old bastard claim you, you might prefer being with someone else. Like me." Fox winked at her and I damn near punched him.

Luciana shook her head so hard I worried she'd crack her neck.

Fox reached for her and Luciana made a sound like a wounded animal before tumbling off my lap. This time, I didn't hold back. I punched Fox in the face, then stood and reached for Luciana. She whimpered and scurried back, her gaze wild and darting around the room. When her eyes became focused again and she realized it was just me, she grabbed onto my leg, wrapping herself around me.

"Luciana," I said softly. "Look at me."

Her gaze stayed on Fox and her grip tightened.

"For fuck's sake. Fox, you're a Goddamn idiot. Thanks for scaring the shit out of her, asshole." I lifted my lip at him in a snarl before reaching down and grabbing Luciana. I tugged her free of my leg and held her in my arms.

"Spider, what's going on?" Casper asked, reminding me he was on the phone.

"Sounds like his VP is pushing his buttons." Torch snickered, making me want to punch him.

"The meeting is over as far as you two are concerned," I said, reaching for the device on the table. "Go handle your own fucking business."

I ended the call and looked at my men.

"Any of you, and I mean *anyone* scares Luciana or Violeta, and I will hand your ass to you. Understood? I might be getting old, but I'm not fucking dead. Until I hand the club over to someone else, my word is law. I would seriously suggest none of you forget it or forget *why* I'm the one in charge." I lifted Luciana into my arms and strode toward the door, pausing a moment. "And for the record, she's mine. I want a property cut by tomorrow morning."

I pushed my way through the door and made my way through the clubhouse. Violeta emerged from the shadows and reached out, grabbing onto my cut. I didn't bother telling her to let go, even though she didn't have permission to touch me. If Luciana had been scared enough to come find me, then it meant Violeta was terrified as well. I still didn't know why she'd come into Church the way she had, but I'd find out soon enough. First, I needed to get her calmed down. Violeta could come with us. Rocket would stop by at some point.

I stopped at one of the club SUVs and placed Luciana in the front passenger seat, then opened the back door for her sister. The keys were in the ignition and I started the engine and drove back to my house. It had been a nice day, so Luciana and I had walked to the clubhouse earlier. No way was she walking back right now. Since I'd just claimed her, I'd have to get some transportation other than my bike. With her being pregnant, I wasn't about to let her ride on my Harley.

I left the SUV in the driveway, then helped Luciana into the house, keeping my arm around her waist. She still seemed a little traumatized and I was ready to kick Fox's ass, even if he had been trying to goad her into saying she wanted me. He was a motherfucker, and I'd deal with him later. Violeta followed us quietly and when I eased Luciana down onto the sofa, she sat beside her sister.

"You're safe," I told Violeta. "I would never hurt you or your sister. She's mine, and that means you're mine too."

Violeta blinked and I realized she didn't understand what I meant.

"In this club, the women we claim are called old ladies. It's like a wife but without the paperwork. Luciana will get a cut." I pointed to mine. "Like this, but it will say *Property of Spider* and she'll be inked with a property stamp."

Violeta still didn't say anything.

"Since you're her sister, that makes you my responsibility as well. Do you like staying with Rocket?"

She gave a slight nod.

"He's been treating you well? Hasn't scared you too much?"

"He didn't like it when I tried to take off my clothes. He looked scared and ran out of the room," Violeta said.

I bit my lip because it wasn't funny, and yet it was. I could just imagine Rocket's horror when the teen started to strip, but the reason why she'd done it was scary as fuck.

"Your sister told me what she's been through. That you and Sofia have suffered as well. Is Luciana the only one pregnant?" I asked.

Her gaze shuttered and that was answer enough. I just didn't know if *she* was pregnant, or Sofia, or both of them. What a fucking mess. Violeta wasn't even at the legal age of consent for most of the states. She should have been in high school, having fun with kids her age, not staring evil in the eye as it did irreparable damage to her physically and emotionally. I hoped Casper took out Mateo Gomez and his entire organization, but I knew another would just crop up. When one fell, another rose. One of Silva's henchmen had tried to take over after Devil's Boneyard had been there saving their man, Havoc, but he hadn't been able to gain enough power to pull it off.

"Violeta, the things your father and his men did, none of that will happen to you here. This club will protect you, keep you safe. No one expects you to spread your legs in payment, or do anything else for that matter." I watched her for a moment. "Did you ever go to school?"

"Tutors," she said. "They can be paid not to ask questions."

"Did you enjoy learning?" I asked, trying to quell the urge to track down the motherfuckers who'd looked the other way when a young girl was being hurt.

She nodded.

"If you'd like to continue your schooling, I'll check around for a tutor. A female tutor if you'd prefer. Would you like that?"

"Yes," she said softly and looked at her sister.

"Violeta, I swear to you that Luciana is safe with me. Could I have a moment alone with her? There's some soda in the fridge and snacks in the pantry. You can help yourself to anything you'd like in there. Except the beer." I winked and gave her a smile. "No underage drinking."

She looked from me to her sister and back before getting up and leaving the room. Luciana had a vacant stare that was scaring the shit out of me. Yes, Fox had been out of line, but this seemed like an extreme reaction. I lifted Luciana, then took a seat and settled her in my lap, holding her close to my chest. I ran my hand up and down her back, just holding her a moment.

"Fox is the Vice President of this club. He's my right-hand man, and while he can be a jackass and do some dumb shit on occasion, he's a decent guy and he would never hurt you. I don't know what he did that caused you to react this way, or if you're under too much stress and finally snapped, but I swear on my life that I will keep you safe. You're mine, Luciana. No one will hurt you at this compound."

She still didn't speak. Didn't cry. Didn't even move.

I glanced up and saw Violeta in the doorway. "What does your Fox look like?"

"He's in his late thirties, bearded, tattooed, brown hair that can look more blond if he's outside a lot." I shrugged a shoulder. "He looks like an everyday biker. Why?"

Violeta stared at her sister before she started to speak again. "One of the men who paid for her was tall, slender, but had muscles. Sometimes he had a neatly trimmed beard and sometimes he shaved. His hair was somewhere between blond and brown, and his eyes were dark and cold."

"How do you know what he looked like?" I asked.

"I saw him once. I'd been bad and was going to be punished. The room where they chained Luciana was open and that man was going inside, removing his clothes. He winked at me before telling her that maybe he'd have me next."

I took a deep breath. Then another. And another. It didn't stop the rage filling me, but I sure as fuck didn't want to scare Violeta.

"Fox would never harm either of you, but I understand her reaction to him now. He flirted and suggested she pick him instead," I said.

Violeta paled and worried at her lower lip.

"He wasn't being cruel, Violeta. He was being playful and didn't mean any harm. I'll speak to him later and let him know that he can't do that shit around either of you," I said. And I just might kick his ass while I was at it. Even if the fucker hadn't known what would happen, he'd been warned the girls had suffered abuse.

It seemed I needed to be a bit clearer about what would and wouldn't be tolerated when it came to Luciana and Violeta. I knew that having women around was a bit of an oddity. Some of the older members, those who were no longer an active part of the club, had old ladies. Those women hadn't hung around much, preferring to live outside the compound. I was the only one still here from the original crew, except Bear.

I cradled Luciana against me. I knew I wouldn't be able to snap her out of this as long as Violeta was here. Rocket would eventually come for his new charge, if only to ensure she was safe. He had a protective instinct that ran deep, and having helped raise his baby sister, I knew he'd keep a close eye on Violeta. It was ingrained in him.

To speed things along, I sent a text to him.

Violeta is with me.

It only took a moment before I got a response.

On my way.

Good. Once Violeta was out of here, I could help Luciana through this. Then we'd discuss why she'd interrupted Church. Something had spooked her, and I wanted to know what, or who, had done it.

Chapter Four

Luciana

One moment, I'd been in Spider's lap, still rattled but not as nervous as I'd been before I'd interrupted his meeting. The next thing I remembered was a man reaching for me, making a suggestion I sleep with him, a man who looked like one of my tormentors, and then… nothing. Not until now. I slowly blinked and looked up at Spider. The water from the showerhead beat down on my back, and his arms were wrapped around me. My naked body was pressed against his, but I saw only concern in his gaze and not lust.

"What happened?" I asked.

"You zoned out. I think when my VP opened his big mouth, you freaked or had some sort of episode. I'd be willing to bet you have PTSD."

"And you thought a hot shower would help?" I asked, gazing up at him in curiosity.

"I was trying to think outside the box. Holding you and trying to talk you through it didn't seem to be helping," Spider said.

I rested my forehead against his chest, then sucked in a deep breath. "Violeta."

"She's with Rocket, and she's fine. What happened, Luciana? What scared you enough that you came to find me?"

"A man came in. We didn't recognize him. Young. Almost too pretty. He stopped and stared, wouldn't take his eyes off us, and Violeta got scared. I was a little worried too."

"Did he have a Prospect patch on his cut?" Spider asked.

"Cut?"

He chuckled a little. "Violeta was confused by that one too. The black vest with all the patches. It's called a cut."

I thought about it a moment. "Yes. It said Prospect."

"Young like you, or younger than you?" he asked.

"I think younger than me. Not the same one that brought us here, though. He was different."

Spider nodded. "Teller. He was probably as scared of you as you were of him. Kid has a traumatic past, but he's got a good soul. Raised in the system until he went to juvie. I found him on the streets and brought him here."

"System?" I asked, not understanding what he meant.

"When a kid in this country doesn't have parents or a legal guardian, they're placed in something called foster care and passed around to people who get paid to take care of them. In Teller's case, they didn't do such a great job. Hurt him pretty bad. He got caught stealing cars and went to juvie, which is jail for someone underage," Spider explained. "No one ever gave him a fair shot. I decided to change that. He's been here for a little over a year. Dropped out of high school and we helped him disappear until he was too old for the state to shove him back into another home."

I looked up at what I figured had to be kindest man I'd ever met. He thought he was bad, but he wasn't. Even if he did break the law, it didn't make him evil, not like my father and the other men I'd known. Spider was a caretaker, even if he didn't realize it. A protector. I'd even go so far as to call him a hero, though I had no doubt he'd scoff and say he was no such thing. But to me, and likely to Teller, that's what he was.

"You're a good man, Spider."

"Call me Trent. At least when the club isn't around. If it's just you and me, you don't have to use the name Spider."

"Trent?" It didn't seem to quite fit him, but if he wanted me to use his given name, then I would.

"Trent Storme." He smiled a little. "Pleasure to meet you, Miss Luciana Gomez."

I dropped my gaze, hating that name. I didn't want a single tie to my father. Spider lifted my chin and gazed down at me with worry in his eyes.

"What did I say?" he asked.

"It's nothing."

His lips twitched like he was fighting back a smile. "Honey, I've been around long enough to know that when a woman says 'it's nothing,' then it's definitely something. I'm old. Not dumb."

I snorted. "You're not old. And it's just that I hate my name."

"Luciana?"

"I guess my first name is fine. But I don't like being a Gomez. I don't want a tie to my father. It's bad enough I'm of his blood, but sharing his name seems wrong. I would completely erase him from my life if I were able."

Spider held me, but didn't say anything for a while. The water started to cool and he shut it off, then wrapped me in a fluffy towel. He used brisk strokes to dry me, then gave me a nudge out of the room while he dried himself. I looked around, realizing for the first time that I'd been in his bathroom. My surroundings hadn't really been in focus until now. The episode I'd had must have been worse than I'd thought.

I started to leave, to go back to the room he'd given me, but he gripped my arm. Not hard enough to hurt, but enough to make me stop. I hadn't even heard him come up behind me. I turned to look at him and could tell he was still worried about me. He wasn't the only one. I'd never had that sort of reaction before. I'd always just dealt with what happened to me, accepted it. It seemed my mind was starting to fight the abuse in a different way now. Or maybe I'd done this before and hadn't even realized it.

"I'm moving your things down here," he said. "I'm not letting you sleep alone. If you had a nightmare, I wouldn't be able to hear you."

"You didn't seem concerned about that before, when you had me placed upstairs."

He pulled me closer. "When I went to pick you up, I thought I was getting some spoiled, entitled little brat. I expected a diva, an overindulged princess. It never occurred to me that your father wouldn't have kept you safe. Men are supposed to protect their children, not abuse them."

"And because I'm damaged that makes you care more?" I asked, feeling a spark of... something. Irritation? Anger? Maybe a bit of both. "Even if I had been spoiled and coddled, I wouldn't have deserved to be brushed off and treated like a nuisance."

"You're right," he said. "And I'm sorry. I only thought about the inconvenience to myself and my club. I didn't think about how you or your sisters were feeling. You were uprooted from your home, your country, and even if you had been kept safe all these years, it still would have been traumatic for you."

I felt the anger drain from me. I couldn't really be mad at him. Spider had to think of what was best for his club, and I'd been an unknown to him. The moment he'd realized I was in trouble he'd vowed to help me. He was keeping me safe. Violeta and I had to hope that Sofia was as well. I didn't know why she'd been given to another club, but if the man guarding her was anything like Spider, then she was better off than she'd been back home.

"You know how you said you're old but not dumb?" I asked.

"Yeah."

"You were wrong. You are most certainly dumb when it comes to women."

He chuckled and held me against him. "You're right, but then, I think most men are rather stupid when it comes to the fairer sex. You don't exactly come with a set of instructions."

"If we did, would you bother to read them?"

His body shook, and then he burst out with a deep laugh that had me looking up and smiling at him. He looked younger, carefree, and really happy in that moment. Not that I thought he was old. *He* might have thought that, but I certainly didn't. Age was just a number, and if he brought it up one more time I'd find a way to get even. He was pissing me off with that nonsense.

"I'm going to assume this means you aren't scared of me," he said, humor shining in his eyes.

His words startled me a moment. I'd never spoken to a man like that before, never teased one or let my temper show. Maybe he was right. I knew he made me feel safe, but perhaps while I was under Spider's roof I would start to heal. I didn't think I'd be so bold with anyone else, but I knew he wasn't going to hurt me. Even though we were still essentially strangers, there was goodness in him. We'd been intimate, but I knew that there was much I didn't know about Spider or his club. Still, if he were going to hurt me surely he'd have done it by now.

"I'm not scared of you," I said, "but I don't think I'm ready to be quite so bold with anyone else just yet."

"Take your time. Everyone heals in their own unique way and at their own pace. It's not a race, Luciana." He frowned. "You don't like your name."

"The Luciana part doesn't really bother me," I assured him.

"Would you like to have your last name legally changed?" he asked.

"Is that possible? I don't care what it is as long as it's not Gomez," I said.

"I'll have Surge work on it. He's fairly new to the club and came highly recommended by Wire over at the Dixie Reapers. The man's a computer genius so you won't even have to leave the compound to have your name changed."

I looked around his room. "You really want me to move in here? You don't want your space?"

"I really want you here. I'm going to get dressed, then I'll bring your bag down. I'll ask a few of the guys to come with us into town. You need clothes, shoes, and whatever other crap women can't live without."

I fingered my wet hair. "Conditioner would be nice."

"Then you'll have it." He winked and brushed a kiss against my cheek.

I held the towel around me as I watched him quickly pull on some clothes. He left and I heard his tread on the stairs. I could have easily gone up after my clothes, but I was learning to like having someone do nice things for me. If my father ever offered to do something or gift me a trinket I'd wanted, then it came with strings attached. That didn't seem to be the case with Spider.

He returned, my bag clutched in his hand, and he passed it to me. While I dressed, he finished getting ready. I cast my gaze his way a few times, watching as he put something in his hair and beard. He combed his beard with a small wooden comb, then put on cologne. Spider came back into the bedroom and slipped on his cut. By then I'd finished dressing and had my hair pulled up in a messy knot. I really wanted to get it cut. My father had never permitted me to do such a thing, saying it devalued me.

Spider looked down at my shoes and shook his head. I stared at the flats but didn't see anything wrong with them. I lifted my gaze to his.

"When you're not pregnant and able to ride on a bike, you'll need boots. For now, we'll just find you some things that will be comfortable during your pregnancy."

My hand went to my belly and my heartbeat stalled a moment. He'd mentioned that keeping the baby was my decision, but that was before he'd claimed me. What if he didn't want the child? I could understand if that was the case. He'd purposely removed any chance he had of creating life again. If his son was older than me, would he want to start over?

"Luciana," he said softly.

I looked up.

"What's going through your mind right now?" he asked.

"You claimed me."

He nodded.

"But the baby…"

Spider took three steps and pulled me into his arms. "The baby is yours, and since you're mine, that makes the kid mine too. Doesn't matter if I created him or not."

"Could be a girl," I said.

"Then I'll buy more guns and ammo."

I snuggled against him. "You said you didn't want more kids."

"I didn't. And at my age, I figured those days were behind me, even if I hadn't gotten a vasectomy. Luciana, just because you and I didn't make the baby together, doesn't mean I will treat it different. I'm the only dad that kid will ever know, and as far as I'm concerned, you never have to tell him, or her, that I'm not their biological father. I'll leave that decision up to you."

"I don't know what I ever did to deserve someone like you," I murmured, holding him tighter.

"I'm no prize."

"We'll have to agree to disagree."

He pressed a kiss to the top of my head. "Come on. We'll take the club SUV for now. I'll have to get a vehicle that's just for you and the baby, but this one will work for now."

I stumbled as he tugged me toward the front of the house. A vehicle for us? Was he going to hire a driver too? I'd never driven anywhere in my life, hadn't been permitted to do something like that. Looking back, I had to admit it was most likely because my father feared I'd have a better chance at escaping. It hadn't occurred to me when I was younger, and I'd have never left my sisters behind.

I'd tell him later. If he brought up buying a car again, I'd tell him that I didn't know how to drive. There was no point in buying a vehicle for me. Even if I were able to learn, I wouldn't want to try it while I was pregnant, and after I'd have the baby to think about.

Spider helped me into the SUV before climbing into the driver's seat. He stopped in front of the clubhouse and reached out to pat my thigh.

"Wait here, sweetheart. Just going to round up a few of the guys to come with us. I'm not taking any chances with your safety."

I nodded and watched as he got out and disappeared into the building. The minutes ticked by and he didn't return. A tap on the window startled me, my hand going to my throat as I jumped. I looked over at the Prospect who had scared Violeta so badly even though he hadn't done anything other than stare. My hand shook as I pressed the button to open the window a little. Not enough he could reach me, but so I could hear him.

"The Pres said I scared you earlier. I wanted to apologize." He shoved his hands in his pockets and took a step back. "Name's Teller. You need anything, let me know. Promise I'm not going to hurt you or your sister."

I gave him a slight nod and watched as he backed up even more before turning and walking off. My heart was hammering in my chest when Spider came back. One of the men who had been at the airstrip was with them. His cut had *Fangs* stitched on it. The others I didn't recognize, but then I hadn't been focused on them when I'd interrupted the meeting before. Spider got into the car, and the other men climbed onto their motorcycles.

"I'm bringing Fangs, Shooter, and Knox with me," he said. "I asked the Prospects to stay behind this time. They're all younger and I didn't want them causing a panic attack. I'll introduce you to everyone later."

"What about Violeta? She'll need things," I reminded him.

"Rocket already has it handled. She wanted to buy her stuff online and have it overnighted. Also spoke to Surge about the issue of your last name. He assured me it would be handled by tonight, although I'm not entirely sure I trust the look in his eyes when he said it. Don't be surprised if you end up with some God-awful name like Sparkles or something."

I blinked at him. He was joking, wasn't he? The look he cast my way told me no, he clearly wasn't joking. Not even a little. Well, I had said that anything other than Gomez was perfectly fine. Looked like I'd be tested on that whenever I found out my new name.

"He's arranging for an ID as well, so while we're out I need to send him a picture of you. Just a headshot, and he said he can alter it as needed."

"An ID? Don't I need to go somewhere for that? Have papers that prove I'm permitted in this country?"

Spider shifted in his seat.

"About that… You technically don't have permission to be here. Casper brought you into the country illegally, but he's working on obtaining the proper paperwork. He has Surge, Wire, and Shade all helping make you, Violeta, and Sofia one hundred percent legal. But as of this very moment? The fewer people know about you the better."

I nodded, a heavy weight settling in my stomach. If his government came for me, wanted to return me to Colombia and my father, there wasn't a single thing Spider could do to stop it from happening. Maybe leaving the compound wasn't such a good idea, but it was too late. Spider pulled into a parking space in front of a long line of stores and shut off the engine.

"This is where we're shopping?" I asked. The shop in front of us had a window display of women's clothing, but I could tell they were well-made and likely not on the cheaper side. I didn't know how much money Spider had, but he'd admitted he wasn't as rich as my father. I didn't want him spending a fortune on clothes.

"Did you notice the sign?" he asked, pointing to the top of the store.

Little Momma. A maternity shop? I looked at the window display again and realized the mannequins did have baby bumps. I was barely showing right now, but with less stress in my life and regular meals? It was a good possibility that I would get bigger a lot faster now. I didn't know for certain how far along I was, but my guess was about four months.

Spider led the way inside, the other men following. Fangs came into the store with us, and the other two remained outside, keeping watch. The woman working the counter and the other helping a customer both stopped and stared, their jaws dropping a little. I looked at Spider, letting my gaze trail from his head to his boots. I didn't know what those women saw when they looked at him, but I was starting to feel that familiar tingle that meant I wanted him. Only Spider had ever made me feel like that.

"May I be of assistance?" the older blonde lady asked, smiling at Spider. She looked old enough to be my mother, and I didn't like the look in her eyes. She wanted him. "Something for your… daughter?"

Spider opened his mouth to answer when Fangs' phone and his both dinged with a message. They looked at their phones, and my stomach clenched, hoping it wasn't bad news. Spider's eyebrow arched and he shared a look with the other man.

"His wife," Fangs said, looking about two seconds from laughing his ass off.

Wife? I stared at Spider until he showed me his phone.

Congrats. You're married and she's now Luciana Storme. You asked for a name change, so you got one. And since I had to work my ass off to make it all legit, that means she's a legal US citizen too.

The message was from Surge.

"He can do that?" I asked.

"My money is on Wire planting the idea," Fangs said. "But yes, he can and he did. So congrats, *mamacita*. You're married to this asshole."

"Wife?" the blonde lady asked, her head swinging from Spider to me and back again.

"Yep. My wife," he said, pulling me against his side and curving his arm around my waist. If he was pissed that were married in the eyes of his government, he wasn't showing it. "She needs some maternity clothes. If you have a problem with that, we'll take our business elsewhere."

The woman opened and shut her mouth several times. The younger one from behind the counter hurried over, stepping in front of the blonde lady.

"I apologize for Diane. My name's Tawny and I'll be happy to help your wife find some new outfits." The woman smiled at me. "Do you know what you're looking for?"

"Something comfortable," I said. I'd worn enough dresses in my life that I didn't care if I never saw another one.

She nodded. "Well, you look to be a size medium." She stopped and eyed my breasts, which had gotten bigger with my pregnancy. "Or maybe a large. Let's see what we have available. You can try on anything you like."

I followed after her and looked over my shoulder, seeing a scowl on Spider's face as he glared at the older woman. If she had any sense, she'd make herself scarce. I certainly wouldn't want to offend the gruff biker, and I'd seen the softer side of him. After a moment she moved on, but I noticed her watching me, a look of hostility on her face with her pinched lips and flashing eyes.

"Ignore her," Tawny whispered. "She's seen the club around town and has been drooling over your husband since she got here about six months ago. She's just pissed he's taken and by someone way prettier and younger than her. Way to go, by the way."

"Way to go?" I asked.

She nodded. "Older men are so hot. Think you could hook me up with the hottie who came in with you? He's not a silver fox like your husband, but he has potential."

"You want me to hook you up with Fangs? Like a date, or…" I was trying not to be rude, but I had to wonder if Tawny was even eighteen. She didn't look it, but then I'd always sucked at judging someone's age.

"A date would be awesome," Tawny said.

"I'll see what I can do."

Tawny smiled widely and helped me gather so many clothes the dressing room looked like it might explode. Spider and Fangs never uttered a word of complaint, even though it took me over an hour to figure out what I wanted to buy. I was even able to change into one of my new outfits before we left the store, and I noticed that Diane was miraculously absent.

We shopped at several more stores, picking up everything I would need, from underthings to shoes and bathroom items. Spider vanished at one point, leaving me with Fangs and the others, but he wasn't gone long. When I couldn't shop another moment, my feet and back aching from all the walking, Spider ordered food to go at the diner before driving us back to the compound. He had one of the Prospects carry my bags into the house while he led me into the kitchen, gently pushing me down into a chair. After we each had a container of food in front of us, and each had a drink, he sat down, gave me a wink, then dug into his food.

"You're not upset?" I asked.

"About what?" he asked between bites.

"That your Surge married us."

He stopped chewing a moment and stared. After he'd swallowed, he reached into his pocket and pulled out a black velvet box. He set it on the table, then reached into his pocket and pulled out something shiny. My eyes went wide as he slid a solid silver band onto his ring finger. When he opened the box and I saw a silver band with sparkling diamonds across the top, I couldn't hold back my gasp.

"If it's not the right size, they said they can resize it for you," Spider said. "But to answer your question, no, I'm not angry. I'd already claimed you, and in my world that's pretty much the same thing. Except once a biker claims you, there's no divorce, no going back. It's a forever kind of thing. What Surge did, that's just paperwork to make it legal in the eyes of the law."

My hand trembled as he grasped it and slid the ring onto my finger.

"Now everyone will know you're claimed even if they don't see your ink, which you'll be getting soon, or your cut, which should be ready by tomorrow. You're mine, Luciana. Forever."

Tears gathered in my eyes as I gazed at the ring, and his hand holding mine. Nothing could have prepared me for the emotions welling inside me. No one had ever wanted me, but he did. A sob escaped me and then another. When Spider pulled me into his arms, it wasn't long before I soaked his shirt with my tears. He rubbed my back and let me cry. I clung to him, wondering how I had gotten lucky enough to be given to a man like him, and hoping I never had to let him go.

Chapter Five

Spider

It had been so damn long since I'd had a woman in my bed. I smoothed Luciana's hair back from her face, admiring her profile as she slept soundly. After she'd cried yesterday, I'd urged her to finish her food before insisting she had a nap. She'd seemed embarrassed over her breakdown, but after everything she'd been through it was a miracle she hadn't bawled her eyes out sooner. She was stronger than she gave herself credit for, and I hoped one day she'd see it.

The diamonds on her finger twinkled in the sunlight peeking through the blinds. She was mine. Not just my old lady, but my wife, thanks to Surge. To me, it was just a legality. Once I'd claimed her, that was it. Didn't matter if she shared my name or not, she was mine. I couldn't remember a time I'd ever felt as protective of someone, or rather over a woman, as I felt over Luciana. I wanted to slay all her dragons, but mostly I wanted to bury her father six feet deep. After torturing the shit out of him. I didn't know what Casper had planned for Mateo Gomez, but I wanted in on it.

I left a note on the nightstand so Luciana wouldn't wake up and worry when she couldn't find me, then I put on my cut, pocketed my phone, and grabbed my keys. I'd never bothered locking my doors inside the compound, but with a pregnant woman under my roof -- *my woman* -- I made sure the house was locked up before I left. My Harley rumbled as I started the engine and drove to the front gates. A Prospect was already there with one of the trucks, as well as Hornet, Slider, and Bear. If I hadn't set up this deal weeks ago, I'd have canceled the damn thing so I could focus on other shit like Mateo Gomez and whether or not he was a threat to my club and my woman. I had a hard time believing he was willingly giving up his daughters, even if he thought he was getting an alliance out of it.

Teller opened the gates, and we pulled through with me taking point. Bear was to my right and half a length behind, then the truck, with Hornet and Slider pulling up the rear. We hit the highway and headed out of town. The pick-up location was outside St. Louis in a spot no one knew about. No one still living at any rate, except my club and now the Quiet Killers. Getting mixed up with organized crime groups was always dicey, but these guys were the new go-between for several arms dealers. Since D.C.A. would only deal with me, thanks to my government connections, providing them with quality guns was a top priority for my club. The Deadly Cobra Association only hired the best assassins, ex-special ops, and other men you didn't want to meet in a dark alley. They were the government's go-to when their military elite got into a bind, or their hands were tied with red tape and a situation needed to be handled immediately.

We were only on the road about an hour before I pulled down a dirt road that looked more like an accident than a true pathway. I slowed my bike, avoiding the pony-sized potholes, and drove through the wooded land, keeping an eye out for trouble. In the clearing ahead, there were two SUVs and a truck. The men waiting were armed, dark glasses hiding their eyes from view. My gut clenched as I came to a stop about four yards away, Bear pulling up next to me.

"What do you think, Pres?" he asked.

"I'm not getting any bad vibes. From what I've heard, these guys are legit and wouldn't want to fuck up this deal."

Bear nodded. We moved in closer and dismounted from our bikes when we were about ten feet away. The truck behind me stopped as well, and I heard Philip get out. The bag of cash was clutched in his hand and I gave him a nod. He walked forward and set it down in front of Miguel Juarez, my contact with Quiet Killers, before backing away. With a snap of his fingers, Miguel had two of his guys sifting through the bag.

"It's all here," one of them confirmed.

I followed Miguel to the truck and motioned for my guys to unload the crates in back. Two crates of M4's and another of CZ 75B's. The head of D.C.A.'s lead tactical team would be very pleased. Mason Parkes could probably get this shit himself, but he was like me and buried up to his neck in fucking paperwork when he wasn't actively kicking the shit out of someone. It was just easier for him to hire me to handle it, and I appreciated the business. D.C.A. was privately funded and money wasn't an issue for them.

"Appreciate it," I said, shaking Miguel's hand.

"If they want more, or need something else, let me know. I can get my hands on just about anything," Miguel said. "Or perhaps you'd like something with a bit more power."

I smirked. "What makes you think I don't have enough firepower already?"

"No such thing as enough," Miguel said. "I'll be in touch."

We pulled away and hit the road, keeping a constant watch for trouble. The first *pop* had me tensing and trying to find the source. With the second,

I felt a searing pain my shoulder. Fucking hell! Bear started firing back as I sped up and left him behind, the truck with our cargo right on my ass. I heard more gunfire and the sound of shots hitting metal. The dumbasses were shooting the fucking truck full of guns! Whoever these guys were, they weren't overly intelligent. Hornet slid up next to me, motioned that he was going to cover the rear, then fell back.

We raced back toward the compound, but I could feel myself growing weaker. The blood had soaked my shirt and covered my arm, but it seemed like it was through and through. I grunted as another round slammed into me, this one lodging in my fucking back. *Enough of this shit*!

I motioned for Philip and Hornet to keep going, and I slowed down. Drawing my gun from my waistband, I opened fire on the assholes trying to steal our cargo. Three rapid fire shots took one out, his bike skidding across the road. He didn't get up, so I focused on another while Bear handled a third. I didn't know how many there had been to start, but we were down to four. After another moment, we'd managed to take them all out, but not before I saw their cuts. *Chaos Killers MC*. Those fucking idiots were a Goddamn menace. Caused a shit ton of trouble for everyone, but thankfully they were too damn stupid to do much other than piss off my club and others in the southern states. They only had one chapter in this area, and with some luck, we'd wipe that one out before it had a chance to spread like a fucking virus.

"Pres, you need to pull over," Bear said.

I shook my head and kept going. It made my vision swim a moment, but I pushed through the pain. When we reached the compound, Teller opened the gates. I brought my bike to a halt just outside the clubhouse, then fell off like a pansy ass. *Motherfucker*!

"Someone get Dread," Bear said as he knelt next to me.

Everything was spinning and getting darker. I fought to keep my eyes open, to stay present. Luciana needed me. I didn't have time for this shit, and I would *not* pass out like some Goddamn pussy in front of my club. I groaned as Bear and Shooter lifted me, carrying me into the clubhouse. They started for the hallway to the back rooms, but I stopped them. If Luciana came here, I didn't want to be in the room where I'd taken the club whores.

"Stop." My command came out weaker than I'd have liked.

They halted and looked at me, Bear's look clearly saying he thought I was losing my mind.

"You need to lie flat." Bear folded his arms and his jaw went tense, as if he were expecting a fight. He would get one too, if he insisted I go to my room down the hall.

"Not in that damn bed I don't."

I heard booted steps, then Fox peered down at me. "Not the bed?"

"No."

He tipped his head to the side and then understanding lit his eyes. "Right. Lay him out on the bar. Won't be comfortable, but Dread can get to him easily there. Once he's patched up, we'll worry about getting him home."

"Should we call Ryker?" Shooter asked.

"Not dying, you fuckers." My voice was getting weaker. I could tell I was losing too much blood. Cold was seeping into me, and it felt like my heart was racing. Shit. "Get Luciana."

Fox's jaw tightened, but he nodded.

"On it," Slider said.

"Dread is on his way," Shooter said. "Just hang in there, Pres. We'll have you patched up in no time. Then that pretty little woman of yours can give you sponge baths and shit."

I managed to lift my arm enough to flip him off, but what should have taken no effort at all made me feel like I'd just run a damn marathon.

"What the fuck did he do now?" I heard Dread's voice boom through the room.

"Got shot. Twice," Fox said.

Dread glared at me and shook his head. "You take too many fucking chances with your life, Pres. You have other priorities now. Can't be rushing off into danger."

"Fuck you," I mumbled.

"Stay with me." Dread checked my pulse, then shined one of those damn pen lights in my eyes.

Someone lifted me enough to ease my cut off and I fought to remain conscious. Dread pulled out some scissors and cut my shirt off, then let out a long whistle.

"Through and through in the shoulder." Dread prodded the area.

"Got shot in the back too," Bear said.

Dread rolled me onto my side and the silence was telling enough. I could feel the cold wetness on my skin and knew it was a fuck ton of blood. Mine.

"This is going to hurt." And that was all the warning I had. I bellowed out my pain and rage as he tried to work the bullet out of my body. It felt like forever before I heard the wet suction of the bullet popping free of my skin. "Missed the important things in there. You got lucky."

"Just stitch me up and shut up," I said.

"You've lost a lot of blood," Dread said.

He wasn't telling me anything I didn't know already, but a hospital was out of the damn question. They'd notify the police, and then I'd have other problems to deal with. No, I'd recover at home like I always did.

"Spider!" I wanted to turn toward Luciana's voice, but Dread's hand, along with Shooter and Fox, kept me immobile. The hole in my back burned like shit when Dread poured something over it. Likely alcohol.

"How close are you to passing out?" Dread asked.

"Not close enough," I said.

"No drugs. Not until we're done. I need you alert, which means…"

"Just do it," I said.

Slider led Luciana around the other side of the bar. She stopped in front of me and gripped my hand. Tears trickled down her cheeks and she looked fucking terrified as she held onto me. I felt like an asshole for scaring her like this. Maybe Dread was right and I needed to slow the fuck down. I fought to not only stay awake but to not squeeze Luciana's hand as Dread started the process of stitching me back together. It felt like hours passed before he'd finished my back and sutured both sides of my shoulder.

"We're never getting all that blood out of the bar," Shooter said.

Luciana turned to him and let loose with rapid fire Spanish that I couldn't follow. Shooter's eyes went wide and he took a step back, his hands up.

"Sorry. I have no idea what you just said, but I'm sorry. Obviously I'm being an insensitive asshole or something."

"He could have died," Luciana said, "and you're worried about a stupid bar?"

"Not dead, darlin'," I said, then coughed, which just made everything hurt even more.

Teller grabbed a bottle of water from the mini fridge and passed it to Luciana. She helped me sip at the cold liquid. As much as I wasn't looking forward to moving, I was more than ready to get off the damn hard wood surface that was digging into my bones. I was too old for this shit. Hell, I'd been too old for this shit since I was forty. I was just too stubborn to back down.

"We need to lay him in the backseat of the SUV. He'll need help getting into his house," Dread said.

"I'll go," Teller said.

"I would, but I don't want to scare your wife," Fox said.

"Just help him," Luciana said. "Don't worry about me."

I braced myself for the pain as they lifted me and carried my ass out to the SUV. Luciana had already climbed inside and they eased me down, but I worried about crushing her with my upper body across her thighs. She didn't seem to care about my weight but ran her fingers through my hair, her gaze full of concern and a bit of fear.

"I'm fine," I told her. "Just need some rest and I'll be good as new. It's not the first time I've been shot."

"It better be the last," she said, then her cheeks flushed.

Shooter chuckled. "Spoken like a true wife. We'll have you home in a moment, Pres. Teller's going to drive you, and the rest of us will follow."

Luciana held onto me as the SUV slowly headed toward our house. Funny. That was the first time I'd thought of the place as ours. When we came to a stop and Teller got out, I was both relieved and dreaded being moved again. I knew I had to be covering Luciana in my blood, but she didn't seem to care. Well, she cared I was bleeding, but I didn't think she minded that it was getting on her clothes and skin. The back door opened on Luciana's side.

"I'll go in and get the bed ready if that's all right," Teller said.

"Yes," Luciana said. "Maybe something to clean him off? He can't be comfortable with the blood drying on his skin. A warm wet cloth?"

Teller nodded and I closed my eyes a moment. I felt Luciana's light touch as she brushed her fingers over my cheeks, down my beard, and then smoothed my hair back. Her hand trembled and I knew she was scared. I felt like an asshole for doing this to her, and for what? More money? I wasn't ready to step down as President, but maybe I could delegate more tasks, not take point quite as often. She needed me, and the kid in her belly would too.

A shadow fell across me and I opened my eyes to see Bear leaning into the vehicle. A glance in the other direction showed Shooter and Fox opening the door with grim looks. Teller came back with the cloth Luciana had requested and she wiped down the front of me, but Fox had to help turn me so she could reach my back. I felt like a fucking infant and hated this shit.

"I'm not dead, you dumbasses. I can get out of the car."

"Sure you can, Pres," Fox said with a smirk. "But we're going to help just the same."

Despite their words, I did my best to get out of the SUV on my own, then staggered my way into the house with Fox supporting my weight. Luciana was within sight the entire time and rushed ahead of us. She smoothed the sheets on the bed and plumped my pillow like I was an invalid or something. I wasn't going to say anything, though, not since she seemed to feel the need to do something to help. Fox helped me sit on the edge of the bed, then Luciana knelt at my feet and removed my boots. I eased my legs up on the bed and leaned back against the pillows.

"Everyone out. My wife will let you know if I stop breathing."

"Not funny," Fox muttered, but he walked out along with the others. Teller hung back, hovering in the doorway.

"What's up, kid?" I asked.

"Maybe I should stay close? In case you need something?" he asked, his gaze skirting to Luciana, then back to me.

I looked at the woman now kneeling on the bed next to me. She didn't seem overly concerned about Teller in the house. Maybe getting shot wasn't such a bad thing after all, if it meant she'd finally trust the men in my club.

"Let him stay," Luciana said, her accent thicker than usual. It was a clue to just how worried she was right then.

"All right. You can stay, Teller, but not in this damn room."

He gave me a salute and walked off. I took Luciana's hand and kissed it.

"I'm fine," I assured her.

"They said you lost a lot of blood. I saw it! You're not fine. You're pale and you could have died!"

"Luciana, my life is dangerous. I'm the President of this club and that means I have to take certain risks. But I'll try to delegate more of those jobs to the others. I know you need me and I don't want to leave this earth too soon. I can't promise I'll never get shot again."

"When that man came and told me you'd been hurt, I think my heart stopped," she said. "I know we're still strangers for the most part, but it scared me. I already care about you, Trent. I don't want to lose you."

I kissed her hand again. "I'm not going anywhere, sweetheart."

"You should rest," she said. "I'll make some soup when you wake up. Or maybe I should check with a doctor? I don't know what to do for you."

"Some Tylenol would be a good start," I said.

She nodded and eased off the bed, careful not to jostle me. She retrieved the bottle from the bathroom, then walked out only to return a few minutes later with a glass of water. I took the pills from her and swallowed them, then guzzled the rest of the cool liquid in the glass.

Luciana took the glass from me and I closed my eyes. I heard her walk out of the room once more, and that was the last conscious thought I had until after night had fallen. I didn't know how I'd slept for so long, but the raised voices in the front of the house were enough to wake me. I groaned as I eased my legs over the side of the bed, then took a breath before rising to my feet. The room swayed, and so did I. After a moment, I took a hesitant step, then another. My head began to clear and even though I hurt like a bitch, I kept going, needing to find out what was going on.

When I got to the living room, it was to find Teller in front of a sobbing Luciana and my son, Ryker, yelling the damn house down. Like getting shot wasn't bad enough! Now I had to deal with this shit. I leaned against the doorframe, more out of necessity than anything else.

"What the fuck is going on?" I asked, my voice not as loud or as strong as I'd have liked.

"You got shot," Ryker said. "And this… this…" He waved a Luciana. "Wouldn't let me see you. Since when do you keep whores in the house?"

I pushed off the doorframe and advanced into the room. I hauled back my fist and slammed it into my son's jaw, then nearly passed the fuck out from the pain. Teller braced my weight as I glared at my son.

"That's my wife, asshole. Watch your tongue."

Ryker worked his jaw back and forth, then looked from me to Luciana and back again. "Is this some sort of joke? She's younger than me!"

"And? What business is it of yours? Your life isn't here anymore, Ryker. Hasn't been for a while. I didn't bitch at you about knocking up Laken. Not much anyway. I'm a grown-ass man, and your father. I don't owe you an explanation."

"I came to check on you because Slider said you were shot twice. Some warning I had a stepmother younger than myself or my wife would have been nice. You should sit down before you fall down."

I grunted in agreement and Teller helped me over to the couch. I sat and propped my feet on the coffee table. Motioning to Luciana, I held her hand as she sat beside me.

"Ryker, this is Luciana. You don't have to like the fact we're married, but she's not going anywhere, so you might as well get used to it. She's also pregnant."

Ryker blinked. Then blinked again. "You can't have kids."

"Doesn't mean I won't claim this one," I said.

"So some whore gets knocked up and you just…" Ryker didn't get to finish his sentence before Teller hit him, landing a solid punch to my son's gut. The kid cast a glance my way, clearly concerned that he'd just technically hit a club member, but my son needed to learn his place.

"Luciana isn't a whore," I said. "You know nothing about her or what she's suffered. So why don't you shut up before I let Teller knock your teeth down your throat? Not sure Laken would appreciate it if I sent you home all banged up."

"This is bullshit," he said, then glared at Teller. "I should call a vote to have you kicked out. You just assaulted a patched member of this club."

Teller didn't so much as flinch. "Go ahead."

I snorted and coughed to cover my laugh. The kid had some balls, that was for certain. "Anyone asks, I authorized that hit," I told him. "Ryker, I love you, but you're a pain in my Goddamn ass right now. Where's Laken and my grandson?"

"At home," he said.

"Right. Home. As in not at the Hades Abyss compound. You might still wear the cut, but you haven't been a true part of us for a while, son. You're always welcome here, and I'm not going to ask you to remove that cut, but you don't get a vote here anymore. You're more Reaper than anything at this point."

That made Ryker pause. "You wouldn't be pissed if I asked to patch in with them? You said something before, but I didn't think you meant it. You'd always wanted me to take over one day."

"Nope. Been waiting on you to ask. The liaison thing was all bullshit, just a way to keep you down there for Laken's sake. You don't need an excuse anymore. They've welcomed you into the fold. If you want to be a Dixie Reaper, I won't stand in the way."

He nodded. "I'll think about it."

"Got a place to stay?" I asked.

"I put my bag in the guest room before your wife found me wandering the house and lost her shit."

"Probably scared her," I said. "She doesn't do well around strange men."

Ryker stared at Luciana hard, and after a moment his gaze softened. The look he gave me was one full of understanding, and I wondered if he'd put the pieces together. With Sofia at the Dixie Reapers, I knew that he had to know about Mateo Gomez by this point. He gave me a nod and eased down onto a chair across the room.

"I won't stay long, but I had to make sure you were all right. I can head out tomorrow if you'd like, but I promised Gabriel I'd have his grandpa call and talk to him. He's worried."

"I'll call him in a bit." My stomach rumbled and Luciana made a sound of distress.

"I forgot to make the soup!" She shot up off the couch, but I grabbed her hand.

"It's fine. Teller can run grab something for everyone. There's a café on the other end of town that has good soup. He can grab me something there, and maybe a sandwich. Just tell him what you want to eat."

"I'm supposed to take care of you," she said, her eyes welling with tears. "I'm failing as a wife."

"No, you're not. It's been a long, stressful day for you. Sit and keep me company."

She nodded and sat back down. After we all gave Teller our orders, he left and Ryker watched me and Luciana like he was trying to figure out a puzzle. I really did love my son, but I'd also been right when I called him a pain in my ass. He had been for as long as I could remember, but I was damn proud of him. He'd served his country, then came home and found a good woman and settled down. Even if he wasn't here with me anymore, I knew he'd grown into a dependable man and a great father. It was all I could ask for.

Now I just had to hope I didn't screw up the kid who hadn't been born yet. The thought of fatherhood to a newborn in my sixties was damn terrifying. Luciana hadn't said for certain she was keeping the kid, but the way she'd hesitated about me wanting to be a father again, I knew she was thinking about it. Or maybe she'd decided and just hadn't come right out and said it yet.

My life was getting too fucking complicated.

Chapter Six

Luciana

When the man had knocked on the door, I'd been too scared to open it. Then he'd said that Spider was hurt and I'd thrown open the door, no longer caring if the man posed a threat to me. All I knew was that if Spider was injured, then I needed to get to him. At the clubhouse, I'd seen the massive amount of blood and I'd worried that he would die. He was still paler than usual, even though it had been five days since the shooting. His son, Ryker, had come and gone, and I couldn't exactly say I was sad to see him leave.

Spider was still taking it easy, but that was mostly due to me fretting over him. The looks he'd cast my way clearly said he'd rather be up and handling club business, but I'd pulled the "worried pregnant woman" card and I wasn't ashamed of it in the least. It hadn't taken me long to learn that he would do what he could to protect me, even if it meant keeping me as stress free as possible.

"Maybe you should go see your sister," Spider suggested as he flipped through the channels on the TV.

"Are you trying to get rid of me so you can sneak away to the clubhouse?"

He gave me a sideways glance. "Maybe."

"Dread said you needed to rest and heal. What part of that is so difficult for you?"

"The part where the asshole club that shot me is still out there. The part where I have no fucking clue what to do about your father and need to meet with Casper to discuss it. The part where I can't stand sitting on the fucking couch watching movies all Goddamn day."

I folded my arms and stared at him with my lips pursed. "Is that all?"

He snorted, then chuckled, only to wince in pain. It proved my point that he wasn't ready to dive back into things headfirst, but I knew he was a stubborn man. A proud man, not being able to handle everything was bothering him. He was a leader, but the kind who liked to get his hands dirty. I was learning that Spider would never ask one of his men to do something he himself wasn't prepared to do, or that he hadn't already done in the past.

"Is it so horrible?" I asked.

"What? Being shot?"

"Staying here with me all day," I said softly.

His gaze locked on me and he reached out a hand, beckoning for me to come closer. I carefully sat next to him, not want to make him hurt more than he already did. Spider reached up and loosened my bun, wrapping the length of my hair around his fingers. I'd noticed he seemed fascinated with it, which was the only reason I hadn't cut it off yet.

He gave my hair a tug and I leaned in closer. When his lips brushed against mine, I couldn't hold back my sigh of pleasure. I'd been so careful not to do anything that might hurt him, but I'd missed his kisses. I worried about him pulling or ripping his stitches, but as his mouth moved against mine, everything faded away except the taste and feel of him.

"I'm sorry," he said. "I never meant to make you feel like I don't want to be here with you."

"I know you didn't exactly choose me, that I was forced on you, but I care about you, Trent. I don't like seeing you in pain, and I'm worried you'll hurt yourself more if you don't slow down and rest."

His thumb caressed my jaw. "Whether I planned to claim you or not, you're mine. That means I have a responsibility to not just keep you safe, but I want you to be happy too. I didn't care with Ryker's mom, and that's on me. I was young and stupid. I also felt like she trapped me with her pregnancy. I went into this thing with you with my eyes wide open, Luciana. I'm here because I want to be."

"I like having you home," I admitted. "Even if we just watch movies or take a nap together. It's nice having you close."

"Then I'll take as much time as Dread suggests and we'll spend those days together. Maybe we can even leave the compound and do something that doesn't require a lot of activity. With my advanced years I can see why everyone is so worried."

I narrowed my eyes. "If you hadn't been shot twice, I'd be tempted to hit you right now. Advanced years? Really?"

He grinned and I knew he'd said it on purpose, knowing how much it irritated me. Ryker had made a huge deal of the age difference between us, and I'd watched it take a toll on Spider. While he was quick to say he was too old for me, I knew it hurt to hear someone else voice that same opinion. It had to be weird knowing his dad would be raising another kid, one younger than Ryker's own son, but it hadn't been enough reason for him to be so rude.

The longer I lived with Spider, the more I found myself speaking out about what I wanted. Not just with the man I was married to, but with the others as well. When Ryker had shown up and gotten loud with me, I hadn't cowered, though that might have had something to do with the fact his dad had been shot and I was too worried about Spider to think about being afraid of everyone else. But I knew a good dose of my confidence just had to do with being out from under my father's thumb. I'd noticed some changes in Violeta as well. The good kind.

"I don't like being cooped up in the house," he said. "We should go somewhere. Is there anything you need?"

I fingered my hair. "I'd thought of getting a haircut."

He stared at my long tresses and a look of longing crossed his face.

"But since you seem to like it so much, I guess I'll keep it the way it is," I said.

"No. If you want to get it cut, then you should. I'm not going to dictate how you style your hair, or what clothes you wear. I want you to do whatever makes you happy, Luciana."

"Being with you is what makes me happy," I said. "You've given me a home, Spider. A place where I feel safe."

He grumbled.

"Sorry. Trent. It's just… you don't seem like a Trent to me. Spider suits you."

"If you would prefer to call me Spider, that's fine. But you're welcome to call me Trent when it's just us." He placed a hand over my belly. "I should take you to the doctor. Make sure everything's all right."

"I think you need more time at home before we venture out anywhere. I know you think you're invincible, but you aren't."

"Luciana --"

I held up my hand. "What happens to me and this baby if you die? I know you think everyone will let us stay here, will take care of us, but they'll pick a new President, right? What if he doesn't want us here?"

He just stared and didn't say anything. I licked my lips and leaned in a little closer.

"Spider, I need you. But it's more than that. I want you. You make me feel safe, feel special. No one's ever treated me the way you do, or made me feel the things I feel around you."

He tugged my face toward his and kissed me again.

"I don't deserve you," he said.

"How much are you hurting right now?" I asked.

"Not much."

I pulled away and studied him. He was a liar, but I knew he'd never admit to being in pain. Maybe I could take his mind off his wounds for a bit. I knelt between his legs. Slowly, I opened his pants and pulled out his cock. His heated gaze tracked my movements as I stroked his shaft. If cocks could be described as pretty, Spider's would be beautiful. I leaned down and lapped at the head before sucking him into my mouth. He groaned and his hand went to my hair, fisting the strands as I wrapped my tongue around him and sucked long and hard. It felt like forever since he'd been inside me, but I didn't want to chance him straining himself or popping his stitches.

I cupped his balls and rolled them in my hand as I licked and teased him. He gave my hair a tug until I'd taken all of him, the head of his cock pushing against the back of my throat. He held me there and my eyes watered. His cock twitched and jerked in my mouth, then he pulled me off before urging me back down again. I let him control my motions and soon his pre-cum was liberally coating my tongue.

"So good," he murmured. "That's it, baby girl. Take every inch."

I could tell he was close, so I sucked harder. It wasn't long before he growled and jet after jet of his hot cum filled my mouth. I swallowed it, then licked him clean.

"Bedroom," he said.

"But we shouldn't…"

He placed a finger over my lips.

"Bedroom, wife. We'll work it out, but I'm not going to leave you unsatisfied."

I nodded and rose to my feet. He still looked paler than usual and I knew he wasn't healed enough for what he had in mind, but telling him that was useless. The man would do what he wanted, for the most part. I'd managed to keep him locked up in the house so far, but I knew time was running out. He'd eventually go back to the clubhouse and take care of business as usual, whatever that meant. I just hoped it didn't involve more bullets.

I stayed close to his side in case he needed me, and when we got to the bedroom, I stripped off my clothes. He'd only been wearing jeans around the house since his T-shirts rubbed against his stitches. Spider quickly dropped them and kicked them away. He got on the bed and knelt, then patted the mattress.

I climbed onto the bed, but I didn't know what he planned to do. With a nod of his head, he directed me to lie down in front of him. Stretching out, I bracketed his body with my thighs and watched to see what he'd do next. Spider reached into the bedside table drawer and pulled out… a pink vibrator?

"When did you get that?" I asked.

"Next Day shipping," he said. "I knew I couldn't properly take care of you for a bit longer. Didn't seem fair to make you wait. If you like this one, I can order more."

He turned on the toy, then parted the lips of my pussy. I gasped and my body tensed when he placed the vibrator against my clit. Spider chuckled and turned up the speed on the toy, causing me to squeal and arch off the bed. It was intense, *too* intense. I screamed as I came in less than a minute. He kept rubbing my clit with the buzzing pink silicone, turning it up even higher. It felt like my orgasm went on forever.

When I didn't think I could take another moment, he pushed the toy inside me.

"Oh, God! Oh, God! Spider!"

He fucked me with it, hard short strokes. The noises coming from me sounded inhuman as I rode the edge of pleasure. Spider pulled the toy from inside me and rubbed my clit with it again. He alternated between teasing me and fucking me, making me feel like I was losing my mind as I came again and again. I hadn't even known such a thing was possible. Spider wrung yet another release from me. My thighs were shaking and my body was slick with sweat.

"Can't," I murmured. "Can't come again. Too much."

He shut off the toy and tossed it aside, then gripped my thighs and pulled me closer. I gasped as his cock brushed against me.

"Spider, no. You'll hurt yourself."

"Let me worry about that. Need you, baby girl. Too damn much."

I bit my lip, not wanting to argue because I needed him every bit as much. He sank into me, his hand gripping my ass. Spider's eyes slid shut a moment, a look of complete bliss crossing his face. He pumped in and out of me, long slow strokes. The push and pull of his cock felt incredible. It wasn't the hard fucking I'd grown accustomed to, but it was just as amazing, if not better. Spider reached for the toy again and turned it back on. He used it to tease my clit as he thrust again and again.

"Spider." I moaned, gripping the sheets tight. "So good. Don't stop."

"Come on my cock, baby girl. Give me that cream."

I whimpered as he turned the toy up another notch. It only took a moment before I was screaming his name. He grunted as he drove his cock into me and I felt his cum filling me up. I came twice more before he stopped, buried inside me and bracing his weight on one hand. His breathing was labored, and his face was flushed. I glanced at his shoulder, happy to see the stitches were holding.

"Not old," I said. "You can never call yourself that again. Any man who can make me come that many times, and get hard twice in the same hour, is far from old."

He chuckled, then shut off the toy. Slowly, he pulled free of my body and rolled onto his side with a groan. I cuddled against him while trying not to hurt him. Spider pressed a kiss to my forehead.

"I'm tingling from head to toe," I murmured.

"I think you can come a few more times," he said.

"No," I said quickly.

"Mmm. Bet you can." He picked up the toy and held it out to me, but I didn't reach for it. "I want to watch you get yourself off."

My mouth dropped open and my eyes went wide as I stared at him. He wanted me to what? He put the toy into my hand and propped himself on his elbow.

"Come on, baby girl. Give me a show." He winked and smiled.

I stared at the toy a moment, then clicked it on. Stretching out on my back, I spread my thighs and teased my clit. I circled the nub slowly, drawing out the pleasure. My gaze locked with Spider's, then dropped to his chest, down his abs, and to his cock which was still wet from our mingled release. I bit my lip and worked my clit harder. When my orgasm tore through me, I plunged the toy into my pussy and fucked myself with it hard and fast.

"That's it," he murmured. "Come for me again."

I pulled the toy out and rubbed it on my clit once more, spreading my thighs wider. My hips lifted and I felt Spider cup my ass with his hand. His fingers slid between my ass cheeks and I gasped as he rubbed the tight hole hidden there. He used my cream to lubricate me, then fucked my ass with his finger as I used the toy to get off again. I was nearly crying the emotions were so intense.

Spider took the toy from me, easing it out of my pussy, then pressing it against that tight ring of muscle. I gasped as he pressed the tip inside. He didn't push it in any farther, just held it there a moment before pulling it back out.

"I'm going to fuck you there one day," he said. "But only when you beg me for it."

"Spider," I said softly.

"Rest, Luciana. We'll get cleaned up after a nap. Or maybe I'll make you come some more."

I sighed and closed my eyes, curling against him.

"Stay?" I asked softly.

"Of course. There's nowhere I'd rather be than here with you." He lightly touched my belly. "Both of you."

"Ryker doesn't like me," I said.

"Ryker doesn't have to, but he does have to refrain from being an asshole when he visits. I'll handle my son. Although, one phone call and I'm sure Laken will sort him out pretty quick. She wouldn't have tolerated his bullshit."

"I'd like to meet her, and your grandson." I smiled sleepily. "Does this mean I'm a grandma?"

He chuckled softly. "Yeah, guess it does. Don't worry. Laken and Gabriel will love you, and Ryker will come around. I haven't had a woman in my life since his mother, even though I couldn't stand her. It's probably a little strange for him to see me with someone, especially someone younger than him."

"He did seem rather hung up on our age difference. And the baby." I rubbed my belly. "I don't want to cause a problem between you and your family, Spider."

He pressed a kiss to my lips. "You're my family now too, Luciana. You and the baby. I'm not letting you go, regardless of whether my son gets his head out of his ass or not."

He grunted as he lay flat on the bed and I leaned over him. The wound in his shoulder seemed to be healing well. With a nudge, I got him to roll onto his stomach and I winced when I saw the one in his lower back. It was angry and red, a little swollen, and when I touched it, it felt overly warm. I didn't know much about gunshot wounds, but I knew the moment he fell asleep I was calling Dread. Something didn't seem right with it, and I'd feel better if the club doctor looked at him. And I'd have to find a way to keep my hands off Spider, and make sure he didn't push himself too hard. We shouldn't have had sex. I'd only meant to relieve some of his tension, not take things even further.

I'd only been his wife for less than two weeks and already I felt like I was failing him. I hoped when the baby came that I'd be a better mother than I was a wife. A soft snore slipped from Spider's lips and I picked up his phone, quickly dialing Dread's number.

"Hello," said a gruff voice.

"Dread? It's Luciana," I said.

"Everything all right?"

"Um, it's Spider. The wound on his lower back looks irritated. I was hoping you might be able to come look at it."

Dread snorted. "He's asleep, isn't he?"

"Yes."

"Figured. No way the Pres would let you call me about his wounds otherwise. I'll swing by in a bit. If he's resting, that's really the best thing for him right now. I'll bring some supplies just in case it's worse than I'm thinking. He's probably just strained himself. I thought he was being a good patient."

My cheeks warmed. "He was. Until today."

"Do I want to know?"

"Probably not," I said.

"Give me an hour. Two tops and I'll be there. Anything changes with him between now and then, call me back."

"Thank you," I said softly, then ended the call.

I stared at the man lying next to me. Never would I have imagined wanting to be intimate with someone or trusting them as much as I trusted Spider. He'd changed my life. My emotions were all over the place lately, but I had just thought it was the surging hormones from my pregnancy. Maybe it was more. Was I starting to fall in love with Spider?

I'd never experienced love before. I had no idea what it looked like or felt like. The love I felt for my sisters was different from what I felt for Spider, but that seemed logical enough. They were my family, my blood. Spider was a man who made my senses come alive, made my body beg for his attention. I was either just deeply in lust with my husband, or I loved him. He hadn't signed up for that, so I would keep those thoughts to myself unless things changed. Maybe one day it would be the right time to tell him. But that day wasn't today.

Chapter Seven

Spider

Three damn weeks of sitting on my ass. Even worse, other than the one day Luciana had surprised me with a blow job that had ended with some of the best sex I'd ever experienced, she'd refused to touch me other than holding my hand or giving me a gentle hug. She'd called in Dread, and I'd been read the riot act on taking better care of myself when it looked like the wound in my back was getting infected. He'd injected me with antibiotics and given me a bottle of pills. Little did my wife realize I'd been given the all clear this morning. She was in for a surprise later.

Fox sat across the kitchen table from me, sipping a cup of coffee as I toyed with one of my own. Having to sit on the sidelines while my club took care of business was starting to piss me off. I was the Goddamn President. I should be out there knocking heads together, not stuck in this house. Despite the fact I was technically healed enough to resume normal activities, I was a little concerned about leaving Luciana for too long. I'd seen the fear in her eyes when I'd been shot and I didn't want to put her through that again so soon, and if I went after her father then I probably wouldn't make it out completely unscathed.

"The Chaos Killers had two chapters in Missouri, not one like we'd thought. As of last night, both have been wiped out. We sent a clear message to any others in the surrounding areas that retaliation wouldn't be tolerated and they would meet the same fate if they fucked with us," Fox said.

"Any word from Casper VanHorne? Fucker is ghosting me."

"From what I've gathered, he's gone dark. Even Torch and Isabella haven't heard anything. I've put out some feelers to see if there's movement on Mateo Gomez, but so far, the man seems to be in business as usual. Whatever Casper is up to, it either doesn't involve Gomez, or he's being so fucking discreet there's not so much as a whisper about it."

"And knowing Casper, that's a good possibility," I said.

"Look, Pres. I know it sucks being housebound, and if you didn't have a pregnant wife then no one would say a word about you resuming your duties."

"But I do have a pregnant wife," I said.

"Yes, and the club is starting to like Luciana. A lot. They don't want to upset her or Violeta. And if Luciana is upset, then so is Violeta. They've been through hell but seem to be settling into life here, and I'd even go so far as to say they're happy. No one wants to fuck that up." Fox blew out a breath. "I know Dread gave you the all clear, but I just think you should take some extra time."

"I'll think about it. A few days wouldn't hurt, but anything beyond that is out of the question. I'd expected to see more of Violeta. She doesn't come visit Luciana that much," I said.

"Probably because Rocket freaks the hell out when he can't find her." Fox smiled a little. "I know she's young, too young for a relationship, but don't be surprised if he claims her one day. He's an even bigger watchdog with her than he was over Rhianon, and you know how protective he felt about his sister. Maybe it's because Rhianon died, but something tells me that isn't it."

"Any word on Sofia? I'm sure Saint is taking good care of her, but he seemed less than pleased about having her around his daughter."

Fox shook his head. "I haven't asked, and the few times I've spoken to Torch he hasn't volunteered the information."

"Just wondered if either of them are pregnant like Luciana. The way Violeta reacted when asked about it makes me think at least one of them is."

Fox hesitated and that was enough to tell me something had happened.

"What?" I asked.

"Violeta *was* pregnant."

"Was?" I asked.

"She miscarried. It's part of why Rocket is keeping her on such a tight leash. If she's out of his sight, he tracks her down. He found her in the bathroom floor, bleeding all over the damn place. No one said anything to Luciana or you. Didn't want to cause either of you more stress than you're already under. She's fine, and it looks like she can still have kids if she wants them in the future."

"What kind of fucking monster rapes and tortures girls? And then gets them pregnant?" I asked. "I want Mateo Gomez to pay, as well as any men who hurt those girls."

"The club is behind you on that one hundred percent. And I know the Dixie Reapers feel the same. I do find it a little odd that Gomez supposedly sent his girls here as a way to make an alliance with the clubs, and yet none of us have heard from him. Shouldn't he have at least checked in by now?" Fox asked.

He was right. I'd thought the same thing, that something seemed off. The man sent his daughters here to smooth things over, create a bond with the clubs, and yet he hadn't called to check on the girls or ask for a single favor. Men like Gomez would strike while the iron was hot. It was unsettling and made me wonder what sort of trouble was on the horizon for us. If he'd planned to use his daughters as moles, I had a feeling it had backfired on him. I didn't see either Luciana or Violeta volunteering information to their father or ever wanting to speak to the man again.

I sipped my coffee and thought about what our next move should be. I didn't have a way to reach Gomez on my own, but it didn't mean that he wasn't doing business stateside. Something I could interfere with, even on a small scale. Maybe not enough to point a gun in the club's direction, but enough to irritate the man and make him slip up. I wanted him to contact us, wanted a way to reach him. Then I'd string him up by his balls and exact revenge for the hell he'd put his daughters through over the years.

"Find out where his shipments are going here in the US," I said. "And I want to know who's handling them."

"You going to steal the man's drugs?" Fox asked.

"Among other things. I don't think he's just dealing drugs. That might be what he's importing into our country, but something has to be going out and I'm betting it's more than money. Have Surge check the missing persons' reports and see if there's an uptick since Gomez came into power."

"Human trafficking?" Fox asked. "You think he's swapping drugs for girls?"

"With the way he treated his daughters? Yeah. Women are nothing but pawns to him, only good for what he can get from them. I also want to find out all we can about every business he owns in Colombia and elsewhere in South America."

"Am I looking for something in particular?" Fox asked.

"Brothels. Luciana said her father's men whored her out for a night when she disobeyed. I doubt he had customers come to his house."

"And for him to have that sort of clientele on the ready it means he knows where to find them," Fox said. "This fucker makes my stomach turn."

"You and me both," I said.

"I know that look," Fox said. "You're not looking for just your everyday brothel, are you?"

"Nope. The girls were young when they were first raped and sold. Too young. Luciana mentioned how much she feared her father getting his hands on her baby, what he'd make the kid do."

Fox turned a little green, and I knew he was following me now. Gomez was a sick fuck, and those under him seemed to be every bit as evil. As much as I hated all this international bullshit that the clubs kept getting involved in, it was time to do something about the fuckers coming into my damn country for this shit. I might sell drugs and guns, but I made damn sure they didn't get into the hands of kids. If I heard someone dealt my drugs to teens, I took care of it. I might not walk on the right side of the law, but I still had a few morals. Since my club had a permanent tie to Colombia now, thanks to my wife, it might be time to do something about the issues over there. Or at least set up a few men to keep an eye on things.

"I'm on it," Fox said. He drained the last of his coffee and stood, but he hesitated before leaving. "I know I'm your VP and you're in charge, but I'm also your friend. When this shit is settled and you know Luciana is safe, you should take a vacation. A real one. Take your woman on a honeymoon or something. Go to a resort somewhere nice. You haven't taken a break in over twenty years that I know of, unless it was medically necessary, and I think Luciana would appreciate a change of scenery."

I nodded and waved him off. Fox was right. He wasn't just my VP, and I knew he made the suggestion for my benefit and Luciana's. The fact he was thinking of my wife, trying to ensure her happiness, made me smile. If anything ever happened to me, I knew Fox would keep an eye on her. She'd found a home here with the club. I just hoped I was around another thirty years to enjoy my time with her, watch that kid grow up. But in this life, nothing was ever guaranteed.

I heard the front door shut and I finished my coffee, enjoying the silence for a moment. I contemplated waking Luciana but decided to get more coffee and let her rest. She'd been so worried about me I hadn't been able to convince her to see a doctor yet. While I enjoyed the second mug of java, I looked up doctors on my phone. As good as Dread was, he wasn't the right type of doctor to ensure Luciana and the baby were doing okay. There were a few OB-GYNs in the area, so I picked the one with the highest rating and called to set an appointment. I'd learned early on that money talked so I offered to pay extra if they'd see her today.

After I disconnected the call, I sent a text to Knox.

Get insurance for the club. Need to make sure Luciana is covered, and Violeta.

It only took a moment for him to respond. *On it.*

I hoped the insurance would cover the baby. From what I remembered of Ryker's birth, that shit was expensive, and probably triple the amount it had been back then. Not that my bank accounts weren't pretty flush, but there was no sense throwing money at doctors when an insurance policy would cover the majority of it. I was frugal, not cheap, or so I told myself. Maybe it came from being born to parents who had lived through the Great Depression. Not that all their lessons had stuck, obviously.

I smiled faintly as I thought about them. My mother would have loved Luciana. Both of my parents would have hated how I turned out, but I knew they would still love me. I'd lost both of them too soon. Even Ryker hadn't had a chance to know them. Luciana's kid wouldn't have grandparents from either side, which was rather sad, but I knew plenty of kids never met theirs. I hadn't. Ryker didn't remember his. If I had any say in the matter, Mateo Gomez wouldn't be drawing breath much longer. Even if he did manage to get out of this alive, I'd never let him anywhere near my family. I'd rather spend the rest of my life behind bars if it meant that Luciana and the baby would be safe.

Speaking of my beautiful wife… she wandered into the kitchen, rubbing her eyes as she blinked sleepily. Her hair was disheveled but she looked adorable, especially wearing one of my shirts and nothing else. Well, almost nothing else I amended as she stretched to reach for a glass and the shirt rode up, exposing a pair of pink panties.

"Morning," I said.

"I didn't sleep too long, did I?" she asked.

"You can sleep as long as you want. You're growing another person, Luciana. It's going to make you more tired than usual."

She nodded and pulled the orange juice from the fridge, then filled a glass. She set the carton down, then stared at it. I bit my lip so I wouldn't laugh. I'd learned that Luciana wasn't much of a morning person and it took a good half hour before she became fully alert. She seemed to shake it off and put away the orange juice, then sat at the table with her glass.

"I made an appointment for you this morning," I said. "Just to make sure everything is all right with the baby."

"Should you --"

I held up a hand and cut her off. "I'm perfectly fine, Luciana. I'm not dying, the stitches dissolved nearly two weeks ago, the infection is gone. I'm plenty capable of driving you to an appointment, but since I still don't know what's going on with your father we'll take a few men with us. Better safe than sorry."

She nodded. "I'm sorry. I've just been so worried about you."

"I know." I reached out and grabbed her hand. "It's nice to have someone worry over me, but I'm perfectly fine, and all the stress isn't good for you and the baby."

She dropped her gaze. "Violeta should have an appointment."

"Because she's pregnant?" I asked, wondering if she'd known about her sister and had kept quiet.

Slowly, she nodded, then chanced a glance in my direction. I gave her what I hoped was a reassuring smile.

"Sweetheart, I hate to tell you this, but Violeta lost her baby. She's fine, and Rocket is taking good care of her."

The tension eased from her shoulders. "Good. Is it horrible that I'm glad she isn't pregnant anymore?"

"No, not considering the circumstances. She's young. Too young. But if she'd had the baby and decided to give it up, we'd have made sure the kid found a good home. And if she'd had it and wanted to keep it, then we'd have helped with that too. Neither of you are alone anymore, Luciana. You have an entire family standing behind you, whether they're blood or not."

"When's my appointment?" she asked.

"You have enough time to have some breakfast, shower, and get ready to go without rushing."

"So I can sit here a little longer?" she asked.

"Of course." I leaned over and kissed her cheek. "Drink your juice and I'll fix you something to eat. Eggs and toast sound okay?"

She nodded and yawned widely.

I smiled as I pulled the eggs and milk from the fridge. I couldn't remember ever thinking a woman was as cute as Luciana. Everything she did fascinated me in some way. I'd be perfectly content to just sit and watch her. Although, that sounded a little creepy now that I thought about it. But I did like watching her twirl her hair around her finger, or the way she bit her lip when she was nervous. The shy smile she gave me at times. Everything about her made me want to learn even more.

Fuck. Me. I was falling in love with my wife. I'd realized a while back that I cared about her, more than I'd ever cared about a woman, but this was more than just caring. I wanted to see her smile, wanted to make her happy, give her everything she'd ever wanted and never had. Yep. I was in love with my wife. I glanced her way, but she wasn't paying me the least bit of attention. I didn't know if she'd be happy to hear that I'd fallen for her, or if it would scare her off. We hadn't entered into this with love on either of our minds. It had been an agreement and nothing more. Yeah, sex had been part of it, but not emotions.

I finished the eggs and stuck the bread into the toaster. I knew she liked hers barely browned, so the level popped a minute later and I slathered the slices in butter before plating them. When I set the dish down in front of Luciana, she gave me a smile and her eyes shone with warmth. Taking care of her felt good. I'd taken care of my club for most of my life, even before I'd been the President, but this was different. With Ryker's mom, we'd tolerated each other, but I hadn't been ready to settle down. I'd run around on her and not treated her very well. I wouldn't make that mistake with Luciana.

"You're not eating?" she asked.

"I had something earlier. Fox came by early to discuss club business so I grabbed a quick meal before he showed up. I didn't want to wake you since you were sleeping so peacefully."

"He doesn't scare me anymore," she said, not looking at me. "If that's part of why you didn't wake me. I know he's not the same man who hurt me. Everyone has treated me really well, and I'm comfortable here now."

"I'm glad. They would lay down their lives for you, or for Violeta."

"I know. It was hard not to see all men as evil. I'd never known anything else. Even Mr. VanHorne left me feeling skeptical. I'd only known that he was working with my father, but I hadn't realized he was trying to make us safe. I thought he was a broker of sorts."

"That's what he wanted your father to think. I believe Mateo Gomez is on borrowed time. Not just as the head of the Colombian cartel, but in life as well. If Casper doesn't end him, I damn sure will find a way to do it. I don't want you to feel like you have to look over your shoulder all the time."

"It's not just him," Luciana said. "You'd have to take down all his men as well. There isn't a single one who is redeemable. All of them are rotten to the core."

I nodded. "I figured as much. I'm hoping we can find enough of your father's businesses that we can rescue any women who might be suffering at his hands, or because of his actions. If not my club directly, then others I trust."

"You're a good man. Honorable. I'm lucky to be your wife, even if we didn't say vows in a church."

I paused, my cup of coffee halfway to my mouth. "You want that? A church wedding?"

She shook her head. "It's not important to me. When I was little, I would dream of my wedding day and finding the perfect prince who would adore me. As I got older and learned about the monsters living in the world, those dreams changed. I only wanted a place where I could feel safe. I have that with you, and more. I'm happy, Spider, and I don't need a dress, flowers, or a church to make me feel any more married to you than I am."

"Surge printed off a copy of a marriage certificate, even if it is completely fabricated by his computer skills, just like our marriage. As far as the state is concerned, we're legally married thanks to his hacking, but you didn't exactly agree to all this. If you'd like, we can frame it and hang it somewhere in the house, or I'll give you a real wedding if you want one."

She smiled brightly. "I'd like that. Framing the certificate. I don't need a wedding."

"You won't have wedding pictures. Don't women want that sort of thing?" I asked.

"Maybe we could just take some together here at the compound," she said almost shyly. "Two houses down there's a pretty tree with flowers. It would make a nice picture."

"The dogwood outside Knox's home?" I asked. Then I wasn't sure she'd know what a dogwood was. Did they have those in Colombia? "Small tree with white flowers?"

She nodded.

"I think that can be arranged. And if you want to plant flowers or anything else around here, you're welcome to. Just let me know what you need."

"I guess if I have an appointment, I should start getting ready." She leaned over and kissed my cheek. "Thank you. For everything you've done for me."

I waved off her thanks, not needing it. If anyone was thankful, it was me. I hadn't realized until now that I'd just been living through one day at a time without any true meaning in my life. My club had been my entire world, and there wasn't anything wrong with that, but Luciana was showing me that I'd been missing out on something amazing.

While Luciana got ready, I cleaned up the kitchen, then browsed SUVs on my phone. With a baby coming, we'd need something other than my bike. Using the club vehicle was fine for now, but we needed a family car that was just ours. Never thought I'd be looking at car seats and shit. It amazed me that I wasn't the least bit bothered by the thought of raising another kid. Ryker had turned out okay. Hopefully I wouldn't screw up this one either.

Chapter Eight

Luciana

I stared at the doctor and blinked a few times. "I'm what?"

"Carrying twins," the doctor repeated. "And you're severely underweight considering how far along you are. The babies aren't developing as well as they should be. I'm going to write you a prescription for prenatal vitamins and give you a diet plan to follow to ensure the babies get all the nutrients they need. I'll want to monitor you closely the next few weeks."

Spider gripped my hand. "She's been under a great deal of stress. I'll make sure she gets plenty of rest and eats properly. Whatever she needs, I'll make sure she gets it."

The doctor looked at his cut and stared down her nose at him. I could have sworn her lip even curled in a snarl for a moment. It was clear she didn't think much of him, and that bothered me a great deal. I gave his hand a reassuring squeeze and hoped he'd give in to the request I was about to make. I knew Spider wouldn't lose his cool with the doctor for fear of upsetting me, especially after the news she'd just given us, but I wasn't about to stand for her to treat him like he was trash.

Now that I was getting more comfortable with my new life, I'd found that I was more outspoken around other people. I didn't cower anymore, or fear being reprimanded for disagreeing with someone. Under Spider's care, I was flourishing, and I loved my new life. With him by my side, I felt like I could do anything. Even take an uppity doctor down a few notches. "Do you think you could give me a minute with the doctor?" I asked.

He glowered at the woman, but kissed my cheek. "I'll be right outside the door in the hallway."

The doctor backed as far away from him as she could as Spider walked out, closing the door a little harder than necessary. She folded her arms over her chest and stared at me, her chin jutted out and her jaw tight. Yeah, she wasn't happy, but I didn't much care. That man had given me a new life, a home where I was safe and cared for, had family other than my sisters. He wasn't a bad guy, and I wouldn't let anyone think otherwise.

"You don't like him," I said.

"I don't like what they stand for. Drugs. Murder. Rape."

I held up a hand. "I can't speak as to whether or not they deal in drugs, but I do know that none of the men in Spider's club, him included, would ever kill an innocent person. I also know they don't rape anyone."

I couldn't say they wouldn't kill *anyone* because I had no doubt they'd all murder my father if they had the chance, and I wouldn't stand in their way. Some people deserved to die, and if Spider and the Hades Abyss wanted to take care of the trash, then I wouldn't utter a word of complaint. One rotten life in exchange for a bunch of innocents? Wasn't a hard decision, not for me.

The doctor opened her mouth, but I stopped her before she could spew more hatred.

"Spider is a good, honorable man. This baby isn't his. Or rather babies," I said pointing to my stomach. "But I'm his wife now and he's accepting these children, even though neither of us knows who the father is other than a complete monster. The scars you saw on my body aren't from my husband. He would never hurt me."

I told her about my father, about what I'd endured since I was just a teenager, and I made sure she understood that Spider had saved me and Violeta. I couldn't stand the thought of her believing such horrible things about him, or any of the men in Hades Abyss. As far as I was concerned, they were saints. Angels. Avenging angels maybe, since I knew every last man I'd spoken to wanted my father's blood for what he'd done to me and my sisters.

"They're good men," I said softly. "If you can't see that, if you can't give them a chance, then I'll have to ask Spider to find a different doctor for me. I won't be seen by someone who's going to treat him like something she stepped in."

The doctor sighed and gave me a slight nod, but not before I saw the sheen of tears in her eyes. I wondered if those were for me and my unborn babies, for my sisters, or if something had happened to her. She'd seemed so insistent that Hades Abyss was full of evil men. It made me wonder if she'd known bikers before, maybe some who weren't as good as the men I now lived with.

"What club hurt you?" I asked, taking a gamble that she'd been mistreated by a biker at some point, or several of them.

Her gaze jerked to mine.

"You're too adamant they're bad people without truly knowing them, which means you've had a previous experience with bikers. A bad one from what I can tell," I said.

"I was gang raped by a club before I moved here about six years ago. They caught me by my car on my way home from med school. I was twenty and completely naïve despite what I'd seen in the hospital. My daughter is the product of that night."

"I knew you looked young," I said with a smile.

She shrugged. "Graduated high school when I was fifteen and went straight to college. Took the max course load and petitioned for more so I could finish my degrees faster. I haven't been practicing all that long, but I pride myself on being the best at what I do."

"You're amazing," I said softly. "But so are the men of Hades Abyss. I understand why you don't want to give them a chance, but I can't keep seeing you if you're going to look at them with hate and contempt."

"Maybe I do have a biased opinion of men like your Spider. If he's as good as you say, then I'll give the Hades Abyss a chance. I wouldn't want anyone to judge me based on someone else's actions, so I'll try to do the same for them."

"Thank you," I said softly.

The doctor crossed the room and pulled open the door, letting Spider back inside the room. He raised his eyebrows as he looked at me, and I gave him a smile and a nod. I was fine. Although, I did wonder if it would be okay to invite the doctor to the compound sometime. Maybe if she got a chance to spend time with Hades Abyss, she'd see how good they were. I didn't fool myself into thinking they were law-abiding by any means, but I also didn't think they would hurt women and children. Assholes like my father were another matter, and I was behind them one hundred percent if they wanted to wipe that type of filth from the face of the earth.

"You ready to go home?" Spider asked.

Honestly? No, I wasn't. I loved being at the house, knowing I was safe, but being outside the gates was nice too. Other than the one shopping trip, and now this visit to the doctor, I hadn't left the compound since Spider had brought me here from the airstrip. I was starting to feel like I lived in a cage. A pretty, spacious one, but a cage just the same. After the life I'd led, I was used to being kept under lock and key, but this time it was different. I wasn't being held hostage by my father and his men. Spider only wanted to keep me safe, and I appreciated that, but I was also ready to experience all I'd missed in my life.

"I'll call in her prescription. The pharmacy on Main Street?" the doctor asked.

"That works," Spider said, observing her.

"I'm sorry," the doctor said, her tone grudging at best. "Your wife pointed out that I was judging you unfairly."

"Bad experience with a biker?" he asked.

I tugged on Spider's hand and shook my head, hoping my look conveyed enough that he'd leave it alone. I'd tell him just enough about the doctor that he wouldn't judge her for her previous behavior, but otherwise it was her story to tell. I just knew my kindhearted husband would do his best to make her feel at ease once he knew that her background with bikers was less than pleasant. She may not have suffered as long as I had, but her experience was no less traumatic. She'd been abused by those men, violated, and I could understand her dislike and fear of Spider.

"Thank you for your time, Doc," Spider said, holding out his hand. The doctor hesitantly shook it, a strange look crossing her face, before she darted out of the room.

"That went well," I said. "Looks like you'll be watching me even closer now."

He snorted, then laughed. "We'll get you back on track. Now that we know there's a problem, we can fix it. Get changed while I go handle the bill and set up your next appointment, assuming you want to come back here."

I nodded. "She had a really bad experience with bikers, but she knows the scars on my body aren't from you. I told her that you and your club were honorable and not like the men who hurt her."

Spider gave me a quick kiss, then ducked out of the room. I started pulling on my clothes and shoved the paper gown in the trash. When I reached the front lobby, Spider had a sheet in his hand with dietary suggestions. He took my hand and led me outside. Teller was waiting for us, along with Marauder and Hornet. Spider refused to let me leave without extra protection, in case we were attacked and he couldn't keep me safe. I thought it was sweet, even though some women might feel stifled by it. I'd gladly go everywhere with a security detail if it meant my father, or men like him, wouldn't get their hands on me.

Having lived through hell, I had a slightly different perspective than most people. Even women who had been assaulted might not appreciate all the muscle surrounding me, but I was more than happy to have them along. They didn't make me feel any less independent, or weak. It just made me feel cherished that the club wanted to keep me safe, even at the possible cost of their own lives. Instead of driving over to the pharmacy, Spider took my hand and led me down the sidewalk. After a moment, I realized we were heading for a park. I couldn't remember ever going to a park before. It was a beautiful day, and even though the news at the doctor's office hadn't been what I'd expected, I felt calmer and more at peace than ever before.

"Any idea what the baby is?" Teller asked from next to me.

"There's two of them, but we don't know the sexes yet," I said.

"Wow, twins?" Teller blinked. "Congratulations!"

"She has to eat better and take vitamins," Spider said. "The babies aren't growing as well as they should, which means they want to keep a close eye on her. She goes back in a week."

Teller frowned. "Will they be okay?"

My heart stopped a moment. I hadn't even thought to ask. Spider had just said he'd do whatever it took to make me better, to make the babies better, and I hadn't questioned it. But now I had to wonder if there was a chance the two children growing inside me wouldn't live long enough to be born or would be born with problems. Was I already a bad mother? I'd been more concerned with how the doctor had treated my husband than over what was happening with the babies.

My stomach churned and I stumbled a little. I placed my hand over my belly and prayed that they would be all right.

"Shut it, youngster," Spider muttered and wrapped his arm around my waist. "She's going to be fine and so are the babies."

Teller nodded. "Sorry. I didn't mean anything by it. It's just that we haven't had any kids around the compound other than when Ryker visits with his family. I was kind of looking forward to it."

I nearly stumbled again as I stopped to stare at Teller. "You want kids at the compound? Why?"

He shrugged. "I like them. They're so innocent and unspoiled by life. You know they mean whatever they say, and there's this look of wonder whenever they discover something new. Until they learn the world we live in is complete shit."

It seemed Teller had depths that no one knew about, since Spider and Marauder were both looking at him like he'd grown a second head. I thought it was sweet, and I had no doubt he'd be a champion to all the kids at the compound -- if mine lived, and if any others came along. As much as I thought Violeta losing her baby was a blessing, I looked forward to raising a family with Spider. Since he'd gotten snipped, the babies inside me were probably my only chance. I knew there were other options like adoption or artificial insemination, but I didn't know if Spider would go for either of those. He'd taken me on with the kids inside me already on board. Asking him to bring in more kids wouldn't be fair. Not after he'd gone to the trouble to never have more.

"Why are we at the park?" Marauder asked.

"Luciana likes the tree out in front of Knox's house. I thought she might enjoy a walk through the park. There's lots of shit with flowers on it right now," Spider said.

I bit my lip so I wouldn't laugh at how eloquent he wasn't. I was thrilled that he'd thought of something like this, but his delivery could use a little work. Then again, he wouldn't be Spider if he had said it any other way. As we walked, I noticed that he no longer winced or rubbed at the gunshot wound in his shoulder, and that his back was looking much better too. It made me happy that he'd healed so well. When I'd seen all the blood, I'd been so scared I would lose him. That moment was when I'd known for sure that I loved him. I was just too damn scared to tell him. What if he didn't feel the same?

"Why don't the three of you give us a bit of room?" Spider asked as he tugged me over to a bench near a small pond.

Ducks paddled across the water and a breeze ruffled the leaves in the tree behind us. Spider slung his arm around my shoulders and pulled me tight against his side. I'd never done something so normal as enjoying the park with the man I loved. If it weren't for the fact my babies were in trouble, my life would be pretty perfect. So perfect it scared me. I was waiting for something horrible to happen, for my father to come for me, or something else to happen to Spider.

"We can come back and bring something to feed the ducks," he said.

"This is nice." I rested my head on his shoulder and just enjoyed the peaceful moment.

"We'll do whatever it takes to make sure the babies are all right," he said. "I know you want to keep them."

The way he said that made me pause. I pulled away a bit and looked at him.

"I want to keep them, but you don't?"

He reached out and twirled a piece of my hair around his finger. "It's not that I don't want children with you, Luciana, I'm just worried. You want these babies right now, but what if they come out looking like one of the men who hurt you? Can you handle seeing that daily reminder? You're starting to heal, to get stronger emotionally and mentally, and I don't want anything to set you back."

I took his hand and placed it over my belly. "It's not their fault they were conceived by rape. They're innocent, Spider. Like me. Victims. You protect the innocent, and I know you'll do the same for them.

They deserve a chance at a good, happy life, just like any other kid."

He tugged me closer again and kissed me softly. The brush of his lips sent a shiver through me, a reminder we hadn't been intimate in far too long, and a public park bench wasn't the best location to start now.

"I was only worried about you," he said as he drew away. "I will love these kids as if they were of my own flesh and blood. I meant what I said before, that they need never know they aren't mine in all ways."

I reached up to cup his cheek, his beard tickling my hand. There was kindness in his eyes, and something else I couldn't quite pinpoint. The way he watched me sometimes made me think he cared for me, or possibly even more than cared, but I wasn't sure I had the guts to ask. What if I said I loved him and it made him pull away? He hadn't asked for my life or affection. He hadn't asked for any of this.

His phone, along with three others, went off at the same time. Spider pulled his from his pocket and swiped to unlock the screen, scowling at whatever message he saw there. I heard the steps of the others as they came close. He glanced at each of them, and the tension increased until my own heart rate picked up. Was something happening? Was it bad?

Spider got off the bench and pulled me to my feet. "We need to go."

"But my prescription…"

"Will have to wait. It's Violeta," he said.

My breath froze in my lungs and the world spun a little. "Violeta?"

"Someone managed to get past Marcus and breached the compound. Rocket was able to keep them from capturing Violeta, but she was hurt," Spider said. "I need to get you out of the open. Now."

I nodded and let him lead me back to the SUV. He raced through town, nearly running a few lights, and went skidding through the gates of the compound. Gates that stood wide open with three armed men just inside. I fought to control my emotions, to lock down the panic that was rising.

One of the men approached the vehicle and Spider rolled down the window.

"They were after your wife and found Violeta instead. Roughed her up pretty good. Rocket has her locked up tight in his house, and Dread is on his way to patch her up and check her out. Make sure nothing is broken."

"Thanks, Patch," Spider said.

"I called in the others," he said. "Yankee, Brazil, and Gunner are all back and they're done with the military this time. They're here to stay. Didn't know where you wanted to put them so they each took a spot in the clubhouse."

"I'll assign them houses later. Ask Yankee and Gunner to come to my house. I want them to keep an eye on Luciana. If those fuckers broke in here once, they'll likely try again, especially since they didn't get what they came for."

Patch nodded. "On it."

Spider pulled away and drove to the house.

"More men?" I asked. "Have I not met everyone?"

"Some of the guys are active duty military, and others are ex-military and have been recruiting our troops from various branches. It's good to have men with that kind of background, those who don't mind getting their hands dirty. Some turn to law enforcement or other civil service jobs when they leave the military, but others need something a bit more, something maybe not quite so legal. They want to get their hands dirty and not have the government staring over their shoulders."

"And Hades Abyss gives that to them?" she asked.

"Yes. I trust every member of this club with your life, Luciana. They'll keep you safe if I'm unable to do so myself."

At the house, he ushered me inside and led me straight to the kitchen. He put some water in the kettle and set it to boil. After he'd learned I liked tea, he'd made sure he stocked the kitchen with a kettle and several types of tea. I didn't have the heart to tell him I'd like a kettle that steeped the tea and didn't like using tea bags. He was trying, and it was one of the sweetest things anyone had ever done for me.

He set the mug of steaming water in front of me and pulled down my favorite tea, handing me a teabag and a spoon. There was a knock at the front door, and he paused only long enough to give me a quick kiss before going to answer it. I heard deep voices, then heavy steps. Two men I hadn't seen before, one incredibly tall and the other of average height, entered the room.

"Luciana, this is Yankee and Gunner," Spider said, motioning to each of them. "Guys, this is my wife, Luciana, and the intended target of the man who broke into the compound. Her sperm donor is Mateo Gomez."

Sperm donor. I snickered a little. I liked that because the man had certainly never been fatherly, even if he'd demanded that title from us. I'd have to share that with my sisters later.

"Violeta. When can I see her?" I asked.

"Dread is checking her over right now. As soon as I have word on her status, I'll let you know," Spider said. "But neither of you are leaving your homes until we get this shit sorted out."

I nodded, my stomach tightening with worry over Violeta. "Sofia? What about her? Did they attack the place where she's living now?"

Spider stared at me a moment, then pulled out his phone.

"Torch, did your compound get hit today? Maybe someone trying to get their hands on Sofia?" he asked.

He held my gaze and shook his head. At least Sofia was safe. I didn't know why my father would want me over my sisters, unless he'd found out about my pregnancy. The thought of him getting his hands on my babies was enough to make me bolt down the hall and throw up in the half bath. Spider knelt next to me and rubbed my back.

"Sofia is safe," he said. "And I'm not letting Gomez get his hands on you."

"You can't stop him," I said. "He has more men than you do. If he wants me, he'll find a way to get me."

He opened his mouth to respond when his phone rang. A strange look crossed his face as he stared at the screen, and when he answered he put the speaker on, then pressed a finger to my lips so I'd know to remain silent.

"Casper, what the fuck is going on?" he asked.

"Gomez has decided that he needs Luciana more than he needs your favor. He knows your club still has Violeta and he's hoping that will be enough to keep you tied to him. Or the imaginary tie that's there."

"His man attacked Violeta and beat the hell out of her," Spider said. "That's not going to endear him to me."

"He doesn't know you have a soft spot for the girls. He thinks you've made them whores and you're passing them around," Casper said.

"Send me the number to Gomez. I think I need to have a little chat with him."

"Spider, be careful. I have plans in motion, and I don't need you to fuck everything up. I know that you're protective of those who are innocent, especially women and children, but don't let that cloud your judgment."

"The fucker came after my wife and kids," Spider said.

There was a beat of silence.

"Wife and kids?" Casper asked.

"Luciana is my wife, and the twins she's carrying are mine as well."

Casper snorted. "You can't have kids."

"Well, I claimed them just the same."

"Gomez isn't aware you married his daughter. Hell, I didn't know about it and this is my fucking mission. Anything else I need to know?" Casper asked.

"Answer the fucking phone and you'd know more, but no. I don't have anything else. Not yet, but give Violeta some time to grow up and I have a feeling Rocket will be claiming her. You think I'm protective? The fucker who hurt Violeta might want to run as far and fast as he can, because if Rocket gets his hands on the guy, he won't be breathing much longer," Spider said.

"Duly noted. I'll send the information for Gomez, but don't do anything stupid. No dick swinging, Spider. I mean it."

Spider flipped the phone off, as if the man could see the gesture, then ended the call. "Fucker," Spider muttered.

His phone chimed a moment later and a sadistic smile slid across his face. A shiver raced down my spine. Not because I feared for myself, but that look didn't bode well for my father. I knew that Spider would end him if he could, and it wouldn't be pleasant.

Chapter Nine

Spider

Mateo Gomez had made a fatal mistake. No one came after my family, and the fucker was about to learn that the hard way. I helped Luciana off the floor, gave her a cup of water to rinse her mouth, then we went back to the kitchen. I wanted Yankee and Gunner to hear this call, and if Luciana needed to stay, then I was fine with that too. She would see a darker side of me, but I was pretty certain she knew I'd never hurt her, never turn that darkness on her or the babies. They were mine, and I would protect them at all costs. Just because I hadn't wanted a wife and kids didn't mean I would leave them defenseless, especially since I'd gone and fallen for the adorable woman who fascinated me more and more every day.

"It seems that Mateo Gomez isn't aware that Luciana is my wife now," I said. "I think it's time he learns what happens to those who fuck with my family. I'm going to put the call on speaker. Luciana, if you stay, I want you to remain quiet. Can you do that for me, baby girl?"

She nodded.

"What about us?" Yankee asked.

"The two of you can threaten the man all you want," Spider said. "He needs to know he didn't just piss me off, but the entire club. And the stunt with Violeta can't go unpunished. I want the man responsible, but no one is to harm him yet. Rocket will want that privilege."

Luciana reached out and took my hand. I knelt next to her chair and smoothed her hair back from her face. She was scared, fear lurking in her eyes, and her lower lip trembled. I wasn't sure if she was worried about her sister, herself, the babies, or if she was concerned something would happen to me. The way she'd looked the day I'd been shot would haunt me for a while. Possibly forever. I never wanted to see that look on her face ever again.

"Everything will be fine," I assured her. "He's not going to hurt me or your sisters. None of us will let that happen. And you're safe, Luciana. I'll put every bullet at this compound into him and anyone else who tries to take you. Understood?"

She nodded and her hand tightened on mine. I brushed a kiss against her cheek, then stood and dialed Mateo Gomez.

The man answered after a few rings.

"Who is this?" he demanded in a thick accent.

"It's Spider, the President of Hades Abyss."

"Ah, yes. Mr. Spider, what may I do for you today?"

"You can start by explaining why one of your men forced their way into my compound, beat the hell out of Violeta, and was apparently trying to take Luciana."

There was a moment of silence.

"I did not authorize anyone to beat Violeta," he said. "I understand she is valuable to you and your men. As for Luciana, I need her to return home."

"No," Spider said. "You gave her to me, and I plan to keep her."

"I can provide another girl for you, Mr. Spider. I have many beautiful girls, much better behaved than my Luciana," Gomez said.

I ground my teeth together and tried not to reach through the phone to choke the fucker. *His* Luciana? Not fucking likely.

"I don't think you understand. Luciana isn't leaving this compound unless she's with me or a member of this club," I said. "She's my property now."

I glanced at Luciana, not sure how she'd handled me phrasing it quite like that, but she was staring at the phone with stark terror on her face. Yeah, no way this dipshit was getting his hands on my wife.

"Why do you need Luciana all of a sudden?" I asked.

"There is a man who wishes to keep Luciana for himself. They spent some time together previously and he's rather enamored of her. She will live in luxury with Pedro Lopez."

Luciana let out a whimper and I quickly gathered her in my arms to keep her quiet. She trembled and clutched at me, her terror a tangible thing. Whoever Pedro Lopez was, I knew he damn sure wasn't going to touch her. I'd cut off his hands and shove them up his ass if I had the chance.

"Spent time together?" I asked. "Were they dating?"

Luciana pressed even tighter to me. I threaded a hand in her hair and held her close. I hated that this call was making those memories come to the surface, and I was wishing I'd asked her to leave the room. I'd thought she had the right to hear what was said, but it hadn't occurred to me that it would frighten her so badly. Sometimes I was an idiot, at least when it came to women.

Gomez didn't answer right away. "I believe they had a sexual relationship."

Yeah, I'd just bet they did. The kind where Luciana was forced to endure whatever the asshole decided to do to her. No fucking way would she leave my sight. I looked at Gunner and Yankee, and could see both were in agreement. I didn't know if they'd been brought up to speed on absolutely everything, but they didn't look the least bit pleased by Gomez's statement.

"I'm afraid Mr. Lopez will have to find another woman," I said.

"I wasn't asking, Mr. Spider. I need Luciana back in Colombia immediately. A jet is already waiting for her at a nearby airstrip."

"I don't think I made this clear enough for you, Gomez. Luciana isn't just my property, she's my wife now. You so much as lay a finger on her, even breathe wrong in her direction, and I will fucking end you and anyone else you send after her. Do we have an understanding?" I was ready to rip the fucker's throat out.

"Wife?" the man asked, his tone biting.

I didn't give a shit if he liked it or not. Luciana was mine, legally thanks to Surge, and I wasn't letting her go. Even if she hadn't been my wife, there was no way I'd send her back to that hell. Violeta wasn't going anywhere either. It didn't matter to me that she was underage. We'd find a way to keep her here, no matter what it took.

"I didn't give permission for Luciana to marry anyone," Gomez said.

"She's a grown-ass woman and doesn't need to ask you or anyone else if she can marry someone," I said. "So if you take her -- my legally wedded wife -- then that's kidnapping. The police in Colombia might look the other way when you sell women or force them into prostitution, but the local boys won't be too happy about it, and neither will the Feds."

"You're threatening me," Gomez said, sounding somewhat amused. "You, a nobody in some insignificant place in America, are threatening the great Mateo Gomez?"

"Spider isn't a nobody," Yankee said. "Probably should have done your homework before threatening the man's wife."

"And who are you?" Gomez asked.

"Yankee. I'm a part of this club, and I can assure you that if Spider comes after you, he won't be alone. You think we're small and easily squashed, but you'd be wrong."

"If I can't have Luciana, then I'll just have to take one of my other daughters and hope Pedro Lopez will be content with Violeta or Sofia. You choose, Mr. Spider. My sweet little Violeta or Sofia? Which will warm Pedro's bed?"

"You sick fucking bastard," I said. "You won't touch either of them."

"We'll see," Gomez said.

The line went dead and I stared at Yankee and Gunner. They both looked as pissed and worried as I felt. Luciana started sobbing and I cursed the man who had ruined our day. I tipped my head toward the door and Yankee and Gunner both made themselves scarce. The doctor's words from earlier had me concerned over Luciana and the babies. She wasn't supposed to be getting upset. She needed rest and good meals.

"Baby girl, I need you to take a breath for me," I said. She did, though it was broken with more crying. "Again. And again."

After a few minutes, the tears slowed and she seemed to have her emotions under control. I ran my hand up and down her back, but I felt her grip on me loosen a little. She tipped her head back and looked up me with swollen eyes and a runny nose. And I still found her fucking beautiful.

"Everything will be fine, Luciana. I meant what I said. You're mine, and I'm not letting you go. Rocket will keep Violeta safe, and I'm sure Saint is protecting Sofia."

"I can't let him take them," she said, her voice a near whisper. "If he has to have someone, it should be me. I've endured Pedro before. I can do it again."

"No. You're not giving up, and you're sure as fuck not turning yourself over to that asshole."

"Not to interrupt," Gunner said from the doorway, "but what if they just think she's surrendering herself?"

"What the fuck does that mean?" I asked. "Because I'm not handing her over to them."

"I meant we could make arrangements to give your wife to Gomez, except we don't actually let him have her. We just need to his ass on US soil, and then we can take him out. Get Surge, Wire, and any of their other hacking buddies to look into Gomez and the disappearance of any underage girls he might have snatched from the US. As much as I know you want to get your hands dirty, I say we gather enough evidence and let the Feds handle this shit," Gunner said.

"Would that work?" Luciana asked.

"I recorded your call," Gunner said, lifting up his phone. "The audio isn't the greatest, but you can hear Gomez clear as day demand you hand over your wife, Sofia, or their underage sister so he can give her to a man. It's implied well enough that he plans to use them for sex. Since Luciana, Sofia, and Violeta are all US citizens thanks to Surge, that should make the Feds sit up and take notice."

"Or I could get the fucker here and bleed him out," I said.

"What happens if your Feds get their hands on my father?" Luciana asked.

Gunner hesitated, but I already knew the answer. I knew he wanted to keep things legal and not bring heat down on the club, but this wasn't the time to toe the line.

"He'd likely be deported and banned from returning to the US. They would probably contact law enforcement in Colombia, but we all know your father has them in his pocket. And since he isn't coming here legally anyway, nothing would stop him from returning, or sending someone after you," I said, which is why I didn't want the damn Feds involved. I wanted Gomez in the damn ground.

She sagged in my arms.

"I'm going to handle it, Luciana. I'll get him here, but I'm not involving the Feds or anyone else. This is club business pure and simple. If taking your father out of the equation helps other people too, then all the better, but that's not my main focus," I said.

"Whatever you need to do, you have my support," she said. "My father is evil. If you need to kill him, I won't think less of you. Just know that another will rise in his place. It's never-ending, Spider. If any of his men who hurt me and my sisters claim his position, they could come for us too. You can't fight the entire Colombian cartel."

"What if we go over their heads?" Gunner asked. "If our Feds can't handle the situation, maybe the government officials in Colombia will be willing to step in. You have a president there, right?"

Luciana nodded.

"Get Surge to put together whatever he can find on Gomez, as well as his top men. We'll make contact with the Colombian president, explain the situation, and see if he's willing to help when we share those files. As long as it doesn't look like he's in bed with Gomez. If that's the case, this whole thing would fall apart pretty fast," I said.

"I'll call Surge now," Gunner said, stepping out of the room.

"One way or another, I'm ending this, Luciana. I won't have you living in fear," I said.

She looked up at me, and the tenderness in her gaze nearly took me to my knees. "I love you. I know it's too soon, or maybe it would always be too soon. You didn't want a wife or children, but I'm so glad you're my husband. I love you, Spider, and I needed you to know that."

I cupped her cheek. "I love you too, baby girl. Never thought I'd let a woman in enough to say those words to her, but you came into my life and tore down the walls I'd erected, one brick at a time. Casper did me a huge fucking favor when he arranged for you to stay with me. But that's between you and me. That bastard is cocky enough already."

She smiled and hugged me tight. My heart ached at the thought of losing her. I didn't care what it took, I'd make sure the threat to Luciana was eliminated. Blood on my hands didn't bother me in the least. Never had, never would. Especially not if I was taking out the trash.

"Let's get you cleaned up and fed, and then you should take a nap," I told her, leading her from the kitchen.

"Cleaned up?" she asked.

"A hot shower will make you feel better. You're tense and stressed. It's not good for you or the babies."

"Only if you join me," she said. She bit her lip. "If it won't hurt your shoulder or your back. I don't want to slow down your healing."

I grinned. That had been my plan exactly. In the bedroom, I shut and locked the door, not wanting any interruptions. While I got the shower set to the right temperature, Luciana started undressing. I waited until she'd stepped under the spray before I removed my own clothes and got in after her. I took my time soaping her hair and body, even put in that conditioner she insisted on having. Her hands coasted over my body as she rubbed soap into my skin. My cock was already hard and aching before she even reached that low.

Her fingers wrapped around my shaft and she gave it a few strokes. Enough to make me crave more, but she just smiled and moved her hand elsewhere. *Tease.* I rinsed us both thoroughly, not wanting soap anywhere uncomfortable, then pressed her against the tiled wall.

"Been too long," I said. "You ready for me?"

She reached out and took my hand, sliding it between her legs. Her pussy was swollen and slick. I slid a finger inside her, pumping it in and out. Yeah, my baby was more than ready for me, but the look of bliss on her face made me want to draw things out a little more. I pressed my thumb to her clit and rubbed as I finger-fucked her pussy, adding a second digit to her tight channel.

"God, Spider. That feels so good."

"*You* feel good," I told her. My cock jerked and pre-cum leaked in a steady stream from the head. I didn't know how long I'd last once I got inside her. It had been too long, and I wanted her too badly.

I tweaked her nipple with my other hand, pinching and twisting the hardened peak until she moaned and spread her legs a little more. I tugged on the tip again before reaching for the other side, giving it the same treatment. I could tell she was close. Leaning down, I kissed her, devouring her lips as I pushed her closer to a climax. I drove my fingers into her hard and fast. Luciana's body went tight and I felt her release coat my fingers.

I groaned as I pulled away, loving the way her cheeks flushed and the heavy-lidded look she gave me. She reached up and ran her fingers through my beard, then tugged me down for another kiss. If Luciana was a drug, then I was definitely an addict. I didn't think I'd ever get enough of her. I hoped like hell I never stopped being able to meet her needs. Hell, I'd pop blue pills if I needed to, but so far that wasn't even remotely an issue. The woman kept me so fired-up that I felt twenty years younger.

I lifted her, urging her legs around my waist, then thrust hard and deep, not stopping until she'd taken every inch. The way she wrapped around my cock, the feel of her slick, tight pussy, was enough to make my heart race. I drove into her as our tongues tangled and she held onto me. There was still a slight twinge where the bullet had entered my back, but it wouldn't stop me. Nothing was going to hold me back right now.

"Yes! Yes! Don't stop," Luciana begged. "So close."

I felt my balls draw up and a tingle started in my back. She wasn't the only one about to go off. I ground against her with each thrust until she was screaming my name and coating my cock with her release, and then I let go. I slammed into her again and again until I filled her pussy with my cum. Even after the last drop had been wrung for me, I didn't want to stop. I kept thrusting until I felt her shudder and come one more time.

"So fucking beautiful," I said. "I love watching you come."

She gave me a shy smile and her cheeks turned a darker pink. Her throat and the upper swells of her breasts were flushed as well from coming several times, and she looked downright delectable.

"You didn't hurt yourself?" she asked.

"All healed. Dread said I could resume normal activities today. There's only a slight pull in my back now and then. Nothing to worry about."

"If you go after my father, you have to promise you'll stay alive. I can't lose you," she said. "Not just because I feel safe here, or because I'm scared to raise these babies on my own. I need you. I…"

I placed a finger over her lips. "I know. I need you too, Luciana."

I pulled out and helped her clean up, then I shut off the water and wrapped her in a thick towel. Quickly drying myself, I took a moment to study her. My wife. My everything. There was still a glow to her, and she appeared a little less stressed. She couldn't hide the worry in her eyes, but as she placed a hand against her belly, I realized she was concerned for the babies. I didn't know how to reassure her that they would be all right. If anything happened and she lost them she'd be inconsolable, but I'd find a way to help her through it. It would gut me as well, but there were always other options if she really wanted kids.

I took her hand and led her into the bedroom, then pulled down the covers.

"Lie down, sweetheart. You rest while I make sure I have all the things on your list of encouraged foods and pick up your prescription. Yankee and Gunner will remain here if you need anything. I need to feed you so you can take one of your prenatal vitamins."

I pulled one of my shirts out of the dresser and helped her into it, then handed her a pair of panties from her drawer. Her head had barely touched the pillow before she was out, her breathing deep and even. Her emotions had run so high, and then I'd physically exhausted her in the shower, that she just couldn't last another moment without some rest.

I leaned down and brushed a kiss against her forehead before getting dressed and leaving instructions with Yankee and Gunner. Teller was on the front steps when I left the house and he gave me a nod.

"I'll help keep her safe," he said.

"Thank you, Teller." I clapped him on the back and removed the keys to the SUV from my pocket. No way was I going grocery shopping on my bike, not with the amount of food and drinks I needed to get. I not only had Luciana's list to tend to, but I also needed to ensure I had sodas, coffee, and food enough for anyone who helped keep an eye on her. There was also an errand I wanted to personally handle, but I was keeping that shit to myself. Luciana had enjoyed the little pink vibrator so much, I wanted to stop by the adult store and pick up another toy or two, and I sure as shit wasn't delegating that to anyone. I'd lucked out with getting a decent one off the Internet before, but I wanted to browse the shop in person this time. Find just the right items without staring at my damn phone.

I'd never done the domestic thing, not even with Ryker's mom, but I had to admit that it felt kind of nice. I liked having Luciana waiting for me, enjoyed waking with her in my arms, but mostly I liked how she'd made my house feel more like a home. She hadn't made any changes to the place, except for her presence, and that was enough. The warmth of her smile could light up any room, and it had quickly thawed my heart.

I only hoped I didn't fail her now.

Chapter Ten

Luciana

I didn't like Spider's plan, not even a little. He didn't know my father the way I did, didn't understand exactly what the man was capable of, and I worried it would get us all killed. We were at the airstrip, meeting my father and Pedro Lopez. I had no doubt that he'd bring others, men he trusted, those who had hurt me. It wasn't just a show of power for Spider's benefit, but to remind me of my place and what would happen if I disobeyed. I'd tried to reason with my husband, had spent the last four days begging him not to do this. I understood that he felt it was the only solution, but I worried that he'd pay a steep price if he followed through. Too many things could go wrong.

I tried to swallow my fear, but my stomach was going to revolt at any moment. I'd already thrown up several times this morning, and I didn't think it was due to my pregnancy. I'd ridden in the SUV with Teller, while Spider and half the club had arrived on their bikes. A rumble in the distance had me looking out the back window and my jaw dropped a little as about twenty other bikers pulled up, none of them wearing the same cut as Spider and the men from Hades Abyss.

"Who are they?" I asked Teller.

He smirked a little. "Didn't think your man would come unprepared, did you? He called in reinforcements. The presidents from four other clubs are here, along with their VPs and a handful of men. He knew your dad wouldn't play by the rules, so Spider didn't either."

"They all came to help?"

Teller nodded. "Torch is the President of the Dixie Reapers, which is where Sofia is living. He's just as vested in having your dad disappear as Spider is. Not to mention Ryker lives with the Dixie Reapers since his wife is the sister of their Treasurer."

"And the others?" I asked.

"Devil's Boneyard has family ties to the Dixie Reapers, and Devil's Fury has ties to Devil's Boneyard. They're all one big happy family. Reckless Kings have put their necks on the line a few times to help other clubs over the past year or two."

"Five clubs," I mumbled. I hadn't realized that Spider was friendly with so many people. Weren't they all supposed to be rivals or something? I still didn't quite understand how all this worked, but I hoped I'd learn one day.

"Doesn't matter how many guys your dad brought with him. We have more."

I nodded and watched as the steps to my father's jet lowered. He came down them, holding his head at a regal angle while buttoning his suit jacket. Heaven forbid he ever wear anything other than his expensive custom-made suits and shirts. Even his shoes were custom.

Behind him, Pedro descended the stairs, and then three other men from my worst nightmares. It was the man who came after them all that almost made me pass out. My father's right-hand man, and my number one tormentor.

"He brought Ricardo," I said.

"The last guy?" Teller asked.

I nodded. "This isn't good."

Teller pulled out a file folder I hadn't even noticed and flipped through it. "Ricardo Sanchez.

Right-hand man to Mateo Gomez, and not afraid to get his hands dirty."

"What's that mean?" I asked.

Teller grinned. "It means we know everything about Mr. Sanchez, as well as your dad and every man he brought with him. None of them are leaving the country -- well, not all of them, anyway. A few pieces will be sent back as a warning to anyone else in your father's cartel. No one will fuck with you after this."

"How?" My brow furrowed as I stared at the folder. "Surge?"

He nodded. "Yep, Surge. Wire, Shade, Outlaw, and Shield."

"Who are the others you mentioned?" I asked.

"Hackers with the other clubs. Wire is with Dixie Reapers, Shade is part of Devil's Boneyard, Outlaw is with Devil's Fury, and Shield is a Reckless King." Teller reached over and patted my hand. "Don't worry, Luciana. They know what they're doing."

Spider walked forward to meet with my father, reaching out to shake his hand. I noticed several other men standing alongside of him, each with a cut from one of the clubs Teller had just mentioned. Were those the other presidents? If they were, I didn't understand what it meant for all of them to be here. Another figure approached and I stifled my gasp when I recognized Casper VanHorne, the man I'd thought was working with my dad until Spider had told me otherwise.

Everything seemed to happen in slow motion, but I watched in horror as Pedro pulled a gun and fired it at one of the presidents. After that, everyone was shooting at someone. With more bikers than Colombians, it didn't take long for Spider and the others to get the upper hand. Or so I'd thought. Ricardo smiled, blood smeared across his teeth, and said something to the men. A man from Devil's Boneyard and Devil's Fury both froze and shared a look.

"What's going on?" I asked.

"No clue, and I'm not leaving you here alone in order to go find out."

"I wasn't even needed. I haven't left the car."

Teller smiled. "Your father's men looked this way a few times so they knew you were present. Probably thought you'd walk out to them all docile and shit. I don't think any of them planned to get shot today."

"Roll down the window or something. I want to know what's going on."

Teller gave me a pointed look then cracked the window a tiny bit, but it was enough to hear since we were so close.

"You had someone take my wife?" the Devil's Boneyard man asked before bursting out into laughter.

"You're so fucked," said the guy from Devil's Fury.

"What's going on?" I asked Teller.

He snickered. "Your father's men took Jordan. She's the wife of the Sergeant at Arms for Devil's Boneyard, and she's batshit fucking crazy. Marched her pregnant ass to Colombia to save her man from what I hear. I think they bit off more than they can chew this time."

"We'll get Jordan back, and if she leaves any of your men alive, we'll take care of them," said an older man from Devil's Boneyard.

"That's Cinder." Teller pointed to the man. "He's their President."

"Wait. Something isn't right." I squinted to try and see on the other side of my father's jet. I sucked in a breath and my eyes widened in horror when I realized what was about to happen. "We're all going to die."

Teller jerked his head my way. "What?"

I pointed, my hand trembling.

A dark figure moved closer to the group, something propped on his shoulder.

"Holy shit! Is that a grenade launcher?" Teller scrambled for the handle on the SUV door, throwing it open. "Everyone run!"

Spider spun our way, saw my frantic look, and rotated back toward the Colombians. He must have seen the man approaching because he turned and started running toward me. Teller slammed his door shut and threw the SUV into gear. I screamed for him to wait as Spider drew closer. My husband was mere feet away when Teller had the tires squealing on the SUV and rocketed through the parking lot, away from the man I loved and everyone who had tried to save me.

I sobbed and fought the seatbelt in an effort to turn and see what was happening. An explosion made my ears ring, but Teller just seemed to go faster. He left the airstrip but I couldn't see through the tears to be able to tell where we were going. I just knew we were leaving Spider, and I had no idea if he was alive or not.

Another explosion sounded and I cried harder. Teller whipped the SUV out into traffic and floored it. In a matter of minutes, we were on the interstate and seemed to be heading south. Teller grabbed his phone and quickly dialed someone.

"Rocket, get Violeta the hell out of there. I'm taking Luciana to the Dixie Reapers." He paused. "I don't know. They could all be dead right now."

I moaned and frantically motioned for Teller to pull over. The SUV came to a jerking halt on the shoulder of the road, just in time for me to open the door and throw up. I heaved until nothing was left in my stomach, then shut the door. Teller grabbed my hand and gave it a squeeze before he started driving again.

"I'm sorry, Luciana. I have to believe that Spider made it out of there, but I knew he'd prefer that I get you to safety. That was my number one mission. Protect you at all costs."

"What's the point of living if he's gone?" I asked.

"Don't think like that. I'm going to call ahead and let the Reapers know what's going on, make sure they have a place for you to stay, and then maybe we can find out what's happening. See if there are survivors."

"Why would he do that?" I asked, thinking of the man I'd seen. "If he was with my father, didn't he risk killing him as well? And all my father's men?"

"Maybe your father thought it was worth the risk. Or maybe the guy wasn't with your dad at all and we're dealing with a completely unknown person. Just try to rest, Luciana. I'm going to get you somewhere safe, then we'll deal with what's happened."

I nodded and shut my eyes, but all I could see was Spider reaching for the SUV before Teller had taken off, leaving him behind.

I didn't know how long we were on the road, but we eventually pulled into a compound that looked different from the Hades Abyss' and yet a little similar. The guy at the gate had waved us through, and I wondered if their security wasn't that stringent or if they had recognized Teller or the vehicle. The club seemed to have a clubhouse and homes, but I also saw what looked like a playground, a pool, and other family friendly things as we drove down a winding road. Teller came to a stop in front of a cute home, and the door swung open to reveal a blond man with a stern expression on his face. There was an adorable little girl wrapped around his leg.

"Who's that?" I asked.

"Saint. Your sister has been living with him. And that's his daughter Delia."

I got out of the car and stretched before slowly approaching the house. The guy didn't so much as smile, but his daughter was adorable as she grinned at me.

"I'm Luciana Storme," I said.

Saint nodded. "Your sister is inside. You'll stay here while someone prepares a place for you. Shouldn't take long."

"Thank you."

He stepped aside, not seeming to even notice his daughter clung to his calf like a monkey. I moved past him into the house and saw Sofia. She looked good, if a bit scared. When her gaze locked on mine, she rushed toward me, wrapping her arms around my waist.

"They won't stop," she said. "We'll never be safe."

"We're not going back, Sofia. Never."

She nodded but didn't seem to believe me. I wasn't entirely sure I believed myself either. I sat with her on the couch and tried to listen to Teller and Saint, but they were speaking too softly. I needed to know if Spider was all right. My stomach clenched at the thought of never seeing him again.

"I miss you and Violeta," Sofia said.

"We miss you too. They're treating you well here, aren't they?" I asked. Just because Spider had said Saint was a decent guy, didn't mean it was true. Even if the guy did have a cute kid, I knew from experience monsters came in all shapes and sizes.

Sofia cast a glance toward Saint and her cheeks flushed a little. "I'm good. I don't think he likes me, though."

"And the little girl?" I asked, knowing how much my sister adored kids.

"She's great. Delia is so much fun, and so sweet. We get along fine. She's four, but she's so smart. I think she's ahead of the other kids her age."

Hmm. That sounded like a little too much pride for a kid that wasn't hers. I looked at Saint and his daughter again, and I noticed the girl was staring at Sofia with a worshipful gaze. Seemed my sister wasn't the only one invested in the relationship between them. Too bad the little girl's daddy seemed like an ass. Would it kill him to smile?

Teller came over, his hands shoved in his pockets. "So, I'm going to stay with you at another house. Rocket will be staying there too with Violeta. Saint said Sofia was welcome to go with us."

Sofia looked heartbroken as she glanced toward Saint again. I could tell my sister felt something for the biker, but I didn't understand why. He didn't seem all that great to me, but then I'd only been in his house less than a half hour. Maybe he had hidden depths. Like way down deep type of hidden.

"Delia doesn't want her to go," Teller said.

Sofia's eyes lit up. "She wants me here?"

He nodded. "I told Saint it would be best for you to stay since you're already set up here. I mean, this isn't my club and even if it were, he outranks me, so... If he says you have to go, then you'll have to go."

Sofia sighed and slowly stood. She walked over to Delia, who still clung to her daddy's leg, and knelt down.

"Delia, my sister is here and my other sister is coming too. I think it's best if I go with them for now, but I'll still be close by."

"She doesn't need you," Saint said.

I shot to my feet, but Teller stilled me with a hand on my arm. I didn't like it, but he was right. While I wanted to defend my sister, this wasn't our home. If I didn't tread carefully, they could ask us to leave. All of us, and then we'd be out in the open.

When Sofia faced us again, I could see the tears in her eyes, and I decided I didn't like Saint very much. Anyone who made Sofia cry couldn't be all that wonderful. I wrapped my arms around my sister when she was within reach and glared at the man across the room. He tipped his chin up and stared me down, but I wasn't going to flinch. In the past I would have, but I was Spider's wife now.

I glanced at Saint's cut and noticed it didn't have a title, which meant he was a member but not an officer. I didn't think I outranked him since I was just a woman, but I knew my husband did. That had to count for something, didn't it? I looked at Teller but he gave a shake of his head and I tried to shove down my annoyance.

"Come on, Sofia. We'll find somewhere else to go until the house is ready for us. And Saint can have your belongings packed." I glared at the man and saw a slight smirk on his lips. "You've been through enough without remaining in a hostile home environment."

That smirk slipped right off his face and he actually looked ashamed for a moment. He glanced down at his daughter and his gaze hardened again. And that is what made me understand a little better exactly what was happening. It wasn't that he didn't like my sister, it was that he was worried about his daughter. The fact he was so protective of her made me soften toward him.

"Spider chose well," Saint said. "I'm sure you're the perfect wife for the President of Hades Abyss. Ryker didn't have too many nice things to say about you, but don't worry. He'll come around."

I glanced from him to Sofia and back again. "The question is whether or not you'll come around. Don't let fear hold you back."

He smiled faintly and lifted his daughter into his arms. "If things were different... but they aren't. I'm not a bad guy, Luciana. But I will die before I let any darkness touch my daughter, and you and your sisters have trouble written all over you. It follows you, stalks you from the shadows, and I don't think it's backing down."

He was right about that. I led Sofia outside and we got into the SUV. As Teller pulled back around to the front gate, I saw another car enter and smiled when I saw Rocket and Violeta in the front seats. Violeta was still bruised but didn't seem to be in a great deal of pain. Her lip was split and she had a blackened eye. If she had more serious injuries, I couldn't tell from here.

I pointed our sister out to Sofia and she gave me a true smile for the first time since I'd seen her today. I didn't know what the future would bring, but I knew that as long as we had each other, and I had the sweet babies growing inside me, then we would be okay. If Spider was gone, my sisters would help me deal with the pain, and my children would give me incentive to keep going, but I still held out hope that he was fine.

"Come back to me," I murmured and toyed with the band on my finger. I'd finally told him I loved him, and now he was gone. My heart felt like it might break, but I was going to assume that no news was good news. As far as I knew, no one had called Teller to say all the men were dead. I would hold onto to any small amount of hope I could grasp.

"Spider's tough," Teller said, catching my gaze and holding it. "Nothing will stop him from coming for you. Not even hell. He loves you, Luciana, more than I think he's ever loved anyone. That's far more powerful than anything on this earth."

"Even a grenade launcher?" I asked.

"He's going to be fine, and he's going to ride through those gates. You'll be together again."

I nodded, knowing he was trying to comfort me, but maybe he really believed what he was saying. He knew Spider well, and if he thought my husband was all right, then I'd have to believe that too. I might be able to go on without him, raise the babies on my own, but I didn't want to. Life held no meaning without him by my side.

We got out of the SUV in front of a pretty blue house and Violeta ran to us, hugging both me and Sofia. Rocket watched us in amusement, a smile gracing his lips. He looked worried, shadows under his eyes and a tenseness to his body that normally wasn't there, but he'd kept my sister safe and I could never thank him enough.

"All right, ladies. Go find your rooms," Rocket said. "The Dixie Reaper women are gathering some things you might need. Except you, Sofia, since your things are already here."

"Thank you," I said, holding Violeta a little tighter.

"She's not getting taken on my watch," Rocket said.

The way he looked at Violeta I knew that he meant it. She might be young, but there was a possessiveness to his gaze. Spider was right. When Violeta was old enough, Rocket would likely make his move and claim her. I was glad she had someone like him. The little interaction I'd had with him, he'd always seemed like a good guy. Laid-back, funny, and protective. Just the type of man Violeta needed in her life.

Now I just needed my protective husband back at my side.

I went in search of a room to temporarily call mine, when a cramp made me bend in half. A sharper pain came, then another. I screamed as I felt a rush of warm liquid between my legs. Something was wrong with the babies! It was too soon, and the doctor had been concerned about their development. I couldn't lose them! "Teller!" I yelled.

He raced to my side and I tried to remain calm. I heard something about an ambulance and miscarriage, but I was focused on praying for my babies, and for Spider. Was I going to lose my entire new family all in one day? I didn't think I could handle much more. I was emotionally, physically, and mentally exhausted. If I lost my children and my husband, I wouldn't have a reason to keep going. My sisters would be taken care of, and I had no one else.

Please. Please don't take them.

Chapter Eleven

Spider

The blast from the grenade launcher had knocked me on my ass. My ears were ringing and the world was spinning. I saw the SUV with my wife go tearing out of the airstrip, and as much as I wished I could be with her, I knew Teller would keep Luciana safe. I got up and brushed myself off, looking around to assess the damage. Most of the bikes were trashed, and at least half the men who'd stood at my back were down.

I picked my way through the bodies, most of the men still alive, and stopped when I stood over Mateo Gomez. His sightless eyes stared up at me. The lower half of his body was gone, and his men hadn't fared very well either. Each were missing limbs, and Pedro had lost his head. I couldn't say I was sorry, but I wished I'd been the one to hand their asses to them.

I felt my phone vibrating and pulled it out, but I still couldn't hear for shit and knew answering would be pointless. I sent Surge a text to tell him I was fine but couldn't hear. I got a response almost immediately.

The Colombian President said he was sending someone to take care of his little problem.

Well, that explained the man in black who had taken out Gomez and all his men. I looked around and noticed most of the clubs who had my back were up and moving, or trying to at any rate. Only two didn't seem to be getting up.

We may have casualties on our side. Going to assess the situation.

I shoved the phone back in my pocket and went from man to man, ensuring everyone was all right. A few were bleeding, but thankfully most just seemed stunned. The two men who weren't getting up belonged to Devil's Fury. I made my way over and knelt next to Grizzly, their President.

One of the bodies jerked and the man started coughing. Badger. No wonder Grizzly looked so damn sick. The guy was married to the President's daughter. He sat up and winced, but didn't seem too worse for wear all things considered. The other man hadn't moved yet, but I saw his chest slowly rise and fall, so at least he was alive. I scanned his cut for a name. Wolf. I looked at Grizzly and he motioned for me to move on. I went club by club, making sure everyone was still breathing. My hearing still hadn't returned when more of my club showed up, along with Dread. He started patching everyone, but I needed answers.

Looking around, I spotted the man in black. He was leaning against the stairs of Gomez's jet, his arms folded as he surveyed us. He didn't seem to be in a hurry to rush off, which wasn't necessarily a good thing. I made my way over to him, not stopping until we were inches apart. His gaze dropped to my cut and then he pulled an envelope from inside his jacket and handed it to me.

Curious, I opened it and then snorted at the words on the paper.

Spider,

I owe you a debt. Mateo Gomez has been a thorn in my side for too long. You provided me the perfect opportunity to rid Colombia of him. Others will be easier to take down now that Gomez has fallen. Congratulations on your marriage to Luciana Gomez. Her mother was a beautiful and kind woman. Your wife is a great deal like her, and I hope you will have many happy years together.

If I may be of service, do not hesitate to reach out to my office.

Harley Wylde   **Flicker/Spider Duet**

President Eduardo Muñoz

I gave the man in black a nod and walked off. Finding my bike was easy enough, or finding most of it. The blast had wrecked it. I wasn't about to sit around and wait for these fuckers to get on their feet. I needed to find my wife and let her know she would never be bothered again by her father or his men.

My hearing started to come back, though there was still a slight ringing in my ears. At least I hadn't gone completely deaf from the blast. Could have been worse.

"Spider," the man called out.

I turned and he tossed a set of keys to me, then nodded toward the other end of the airstrip. I looked at the keys, then in the direction he'd indicated.

"The President thought things might get messy. Even though Gomez was his main concern, we knew there was a chance that in taking out all of them at once there might be casualties with your men as well. He apologizes and wants to make sure you are compensated. I was ordered to ensure the latest Road King Special, with some extras, was gifted to you to show the President's appreciation for your assistance with this matter. Think of it as a bonus. The President will also be transferring some funds for a job well done."

"Bonus, my ass. You killed my motorcycle."

The man shrugged. "I'll make sure it's repaired and returned to your compound."

"Thanks. What do I call you?" I asked.

"Specter."

Holy fucking shit.

The man smirked, knowing I'd recognized his name. Specter was legendary. Ex-military turned mercenary, but the man had made a name for himself from the very first mission he'd been assigned, and his reputation had only grown over the years. He walked off, and I headed in the direction of the new bike, intent on getting to my woman as quickly as possible. I grabbed my phone from my pocket and pressed the speed dial for Teller, only for my damn phone to go black. I cursed my rotten luck and shoved it back into my pocket. I swung my leg over the seat of my new ride and started the engine. The bike roared to life and I couldn't help but smile.

Fox gave me a wave and I left everything in his capable hands. Once I hit the open road, I opened up the new bike to see what she could handle.

As much as I wanted to go straight to my wife, I needed to check in with everyone at the compound first. Since my phone was out of commission, I'd need to go in person to send more help Fox's way. Marcus was working the gate, and he looked relieved when I rolled through.

"I need you to stay on the gate, Marcus. I'm going to send some men to help Fox and then I need to go after my wife."

"Pres, there's a bit of a problem," he said.

"Problem?"

He nodded then pointed out two men in suits. Fuck my life. They had government written all over them. With a sigh, I drove the bike over to the clubhouse and parked in front of the agents. What kind of agents they were was still to be determined.

"What can I do for you, gentlemen?"

"We need to talk about some drugs that made their way into the local high school," the taller one said. "Tracked down the dealer and he said the shit came from Hades Abyss."

"No fucking way."

"Is there somewhere we could have this discussion?" the shorter one asked.

"Soon as you tell me who the fuck you are."

"Agent Parkes," said the tall one, "and this is my partner, Agent Phelps. D.E.A."

Fuck. My. Life.

It took me four fucking days to sort out the shit with the D.E.A. and help them find the real culprit behind the drugs at the school. Some days my connections were a pain in my ass. If I had been your average biker President, they wouldn't have dirtied their hands by asking for my help. The second they left the compound, I got on my new ride and hit the road. The tires ate up the miles as I headed south toward Alabama.

Night had fallen before I reached the Dixie Reapers' compound, and I had started feeling a few aches along the way. The blast had bruised me and I had a few scrapes, but nothing that would keep me from getting to my wife. I hadn't been able to reach Teller, or anyone at the Reapers' compound except for a brief conversation with Torch over a landline in my office, and I was getting worried. It was probably my fucking cell phone, and I'd need a new one, but right now I just wanted to get to Luciana as fast as possible. As I pulled up to the gates, a Prospect I hadn't seen before stopped me.

He eyed my cut and gave me a smile. "Someone will be really damn happy to see you."

I raised my eyebrows.

"Your wife has been rather worried, fearing the worst. Go right once you're in the gate and follow the road. She's staying in a blue house with a red door.

Can't miss it. I'm sure you'll recognize your club's SUV in the driveway."

"Thanks."

The man held out his hand. "I'm King. It's a pleasure to meet you."

I shook his hand and made my way inside the compound. He was right. The house was easy to find. I parked my bike and walked up to the door, taking a moment to run a hand through my hair and smooth my shirt. I probably looked like hell, but I needed to hold Luciana, to see for myself that she was all right.

The door was locked, so I knocked and waited. Teller opened it and grinned.

"'Bout damn time," he said. "Get in here, Pres, and see if you can get your woman to eat something. She's worried herself to death."

I stepped inside and followed the sound of female voices. Luciana and her two sisters were at the kitchen table. Violeta and Sofia had nearly cleared their plates, but Luciana didn't seem to have taken a single bite. She was smiling, but it didn't reach her eyes. Teller moved farther into the room and I followed. Luciana didn't even look my way. I smiled as I went closer and knelt by her side.

"Luciana," I said.

Her head whipped around in my direction and her jaw dropped, then the tears started. She sobbed and threw herself at me, her arms going around my neck.

"It's okay, baby girl. I'm here."

Even though I hadn't been able to reach Teller, I had spoken to Torch. Once, at any rate. If she'd been so scared, why hadn't someone told her that I was all right? It was ridiculous that she'd worried herself sick when I was perfectly fine, and if Torch knew, then it was likely that several Dixie Reapers had known that as well. His officers at the very least. I'd be having words with Torch before the night was over, whether I was on his territory or not.

"I-I thought you were d-dead."

"Gonna take more than that to kill me," I said.

"I convinced her to take the master bedroom," Teller said. "I think the two of you could use some alone time. The girls and I will head out for a walk."

I gave him a nod and lifted Luciana into my arms, then carried her to the back of the house. I opened two doors before I finally found what seemed to be her room. The clothes she'd been wearing the day we'd met her father were washed and folded on the dresser. After I shut the door, I carried her into the bathroom and eased her down onto the counter. There was a stack of folded cloths so I grabbed one and ran it under some cool water, then pressed it to her face, dabbing at her tears and hoping it would calm her down.

"I had a reason to stay alive," I told her. "Three of them."

Her lip trembled and she started crying again, gripping my arms tight.

"Luciana? What's wrong?"

"I lost them," she said softly. "I lost the babies."

I gathered her close and breathed in her scent. "I'm so damn sorry, sweetheart. I know you were looking forward to having them."

"Now I'll never be a mother," she said, her words cutting me deep. It was my fault she felt that way. If I hadn't been snipped, then I could possibly give her some kids.

"We'll adopt," I said. "Lots of kids out there need a home. Look at me, Luciana."

She pulled back and her gaze held mine.

"I love you. So damn much," I said. "The doctor warned us the babies weren't doing well, hadn't developed properly. Maybe it's for the best. You could have gotten into the delivery room and had two stillborn kids. Or maybe we'd have been lucky and they'd have lived. Everything happens for a reason, Luciana."

"Everything?" she asked, and I knew she was thinking about her past.

"I hate what happened to you. If I could wipe the earth of all rapists, then I would. But the fact your father didn't want you, treated you so badly, is what brought you to me. I'm so fucking glad to have you in my life, Luciana. You're my entire world."

She snuggled against me. "You'd really be willing to adopt?"

"Of course. Anything you want." And I did mean anything. When I'd had my vasectomy, the doc had mentioned it might be possible to reverse it. There was no guarantee, and I'd had it done so damn long ago I didn't think the chances were good, but I could always look into it if that's what Luciana wanted.

I kissed her, soft and slow. Luciana moaned and leaned in closer, then stopped. "We can't." She placed her hand on my chest. "Not yet. The doctor said I'm still healing. He suggested I wait two weeks. There's still a bit of bleeding."

"I wish I had known, had been here."

"Where were you?" she asked.

"The D.E.A. was on the clubhouse doorstep when I left the airstrip. I had to get that shit sorted out before they decided to arrest all of us. I tried to call Teller, but he never answered."

She ran her fingers through my beard. "I'm just glad you're here. I missed you, and I love you so much."

"Love you too, baby girl." I kissed her again. "Let's take a shower, then rest a bit. It was a long-ass drive down here. I promise I won't do anything I shouldn't."

She smiled and nodded.

I started the shower, letting the water get nice and hot. I helped Luciana out of her clothes, then removed mine. We stepped into the shower and I shut the glass door. I took my time washing her, being as gentle as I could for fear of hurting her. After she rinsed, she grabbed the soap and started cleaning me. A mischievous look crossed her face as she neared my cock. Her soap-slicked hand wrapped around my shaft, and she stroked it hard, tugging just the right amount. When she added a twist to her stroke, I damn near came.

"Have to get you good and clean." Her lips tilted up in a smile. When I was seconds from spilling my release all over her hand, she rinsed me off, then dropped to her knees.

"Luciana. You don't have to do this."

"I want to," she said, lapping the head of my cock. "Now use me, Spider."

"Use you?"

She nodded. "Take what you need from me."

I groaned as she licked my shaft. Fucking hell. She was trying to kill me.

"Open up, baby girl. Open wide."

Her lips parted and I fisted her hair, tipping her head a little. I pushed my cock into her mouth.

"That's it. You're going to take it all, aren't you?"

She hummed her agreement.

"This is going to be fast and hard, baby girl. Need you too much. Relax your throat."

She placed her hands on my thighs and I started fucking her mouth with long, deep strokes. She greedily sucked me and it wasn't long before my balls were drawing up and I was seconds away from exploding.

"Fuck, baby girl. Gonna come."

She hummed at me again.

"Swallow for me."

Her hands gripped my legs tighter and I thrust hard and deep, unloading jet after jet of cum into her mouth and down her throat. She swallowed every drop, then licked me clean. I helped her to her feet, hating that I didn't get to please her too. I'd make it up to her, when she was healed, and ready. I wouldn't push. Losing the babies, and fearing that I was dead, had been hard on her.

"Come on, sweetheart. Time to rest. Tomorrow we'll start planning our return trip home."

I shut off the water and dried both of us, then led her to the large bed. I slid under the covers and made room for Luciana, tugging her down next to me. She curled against my body, and I held her close. It hurt, knowing she'd lost the babies, but as long as I had her, then I didn't need anything else. But if she needed more than just me, I'd do anything to give it to her. Whatever it might be.

Epilogue

One Month Later
Luciana

My hands twisted in my skirt and I danced from foot to foot. Today was the big day. I didn't know how Spider had pulled it off, but he'd told me about a little girl who needed a new home. We weren't going through an adoption agency, and I'd decided I didn't want to know the details. I wasn't going to question the wonderful gift we were receiving.

Teller pulled to a stop in front of the house and got out of the club SUV. He smiled and gave me a wink as he opened the back door and pulled out a little girl dressed all in pink. Carefully, he brought her around the front of the vehicle and handed Spider a folder and a bag, then gave the little girl to me. I gazed down at the beautiful little girl in my arms and loved her instantly.

"Spider," I said softly.

He wrapped an arm around my waist. "She's ours, Luciana. Her mother signed away her rights, and Surge is working on getting everything in order. Her name is Marianna, and she's a year old."

I reached and down and stroked Marianna's baby soft cheek.

Spider smiled at our new daughter. "She has a few developmental delays. I didn't think you'd care. The mother didn't want her, claimed she was too much trouble. Honestly, I think the mom was doing drugs when she was pregnant, but I had a pediatrician check her out and she seems healthy."

I rubbed her cheek again, marveling at how perfect she was. "She's beautiful, and the most precious thing I've ever seen."

"Marianna," Spider said, "Meet your new momma. I have a feeling you're going to be one spoiled little girl."

"Let me know if you need a babysitter." Teller grinned. "Kids love me."

Spider wrapped his arm around my waist and led me inside the house. Marianna clung to me, and I was loving every moment of it. She was perfect. And ours.

"I love you, Marianna," I murmured.

She grinned and reached up to pull my hair. Spider nodded toward the hallway and I carried Marianna as we went to her bedroom. Spider had painted it lavender and quickly put together a baby bed and changing table. We'd decorated with butterflies and flowers. She gazed around her room, as if she was taking everything in, then babbled a bit.

"She's really ours?" I asked, almost afraid someone would come snatch her out of my arms.

"Yes, Luciana. She's ours. No one will ever take her from us." He looked around the room. "She may need to remain in the crib longer than most kids. I'm not sure what she is and isn't capable of right now, but we'll figure it out."

"Thank you," I said softly, leaning up to kiss him.

The little girl, my new daughter, had dark hair just like me, but her eyes were a lighter color. Somewhere between blue and gray. Her skin wasn't as dusky as mine, and I wondered about her heritage. Not that it mattered to me, but I wanted to be able to tell her one day about where she came from. Maybe just leave out the druggie mother.

"You have a home. A husband. And now a daughter. What else does my sexy wife want or need?" he asked.

"Nothing. I have everything I could ever want or need right here."

Spider kissed me, long and slow, until Marianna giggled and started to squirm. I set her down and let her explore her new room. Spider tugged me into the hall and put a baby gate across the doorway to Marianna's room. Making sure we were just out of sight of our new daughter, he pressed me against the wall, grinding his cock against me.

"When she goes to sleep, I'm going to show you just how hot you are as a mom. Seeing her in your arms made me wish I could give you a dozen more."

I nipped his lower lips, then kissed him quickly. "I don't think we have room for a dozen. Besides, I have a feeling that Marianna will keep us busy enough."

Spider kissed me a while longer, until our daughter caught our attention. She reached through the bars of the baby gate and babbled at us. Spider reached over and picked her up, holding her close to his chest. My eyes misted with tears at how sweet they looked together. My big, gruff biker and the adorable little girl in pink.

I pulled his phone from his pocket, unlocked it, and snapped a picture of the two of them together. Spider reached out and brought me over to his side, then took a selfie with me and Marianna. Our first family picture.

"I love you," I told him.

"Love you too, baby girl. I thought I had everything I needed. Then you walked into my life and I learned exactly what I'd been missing. I don't want to live a second without you, or without Marianna. This club has always been my family, but now I have a wife and daughter as well. You tore down the walls around my heart, and showed me what it was to fall in love."

"Spider." I pressed my lips together, afraid I'd burst into tears if I said anything else. I tried to compose myself, then blew out a breath. "You are the most incredible man I've ever met. I was scared at first, thinking you were like the others. Then you proved me wrong, and I saw your big heart and experienced kindness from a man for the first time in my life. I'm so glad that Casper gave me to you because you're the best thing that ever happened to me. I love you. Always and forever."

We shared another kiss, then spent the rest of the day getting to know our daughter. I didn't care if other people didn't see her as perfect. Marianna was beautiful and sweet, and she was mine. That's all that mattered.

I thought I'd lost everything, had no reason to keep living, and then Spider had given me the world. My big, tough biker with the heart of gold and the squishiness of a teddy bear, at least when it came to me and his daughter. The only man I would ever want or need. And he was mine.

Dixie Reapers MC

Dear Reader,

Thank you for purchasing a copy of *Flicker/Spider Duet*! I hope you enjoyed the book. For those of you who have read the series from the beginning, you know that Flicker's story was long overdue. I had to pair him with just the right woman, and I think Pepper is perfect for him in every way. She can go toe to toe with him when necessary, but also knows when to let him take care of her.

As usual, I've taken a few liberties while writing Spider's story. But then, it wouldn't be fiction otherwise. There is a president of Colombia, but I used a made-up name and in no way does my character represent the true Colombian president. The characters in this story are completely made up and are not based off real-life people.

I appreciate your support! If you love the Dixie Reapers and their related series, Devil's Boneyard, Hades Abyss, Devil's Fury MC -- the list keeps on growing! -- as much as I do, please check out Harley's Wyldlings on Facebook! We have a lot of fun in there, but be advised it is an adult group.

Until next time...

Harley

Harley Wylde

When Harley is writing, her motto is the hotter the better. Off-the-charts sex, commanding men, and the women who can't deny them. If you want men who talk dirty, are sexy as hell, and take what they want, then you've come to the right place!

An international bestselling author, Harley is the "wilder" side of award-winning scifi/fantasy romance author Jessica Coulter Smith, and writes gay fantasy romance as Dulce Dennison.

Harley Wylde at Changeling: changelingpress.com/harley-wylde-a-196

Jessica Coulter Smith at Changeling: changelingpress.com/jessica-coulter-smith-a-144

Dulce Dennison at Changeling: changelingpress.com/dulce-dennison-a-205

Changeling Press E-Books

More Sci-Fi, Fantasy, Paranormal, and BDSM adventures available in e-book format for immediate download at ChangelingPress.com -- Werewolves, Vampires, Dragons, Shapeshifters and more -- Erotic Tales from the edge of your imagination.

What are E-Books?

E-books, or electronic books, are books designed to be read in digital format -- on your desktop or laptop computer, notebook, tablet, Smart Phone, or any electronic e-book reader.

Where can I get Changeling Press E-Books?

Changeling Press e-books are available at ChangelingPress.com, Amazon, Apple Books, Barnes & Noble, and Kobo/Walmart.

ChangelingPress.com

Printed in Great Britain
by Amazon